THE BREEZE
HORROR

By Candace Caponegro

READ UNTIL YOU BLEED!

THE BREEZE HORROR

CANDACE CAPONEGRO

In memory of my mother,
Frances Beverly Adcock Calnan

PROLOGUE

The odds were a million to one against anything going wrong. The space shuttle had been tested and retested, probed and reprobed, studied and restudied. Environmental-impact reports concluded that disposing of highly toxic waste in space was unquestionably safer than any option on Earth. Of course, no one could have foreseen the space shuttle colliding with an untested, unprobed, unstudied and very unaccountable meteor.

The odds were a million to one. But the small explosion in Earth's stratosphere beat the odds, and in one small New Jersey beach town, a new kind of life began to evolve... into a new kind of death.

Mason sat on a cold bench in a deserted New York City cement park feeding pigeons. His watery eyes were as gray as the cloudy dawn, and his hair hung in blond clumps around his dirty face. He stopped flinging the stale popcorn, and his hands hung limply between his thighs, his shoulders hunched.

And Mason was happy. He didn't feel the brisk early morning breeze that kept the bag ladies hovering in doorways. He didn't hear the cacophonous commuter traffic from the nearby Holland Tunnel. He wasn't hungry or thirsty or in need of any material thing. He felt like a stone embedded in tons of rich, moist earth, or a translucent soap bubble adrift in quiet waters.

Thank God for the mental health clinic where they dispensed the pills that made him feel so good. He loved every one of the people who worked there.

Pangs of love shot through his body and he stiffened and smiled at the warmth. He flung the remaining kernels to the cluster of birds at his feet. He loved the pigeons. They did their best to peck out a living, just like he tried to do.

That's profound, he thought as he started nodding his head to the pecking motion of the birds.

I love you, Cassie.

He halted abruptly as the familiar words reverberated in his mind. They were the same relentless words he'd been hearing every day for the past ten years. He was never too doped up to forget his one love, forever love.

Then the ache washed over him, starting as a choking wave in his throat and thrusting its way in, tightening his chest. Hazily, he tried to scramble his thoughts, before the pain and desolation set in.

A pigeon in search of more popcorn perched gracefully on the bench next to him. He channeled his attention to the bird and away from the ache. The pigeon resembled a big-busted, prim-and-proper matron and seemed oblivious to the fact that a kernel of sticky corn was stuck to its beak.

"Poor little bird," Mason muttered. "All alone and no pills to ease the pain."

Taking a black capsule out of his pocket, spilling the contents into the cup of his hand, he enticed the bird to draw nearer. It did. In a flash, the bird was between Mason's two big hands, its head jerking wildly around. Its eyes bulged, staring up at its captor.

Mason slowly rubbed the feathery head against his cheeks, down his chin and around his mouth. He gently kissed the top of the bird's head and crooned an off-key lullaby.

It was Cassie's song.

When he had finished, he kissed the bird one last time before ripping its head from its rigid body. It felt just like popping open a can of soda. He threw the headless torso violently to the ground and began examining the sticky pulp that hung from its neck. The kernel of corn was, somehow, still stuck to its beak, and Mason lovingly removed it.

He began rolling the bird head around and around in the palms of his hands as if making a ball out of Silly Putty.

The warmth returned and Mason shuddered with desire.

He was happy.

ONE

RED RAIN

1.

6:30 AM

Sandy Galotti was speeding along the New Jersey turnpike when her radio went berserk. She was taking her two-year-old son Jesse to her mother's house in down-neck Newark before going in to her Manhattan office. She didn't even know the radio was on until it began buzzing and blasting static. Jesse started howling at the piercing noise and Sandy quickly shut it off.

She stole a glance at her crying son's glassy eyes and red face, then felt his forehead. It was warmer than when she'd left her house twenty minutes ago, and she felt guilty as hell. This would no doubt be one of the days her mother would deliver a fifteen-minute lousy-parent lecture, and she would get to work even later than usual.

Maybe she deserved the lecture.

With a deep, well-worn sigh, she pulled a juice bottle from her diaper bag and quickly pacified Jesse. It would be lovely if she could pacify Mrs. Strinberg so easily. The thought of her boss greeting clients with a Fred Flintstone-shaped baby bottle dangling from her lips made Sandy smile.

She turned her attention back to the road, noticing that traffic was unusually light for a working day. But something else was wrong. Cars were pulling to the shoulder of the road and stopping.

Her first reaction was to check the windows to make sure they were tightly closed. She was on the northbound section of the turnpike, passing what was better known as the "Toilet Bowl of the Garden State." It was a plumber's nightmare of thick, grimy, steel tubing; a network of huge Tinkertoy structures, long phallic chimneys, black meadows and oily factories, all oozing ominous vapors. Skies were dirty and the air was thick.

Sandy had often wondered whether this polluted doorway to New York City would cause some horrendous health crisis before the media and politicians would take action. She could picture the headlines: *Thousands of Motorists Perish from Pestiferous Fumes*. A controversial political film would surely follow with Jane Fonda as the gutsy heroine.

A light-blue Volkswagen Rabbit started passing her in the right lane, blaring his horn continuously. When she glanced over, she saw a young-executive-type rolling down his window.

"Your radio," he yelled, making a turning gesture with his hand. "Turn on your radio!"

Without further explanation, he accelerated and sped toward an exit. Sandy immediately jerked the station wagon to the shoulder and shoved it into park.

She tried the radio again. It was a cheap AM model that had been in the Pontiac wagon when she'd bought it secondhand. On a good day, which was rare, she could tune in five stations: one rock, two news, one country, and one Spanish. On other days, the radio faded in and out like a tortured phantom, rattling bits of commercials and weather reports or wailing a few lines of a song before hiding silently in the dashboard.

She clicked the dial off and on. There was complete silence. Sandy bit her thumbnail and looked at Jesse sitting quietly, oblivious to her growing nervousness. She took a deep breath and decided to stop the next car she saw and ask for information.

Just before she opened her door she heard a faint wisp of static. A lot of fine tuning and some well-aimed kicking—which made Jesse stop slurping apple juice and stare quizzically at her—and she finally zeroed in on a station.

". . . all citizens are asked to remain calm during... [static]... We repeat. There has been an explosion on the Galaxy IV Space Carrier Shuttle... [static]... lethal elements released into the earth's... [static]... studying the immediate health hazards... global implications involved. Until all information is carefully studied we recommend that residents remain calm... All police and firemen... [static]..."

Sandy changed stations and tuned in an announcer's voice faltering on the edge of hysteria. Instinctively she reached over and held Jesse's hand.

"We have just now been informed that Mayor Koch has called a news conference to institute an immediate evacuation plan for New York City. We are switching you now to Gracie..."

Sandy's mind reeled. She was only ten minutes away from the city. Cars sped by to the exit ahead and she knew she should do something. But her mind went blank and she couldn't move. It was always her first reaction in an emergency: mental flight before fight. It was exactly what she'd done the day her husband had died.

It was almost a year ago. Jesse had just been put in for his nap and she lay languishing on satin sheets reading a play when the police called.

"Mrs. Galotti? This is the State Police Highway Patrol. Is there someone there with you?"

"Yes. My son, Jesse," she'd stammered, not realizing why they'd asked.

The hideous details of the car accident sent her mind spinning. Sounds grew dimmer and dimmer and she felt that her body was a camera lens zooming away from the rest of the world.

Poor loving Matt—so kind, so dependable, and probably the only person in the world that could ever put up with her. Matt was gone. She hung up the phone and the camera lens zoomed back to the ridiculous fight they'd had that morning.

"But it describes me perfectly," Sandy had pleaded, thrusting the script at her red-faced husband.

"Leslie: early twenties, blue-eyed blond, vulnerable, and not too bright. Well, the last part would definitely be typecasting," he quipped.

Sandy grabbed the script from him and struck her hand-on-hip actress pose.

"Dumb blond has always been my specialty and I don't see what's wrong with earning a hundred and twenty-five a week for a few hours' work at a dinner theater."

"What about all the hours you'll spend rehearsing? What'll you do with Jesse?"

"I'll get a babysitter. My mother would jump at the chance to stuff him with as much food as possible, like any self-respecting Italian grandma."

At Matt's grimace, Sandy put her arms around his neck and tried a softer approach. "Oh, I know we agreed I'd give it all up and be a fulltime mother until Jesse starts school, but I didn't know I'd miss acting this much. Besides, it's only an eight-week run."

Sandy stroked the hair on the back of her husband's neck.

Matt brushed her hand away and stepped back. "Be honest. What you really miss are the parties after the show and your crazy friends... and then you'll get a part in a road company headed for Wisconsin. You'll go off, have a great time, and where will that leave me and Jesse? Forget it! We've been through all this before and I don't want that kind of marriage or that kind of life."

"Well what about my life? In five years, I'll be too old for any decent roles. I've tried the devoted-wife-and-mother bit and it's not enough. I need something more... and not more friends or more parties. Acting isn't something you can do by yourself. You need a stage and an audience—"

"Look, hon," Matt interrupted. He glanced nervously at his watch. "Let's take five and continue this scene tonight. We can stand on the dining room table and invite the neighbors to come over and applaud."

He threw open the door and slammed it shut behind him. She never saw him alive again.

Ironically, she never gave another thought to an acting career and was truly content with a nine-to-five secretarial slot at the Strinberg Talent Agency. Her salary, plus Matt's insurance money, was enough to support Jesse and herself without her family's assistance or restrictions.

The thought of her family snapped her back to reality again.

Northbound lanes of the turnpike were now deserted. Sandy debated with herself as to how quickly she could speed to the exit, through the Ironbound section of Newark, to her parents' house.

The radio crackled on for one final blast.

"...residents of Thirty-fourth to Sixtieth streets west of Fifth Avenue go directly to the Port Authority Terminal.

Buses are on hand to drive you safely through the Lincoln Tunnel. Residents of Sixty-first Street to..."

Sandy wondered where all the people would go.

And then she noticed the cars already jammed bumper to bumper in the turnpike's southbound lanes. It looked like five P.M. the Friday before Labor Day weekend.

Questions echoed through her mind, and the radio answered with a deathly silence. Surely her family had heard the news and were heading away from the area.

Glancing over the metal road dividers to the south-bound lanes, she saw traffic now at a standstill. Where were they all headed?

Damn the radio!

The only place south she could think to go was the beach house, a good ninety miles down the Jersey shore. Her family had owned the bungalow for fifteen years and she'd spent fifteen summers vacationing there.

Of course, it might not be safe there either. On the other hand, if it wasn't safe, she could just keep driving south until she found a place that was.

"Mommy."

Jesse fumbled with his bottle and let out a few whimpers before Sandy plugged it back into his mouth.

There was no time to waste. She couldn't risk creeping along the entire ninety miles to Sea Breeze Island when she had a sick baby that needed care.

She swallowed hard to stem the panic in her throat before jamming the car into drive. She swung the wagon into a wide U-turn and sped south in the empty northbound lanes. Flying at seventy miles an hour was exhilarating—like an audience of a thousand applauding fans.

2.

9:30 AM

Hideous air raid whistles pierced the deadly silence of Manhattan's streets.

Oblivious to any type of crisis, Mason finished playing with the pigeons and stalked down Hudson Street to the mental health clinic. He listened to the sirens and wondered briefly where the fire was. Maybe it was in the clinic and good old Nurse Dawkins was roasting in the middle of it. Mason grinned broadly at the thought.

It was she and that whacked out psychiatrist who had cooked up his early release agreement from Overbrook Asylum. Every day, including Sundays, he had to waltz down to the clinic to gobble a bunch pills "under supervision," so he'd be too stoned to act violent again. Then he had to sweep up around the clinic and suck up to Dawkins for a few measly dollars to pay for room and board at the welfare hotel he was supposed to call home.

With fists thrust into the pockets of his filthy jeans, he reached the clinic storefront and tried the door. It was locked. The fat cow was late again. He leaned back against the door and banged the heel of his shoe stubbornly into the clinic stoop.

Sirens still blared full force in the nearly deserted city streets: Mason fiercely scanned the area and for the first time realized that something unusual was going on.

The warehouses towering above the clinic were usually bustling with activity at this time of the morning.

They were as motionless as store mannequins now. Even the twenty-four-hour coffee shop on the corner looked closed. The only sign of life was an overloaded, rusty '69 Chevy that sagged miserably to the right with a flat tire. Two Puerto Ricans, an elderly man and woman, were arguing vehemently around it.

As quickly as they'd 'begun, the sirens fell silent. The couple stopped arguing and Mason heard a scream, a howling, that sounded like a she-wolf in heat. Mason wondered why the crazy Ricans were suddenly frightened until he saw a stiffly pressed, starched white figure plodding around the corner.

The Puerto Rican male started toward the nurse, waving his arms wildly, shouting in Spanish staccato fury, but' Nurse Dawkins shooed him away with a flick of her plump black wrist.

"Oh, thank the Lord you're here, Mason," she gasped between gulps of air. Reaching him, she leaned her heavy bulk against his chest and attempted to catch her breath.

"I jes knew you'd be the only one in the whole city that wouldn't know we's all being evacuated. I swear I couldn't wait on that boat on South Street for thinking of you waiting on me here, like always. No way I could leave my poor pretty white boy to die all alone."

Mason gritted his teeth but forced a smile on his lips.

"You're late today, ma'am," he said politely.

"Late? Haven't you been listening to what I been telling you?"

"Yes, ma'am."

"I jes said I have risked my life to come and get you. It's been on the radio all morning long about some space rocket they been using as a fancy garbage truck to send toxic junk and nuclear gook and who knows what other mean stuff, to outer space. Only the whole mess done blowed up and it's heading straight for us."

Mason stared at her with a deadpan expression.

"And you best believe all the roads are crammed with people trying to get out of here—and why am I wasting my time trying to explain anything to a downed-out junkie?"

She turned from him to rummage in her purse for the clinic keys. "Look, honey, never you mind. I got it all worked out. I'm jes gonna run inside and grab you one of them white lab coats I sometimes wear, and I got me a black doctor bag stashed somewheres around here."

Mason watched her waddle across the floor, grab a lab coat, and begin throwing things out of a cabinet. The clinic rooms and Dawkins reeked of the same smells: sterilized needles and foul breath; week-old garbage and Lysol; carbon copy ink and roaches. He had once watched in fascination as a plump crispy-looking roach climbed over her shoe, up her leg, and under her uniform. He kept waiting for it to reappear, but it never did.

Sometimes he felt like that roach—engulfed by Dawkins and the rest of the filth in New York City. If it all was going down the drain, so be it. He couldn't care less.

But it was impossible.

"Ma'am? Just what kind of con job is this?"

Her fat ass widened as she bent to free a dusty, weathered doctor's bag from behind a cabinet. "Good Lord, Mason! Let's not go over this again. You had to have heard them air raid whistles. Now come on, put the damn coat on so you look something like a doctor and I can get you on that boat."

Mason shook his head and started to giggle. Soon he was consumed with laughter.

Nurse Dawkins tried to shake him out of it. "Don't go crazy on me now. We ain't got time for it."

Mason roared even harder. Tears streamed down his face.

"I warned you, boy," she yelled, and then she slapped him hard across the face.

Mason immediately silenced.

"Now go wash your face and put on the lab coat while I find you some pills to make you normal again."

Nurse Dawkins unlocked a cabinet, extracted two black capsules from a pill bottle, and handed them to Mason. Then she dumped a shelf full of pill bottles into the doctor's bag.

Mason received the pills stonily, his face a mask of non-expression. The slap had shocked him back to reality and he realized Dawkins was telling the truth. It was no con. He also realized she no longer held any power over him.

When she approached him with the stethoscope she'd retrieved from a bottom desk drawer, he arched forward to allow her to drape the instrument around his neck.

"This is perfect," he said. The pills in his hand dropped to the floor.

"Oh, Mason, take your pills like a good boy so we can get going."

Mason took off the stethoscope and flung the bell part over her head and down her back. He tugged gently at the instrument and pulled the nurse toward him. "I don't have to be a good boy anymore. It's a new world starting today," he whispered.

"Honey, there's going to be no world for either one of us if we don't get our asses to South Street and catch that boat to Sea Breeze Island. So, quit this fooling. We got plenty of time for that later," She added with a wink.

"No, now," he demanded. He slid the stethoscope against the back of her neck, grasped her closer, and began kissing her cheeks. He hummed a song as he moved to her hair and eyes. Seductively he moved the stethoscope side to side on her neck. Then, pausing to lock eyes, he attacked. With incredible strength, he crossed the metal arms in front of her neck and squeezed tighter...and tighter.

Nurse Dawkins flung out her arms and lost her balance. Mason forced her to the floor and pinned her down with one knee. The stethoscope arms twisted and he tightened his hold around her neck. For several long minutes, he felt her body flop around like a beached whale.

When her eyes had substantially protruded from their sockets, and her tongue had stopped flicking like some frenzied, hungry snake, he released his hold and stood away from the body.

Her foot continued jerking against the side of a desk, and Mason desperately wished for a knife. He searched the clinic cabinets for something sharp like a scalpel, and his hand closed around a long, thin hemostat. He walked toward the body. He paused. Hadn't the fat bitch said something about the medical boat going to Sea Breeze Island?

Cassie had lived on Sea Breeze Island. Warmly he remembered the summer paradise of beaches and bungalows where he and Cassie had met and fallen in love. It had been the only happy time in his life.

Next winter he'd had his first nervous breakdown, and everything stood between him and Cassie. It had nearly driven him out of his mind.

The nurse's massive body was motionless. He stepped over her and started gathering the things he'd need from the clinic. Daydreams of a chance like this had filled his head so often, he'd almost failed to see the real thing when it occurred. If the medical boat was headed toward Breeze Island, it must be considered safe from the shit coming down in New York City.

Got to get there and save Cassie.

Her parents had that house on the island, so it was the logical place she'd go. He'd arrive like a knight in shining armor to protect her and redeem himself.

I'm coming, Cassie. I'm only a boat ride away.

3.

On a map of New Jersey, Sea Breeze Island is shaped like the side view of a pancake. Nine miles long and three city blocks wide at the center, it is an oasis of sand on the Atlantic Ocean.

On its western side, a mile-long antiquated bridge connects the island to the rest of the continent. Mean, jagged rocks guard its northern and southernmost tips. Its only claim to fame, the Sea Breeze National Armory, was built in the '30s and became a regular beehive of activity during World War II. Barbed wire and armed guards had cut off two miles of sandy marshes that flanked the armory. A president's mansion peeked from behind sand dunes. Long black cars with shaded windows had traveled silently to and fro across the island bridge.

After the war, the barbed wire was dismantled and the wild sandy marshlands were declared a national park. The mansion was boarded up and the black cars were rarely seen again.

The rest of the island quickly developed into a working man's vacation haven. Modest bungalows and rental units, resembling the houses in a Monopoly game, were squeezed together, only inches apart. The huge public beach that faced the Atlantic was surrounded by a spectacular boardwalk. There were skill games, wheels, rows of cheap, fuzzy animal prizes, video arcades and miniature golf. Vacationers were treated to the aromas of salt water taffy, popcorn, suntan oil, and fried sausage grease.

In the late 1950s an amusement pier was added, jutting out from the boardwalk into the ocean. Screams from the giant Zipper Wheel ride could sometimes be heard across the whole island, piercing through the general din of roaring surf, beach blanket radios, lifeguard whistles, and laughing children.

Families spent their summers on Sea Breeze Island. They came back year after year. Rental units were clean and cheap and included kitchens so Dad wouldn't go broke taking the family out to eat each night. Clotheslines were provided so Mom could wash out the baby's clothes. And the boardwalk was easily accessible so the kids could spend their change and stay out of their parents' hair.

Some mothers might complain that it was hardly a vacation, for them, but it perfectly suited the many Italian families who bought houses on the island. They cleaned and cooked all day and set up tables on their cement yards at night. Cards and gossip were tossed back and forth after dark as they relaxed with their extended families.

At the end of the summer the resort community of thirty thousand would dwindle to a ghost town of less than one thousand permanent residents. Houses would be boarded and bathing suits stored until the next year.

It was the workingman's haven that was soon to become every man's nightmare.

11:30 AM

"Do you have any identification?"

Sandy eyed the cop, a sort of sexy, grown up version of a Campbell's Soup kid, and quickly handed her license to him. Her car, along with hundreds of others, was stopped at the police barricade blocking the mouth of the Sea Breeze Island Bridge.

"I'm sorry, miss." He handed the license back to her. "If you'll follow the car in front of you, you'll see a detour sign on the left. Make the left turn and signs will lead you to the next available shelter."

Speech over, he headed toward the next car.

"Wait a minute," Sandy. called to him, "I don't understand, I'm not looking for any shelter."

The officer turned around and looked into her face for the first time. His voice softened. "Aren't you on your way to the armory on the island?"

"Why would I want to go there?"

"Radio says it's a safe place to be."

"My radio's broken. Is it?"

"Is what?"

"Is it a safe place?"

He shrugged. "A lot of people must think so. Forty or fifty thousand cars must have crossed this bridge today. Trouble is, there's no more room. That's why we have to turn away all but the permanent residents. Sorry, miss."

"But I am a permanent resident."

"Not according to your driver's license."

"I've been a permanent resident every summer for the last fifteen years. My parents live at 377 Kearny Avenue and—"

"Look, I'd like to help you, but like I said, the armory is full and the island is already bursting from too many people with no place to go."

Sandy decided she'd do better if she'd slip into one of her old characterizations. Praying she wasn't too rusty, she bit down hard on her lower lip and began twirling a strand of blond hair around a finger. She blinked until she could feel tears in the corners of her

"I just don't know what I'm going to do if I can't cross the bridge and meet my parents at the house. They're quite helpless without me," she lied. ' 'My father's in a wheelchair and my mother has a heart condition. I know I shouldn't have left them alone, but Jesse had to go to the doctor today."

The cop looked unconvinced. She lifted Jesse to the window.

"Just feel his head and tell me he's not burning with fever." Sandy took one of the policeman's hands and placed it on Jesse's forehead.

"Really, I wish I could help you." He scratched at his shocking red hair. "Do you have anything that'll prove where you live on the island?"

Sandy let her lower lip quiver slightly before covering it with clenched fingers, as if attempting to conceal her distress.

"No. Nothing. But I swear on my dead mother's grave, I'm not lying. Look, you can call the house and check with my parents. The number is 793—"

"Never mind," he cut in. "What kind of cop would I be if I couldn't tell when a person was lying or not? Pull your car over to the right. As soon as the boat traffic clears, we'll get the bridge down and you can follow those cars across."

"Thank you, Officer." Sandy beamed at him. Impulsively she grabbed his hand again and kissed it.

He flashed an even white smile and winked as he backed away. "You just take care of that baby now," he said, "and remember me to your dead mother with the heart condition."

She steered to the short line of cars on the right and Jeremiah Stafford watched with amusement, wondering why he'd always been a sucker for a blonde.

"Thanks again, Red," he heard her yell, and he had to smother a laugh.

"Three-seven-seven Kearny Ave," he repeated to himself. "Oh, hell, she's married."

He turned his attention to the next car in line.

───────

Exuberance was quickly replaced with impatience as Sandy waited for the bridge to close.

"Come on let's get moving," she said aloud. Now that she was so close to her destination, her body was ready to give up the fight. Every muscle, every joint, felt ragged. Her mouth tasted cotton-dry and she knew when she stood up she'd need a bathroom within ten seconds.

Jesse wasn't faring much better. Perspiration gleamed at the edge of his hairline. His bottle. had run dry and was slipping from his sweaty hands. For the last hour he'd slept fitfully. He'd wake and gaze at her, raise the bottle to give it to then hold out his hand to retrieve it. After a few shakes to convince himself it was truly empty, he'd drift back to sleep.

Sandy bent over and took his temperature using the kissing-the-forehead technique.

"Oh God, it must be a hundred and four degrees," she mumbled to herself. "I'm a lousy mother." Jesse gazed forlornly at her and handed her the bottle. Sandy looked around for her redhead policeman, but he was too far away and she didn't want to attract attention to herself by running after him.

There were no cars behind her. The car in front, a brown dusty sedan, sprouted what appeared to be a short elderly man, wearing a hat. Sandy sized him up as the type of driver who would lead a parade of cars at fifteen mph through the center of town on a Sunday afternoon. Maybe he was just the type to carry around a spare aspirin. She'd give it a shot.

"Excuse me, I'm waiting in the car behind you and my baby's sick. Would you, by any chance, have an aspirin I could give him?"

An old wizard-sly face peeked out from under the hat and smiled at her.

"Too late for an aspirin," he said.

"What?"

"It's in the air," he whispered. "It's all around us, and no matter where we run we can't escape it. We're all doomed."

"Look, if you don't have an aspirin, do you have any water I could put in his bottle?"

The old man laughed and shook his head no. Sandy stared at him dumbly.

"There'll be plenty of water if it rains tonight," he said, "but who'll be around to drink it?"

Sandy decided to give up on the crazy geezer and try the car in front of him, when she heard the rickety sounds of the old bridge. Police ran in all directions. Engines were started. The bridge locked into place. Barricades were removed.

Minutes later she followed the old geezer's car across the bridge. There were screams and a loud crescendo of horns behind her. Sandy thought she heard shots, but a glance in her rearview mirror showed only police cars serenely following her.

Across the bridge, she carefully maneuvered her car through the hordes of people in the street. As she crept toward Kearny Avenue, she thought she heard the bridge being raised again, the cranking of steel into water.

But it could have been thunder. The skies above Sea Breeze Island hung dark and heavy with storm clouds.

The rain that saturated Sea Breeze Island was a gurgling sea ghoul whose bowels excreted black water. Her mouth blew winds of incredible force. Her lightning eyes pierced the skies and sent bolts of fire to many island structures. Her foreboding arms encircled the island with paralyzing power. Her victims—anyone touched by her waters—felt a deadening, not unlike being swabbed by Novocain.

Lightning struck first at the old raised bridge that was the vital link between the island and the mainland. The island's fire department attempted to respond to the ensuing inferno, but machinery exposed to the rain broke down within minutes. Rather than dousing the fire, the rain seemed to feed the flames until the bridge was a smoldering obscenity.

Boats were not immune to the rain ghoul's tantrums. The medical ship, untouched by her lightning, fell victim to the tremendous force of her winds and crashed into the rocks that lined the northern entrance to Sea Breeze Bay. Debris littered the waters.

In the Sea Breeze Island National Park, the squat, box-like armory was bloated with refugees. Cracks in its ancient roof soon gave way to holes of gushing waters. Volunteers rushed to make repairs but were driven back by the rain's fury. When the roof caved in, many were instantly killed.

They were the lucky ones.

Hundreds of others. struggled and clawed in the streets to find shelter from the searing rain, to keep it from crawling into their mouths, slithering into their eyes, festering on their skin.

The rain ghoul ruled for three more days.

TWO

THE FALL OF THE NORMS

4.

The tapping sound grew louder and louder as each coffin nail was hammered into her casket. When she opened her mouth to scream, she found she couldn't. Breathing was becoming difficult. She knew she had to make her move now. If she didn't alert the undertaker she was still alive, she'd suffocate and die alone in the damp, dark tomb.

Sandy stretched out her arm to bang on the lid of the coffin and touched the windowsill on the side of her bed. The reality of the cold sill shocked her awake, and she bolted upright in bed. Gradually the dream slipped away and she remembered why she and Jesse were alone in the beach house in the dark.

The tapping resumed on the far side of the bungalow. There were three short taps, then silence. Then four taps and silence. Sandy took a deep breath and decided it was a tree branch hitting the window.

She listened intently for the tapping to continue but heard only Jesse's even breathing as he slept in the crib across the room. Though the storm still raged outside, Sandy was no longer aware of the noise. For three days the small cottage had rocked and heaved from the continuous onslaught of wind and rain.

Sandy groped in the dark and felt the window just above her bed. She parted the curtains and raised the shade. Face pressed to the glass, she peered outside.

Although she knew her bedroom window looked directly into a four-foot alley that separated her house from the Morelli cottage next door, she saw nothing but rain— streams of black, oily rain, a wall of rain. Nothing else was visible.

The tapping started again. Sandy jerked away from the window. Automatically, she reached for the lamp on the night table and turned the switch.

Nothing happened.

Then she remembered how the electricity had flickered off the first day of the storm. She had assumed the power lines were down, and did not expect them to be fixed until the rain stopped or at least let up. She had not attempted to open her front door. The rain was too blinding, too powerful.

The tapping grew louder and seemed to be moving around the outside of the house. As it came closer, Sandy decided it sounded less like tapping and more like knocking or banging. She felt like a rabbit whose cage was being rattled by a predator looking for a way to get in.

Maybe it was her family.

She immediately rejected the idea. Her family certainly had keys, and even if they didn't, they would be at the door calling her name. They were definitely not the types to go banging around the house in the middle of the night.

After the initial disappointment of not finding her family waiting for her, she had immediately set about locating the aspirin and running a cool bath to bring down Jesse's fever. By the time that was accomplished, the rain had started. There was no radio or TV. For all she knew, she and Jesse might be the only people alive in the world.

The banging stopped.

Fumbling out of bed, Sandy felt for the wall and followed it to the crib where Jesse lay sleeping. She touched his forehead. It was warm, but not burning. She tucked the covers around him.

Halfway back to her own bed, the knocking started again and seemed to come up behind her, pounding on the wall of her bedroom. Falling, slamming her knee on the night table, she dived toward her bed and scrambled under the covers.

Take deep breaths, she told herself, deep breaths from the diaphragm. If they're good for stage fright, they must be good for any kind of fright.

It had to be the storm... and the wind in the trees... branches of trees banging on the house. Then she froze. Under the blankets her body went as cold as a slab of stone as she realized it couldn't be trees. There were no trees. There was sand, there was cement, but there were no trees anywhere near the beach house.

When the knocking started on the window directly above her bed, Sandy jumped, but she wasn't surprised. She was too terrified to be surprised. The surprise came when she finally slid the covers slowly from her head and stared with her mouth hanging open at the window that was inches away from her face.

Unlike her dream, however, she was able to scream. She screamed uncontrollably and hysterically. She screamed loud enough to wake the dead and long enough to make sure the dead stayed awake. She screamed until she was too hoarse to make any sound whatsoever.

Yet, even then, her mouth remained open, frozen in a silent scream, while her eyes remained glued to the apparition with yellow eyes and a flattened, distorted face that was pressed against her window. The eyes dripped black, oily blood. And there was a hand—a hand that was banging on the glass with what appeared to be the heel of a bleeding red shoe.

Sandy's silent scream was suddenly pierced by the cries of her son. Jesse was wailing in the crib behind her. Finally able to break her paralysis, she lurched out of bed, tripping over her blankets, and crawled toward his crib.

Only when Jesse was safely held against her breast and she was halfway out the bedroom door, did Sandy dare look back toward the window. The apparition was gone. The banging had ceased. There was only the streaming rain outside.

Sandy carried Jesse to the other side of the bungalow before it dawned on her. The face at the window had been screaming with a terror even greater than her own.

5.

Mason knew what hell was like. Hell was pain, teeth-gnashing, heart-wrenching pain. He lay spread-eagled on the beach. The needles of rain impaled his body. He was immobile. Mason tried again to turn himself over but failed. Was it yesterday he had dragged himself to the shoreline after the medical boat crashed on the rocks?

He remembered how easy it had been to walk right onto the boat, where everyone thought he was a doctor. But the next thing he remembered was diving into the water while his fellow passengers called for help on the sinking ship. He remembered being tossed about in the waves, one hand glued to his medical bag while the other hand clutched a piece of floating debris. But how long had he been in the water? When had he touched land? Time had lost all meaning. The rain blinded his eyes so he didn't even know if it was night or day.

He heard moaning. Fellow sufferers were groaning all around him. Although the pain had been excruciating, earlier he had stretched his hand as far as it could reach. In the dizzying rain he'd hoped to touch the medical bag that was filled with pills. Instead, he touched human flesh.

The medical bag was a remote daydream. He doubted he could swallow a pill anyway. His throat felt like a lighted torch that sent flames through his entire body each time he gasped for breath—flames that consumed his veins and arteries, inch by agonizing inch. He was burning in the eternal fire of damnation and no pill could douse the blaze.

His only hope was to push the pain from his conscious-ness—refuse to acknowledge it and concentrate on something else. This trick, a form of self-hypnosis, had been essential for his survival. It enabled him to withstand the therapy in the asylum, and it made it possible for him to endure the perversions of Nurse Dawkins. Like hell and damnation, he'd learned the trick from his parents.

The thought of his parents filled him with a hate almost as intense as the pain. He shifted attention from the pain to his earliest recollection of his father and visualized the well-pressed man in gray as he stood on a busy corner shouting a sermon called, *"The Total Destruction and Annihilation of All Sinners in the Entire Inhabited World."* Occasionally he interrupted his sermon to thrust pamphlets at disinterested commuters as they hurried past. Mason's pinch-faced mother stood nearby and maintained a steady supply of the leaflets. Mason held the Bible.

The memory blurred and faded, replaced by a vision of his father's hand reaching down for him. It moved slowly forward, then swung out violently and came cracking across his face. Mason was thrown to the floor and his nose began to bleed on the cold tile. His cries were a mixture of pain, frustration, bewilderment, and hopelessness. He looked up at his father and saw that he was removing his gray suit jacket and carefully rolling up his sleeves. Mother sat at a piano and played a hymn.

"Exodus 20:12 - Thou shall honor thy father and thy mother." Father's voice boomed louder than the piano music, louder than Mason's screams, and the first of countless beatings continued.

By the time he reached his teens, Mason had become a dutiful, preaching robot who had mastered the trick of separating himself from the pain in his world. In the evenings, he quoted Scriptures and expounded on them as easily as his father. He held hands with his mother, swaying in rhythm with her, as they beseeched the Holy Spirit to enter and bless them. He began talking in tongues. His parents were delighted.

Then he met Cassie and his world turned upside down. She became his god, his light, his reason for living. He burned with only one desire: to possess her. His parents had tried to interfere. They beat him, locked him in his room, sermonized and exorcised him, until Mason knew he had only one option left.

They took three days to die.

Mason smiled as the rain entered and consecrated him.

6.

Jesse awoke bright and bubbly and climbed on his mother's sleeping back. "Mommy, you sleeping? You sleeping, Mommy?"

Sandy rolled over and felt his forehead. It felt normal. Jesse seized the opportunity to jump hard on his mother's stomach. "Mommy play horsie? Play horsie? Huh, Mommy?" He bounced up and down and giggled when she moaned.

"Whoa there, cowboy," she said. "You certainly act like you're feeling better. How about giving horsie a break so we can rustle up some breakfast?"

He tumbled gently onto a pillow as she raised herself up to try the lamp switch, but there was still no power.

"What doing, Mommy?"

"Nothing."

"Mommy get up?"

"Yes, I'm getting up. Now, no more questions." Her feet touched the cold linoleum and she looked around for her slippers. Unable to find them in the dimly lit room, she reached for the window shade... and Stopped. The contorted face of the previous night was still vivid in her mind. But that was in the downstairs bedroom, she reminded herself. She was upstairs now.

The beach cottage attic consisted of two bedrooms, all odd angles and sloped ceilings. Windows faced the street and the alley. Sandy knew it was unlikely anyone would climb the pitched roof to gawk at her through a window on the second floor, but still she hesitated.

"What matter, Mommy? You scared?"

"Jesse, if you don't stop asking questions I'll go crazy. How come you're only quiet when you're sick ' or sleeping?"

Jesse clamped his mouth closed and pouted.

"I'm sorry, baby. I didn't mean to snap at you." She pulled him on her lap and cuddled him. "Go ahead. Ask your questions."

Jesse shook his head.

"Didn't you want to know if Mommy was scared?"

Jesse looked up at her. "Me scared, too," he said in a quiet voice.

"You? What are you scared of?"

Jesse pointed slowly toward the window. "Mommy scared?" he asked.

Sandy looked at her son for a moment before she answered, "Me? Are you crazy? This is Fearless Mom you're dealing with here."

She took a deep breath, held it, and flipped up the shade. Murky sunlight filled the room. The rain had finally stopped.

Jesse crept nearer to the sill and together they peered through the glass for a closer look.

The street was deserted. Garbage and broken glass were strewn everywhere. Sandy strained to see the boardwalk located a half a block from the cottage, but her view was blocked by a telephone pole smashed into a Volkswagen on the sidewalk. Wire lay tangled on the pavement.

Sandy raised the shade on another window and looked down into the alley. Her mother's clotheslines near the outdoor shed and shower stall had caved in, but otherwise everything was in place, quiet and deserted.

She turned back to Jesse. "Are you ready to conquer the downstairs with Fearless Mom?"

Sandy draped a chenille bedspread over her shoulders, Indian-style, and led giggling Jesse down the stairs into the main room of the house. Flanked on two sides by eight windows, the huge room was a combination kitchen, dining room, and living room. In front of this room was a small porch. In back, through a connecting door next to the pantry, was an adjoining apartment of two bedrooms and a smaller kitchen.

With Sandy's wide assortment of uncles and aunts, cousins and second cousins, the back apartment had often handled the overflow of visiting relatives that descended on the house each summer.

Sandy missed the hustle and bustle of their activity. She missed her family. Standing in the silent, empty room, she tried to keep from crying.

"What's matter, Mommy? You scared?"

Sandy looked down at her son and forced herself to smile. "Fearless Mom doesn't know the meaning of the word," she assured him. With an exaggerated air of bravado, she flipped the shades up on all the windows. Then, Jesse trailing behind her, she surveyed the other rooms.

The beach house was decorated like a glorified cellar. Nothing matched. Relatives had donated odds and ends. A flamingo lamp sat on an Early American end table. A red shag rug was spread on new green-and-gold-striped linoleum, Budweiser beer mirrors lined the stairway. Red, white, and blue eagle wallpaper covered all the downstairs walls. And in the center of the house, dwarfing the entire thirty-by-fifteen-foot main room, was a huge Art Deco pedestal table that was covered with three different floral tablecloths. It seated fourteen (twenty in a pinch).

After exploring each room and finding nothing amiss, Sandy settled Jesse into a chair at the table. She poured two bowls of Count Chocula cereal and was just adding evaporated milk when someone knocked at the front door.

Both Sandy and Jesse jumped.

"Me scared," Jesse yelled.

"Who is it?" Sandy asked nervously. Her Fearless Mom courage was forgotten until she heard a familiar voice say, "Can you help me? It's Mrs. Morelli from next door."

Then Fearless Mom opened the door.

"Your parents didn't come down here with you?" Mrs. Morelli asked after she was seated at the table. Mrs. Morelli reminded Sandy of a grandmother on an old-fashioned Christmas card. Although she was a year-round resident of the island, her complexion was always untanned and creamy clear. Silver-gray hair was tucked into a neat bun on top of her head. Lively blue eyes and laugh lines around her mouth were testimony to her happy outlook on life. Today, however, the lines on her face were creased with worry.

"I've heard nothing from my parents. In fact, I've heard no news at all. Have you been listening to a radio or...?"

Mrs. Morelli shook her head sadly. "No, the electricity's been off for three days now. Phone's dead, too. The last call I received was for my Danny to report to the armory."

A picture flashed into Sandy's mind of the husky, soft-spoken Danny, overloaded with grocery bags as he trailed behind his petite seventy-year-old mom.

"Danny, God bless him, is a volunteer fireman," Mrs. Morelli said proudly, "and they needed him to help settle all those people evacuated to the armory. He promised he'd call me that night but... he never did." Mrs. Morelli removed a hanky from a pocket in her trim housedress and dabbed at the tears gleaming in the comers of her eyes.

Sandy remembered the way Mrs. Morelli treated her forty-five-year-old son. To her, he would always be her baby.

"How can I help you?" She sat back at the table and took Mrs. Morelli's hands into her own. "Do you want me to try to find Danny?"

"No," she cried, "if he's not at the armory you wouldn't know which of his friends to ask, where they live, or whatever. I'm too nervous to just sit around and wait any longer. But Mr. Morelli" — she lowered her eyes — "I hate to leave him all by himself."

Sandy recalled why she had always admired Mrs. Morelli's happy outlook on life. "How is Mr. Morelli doing?"

"Just fine, God bless him," Mrs. Morelli replied. "The Parkinson's has him pretty much confined to a wheelchair now, but he can still take a few steps leaning on his cane when he has a mind to. He can probably manage by himself, but I don't know how long I'll be gone. I thought if you could keep an eye on him, like your mother does sometimes in the summer..."

"Don't say another word. I'll be happy to."

"God bless you, Sandy." She hugged Sandy and headed for the door before hesitating.

"By the way," she said, turning back. "Don't let Mr. Morelli bamboozle you. His doctor said liquor is no good for him, so don't let him talk you into giving him any." With a wink and a wave, she left.

Twenty minutes later, Sandy and Jesse were sitting on the Morelli stoop. The air outside was foggy and warm. The streets were littered with debris, deserted except for her and Jesse, and of course, Mr. Morelli.

Mr. Morelli's hand shook as he lowered the cup of orange juice from his lips.

"Can you put a shot in it?" he asked in a hoarse whisper that reminded Sandy of Marlon Brando in The Godfather.

"I don't think you're allowed to have alcohol, Mr. Morelli," Sandy yelled in a voice people reserve for the elderly or feebleminded. "It's not even lunchtime yet."

She made a big show of pointing to her watch before turning her attention to her son. Jesse was in his glory trundling up and down the Morelli ramp.

The Morelli house, a bleached white cement cottage with its four-by-ten-foot cement stoop stuck on the front, was almost identical to Sandy's house next door. The only difference was a newly constructed wooden ramp on the Morelli house that led to the sidewalk.

"Danny must have had a busy spring," Sandy said aloud but to herself.

"Danny don't do nothing for me." The old man lurched around in his wheelchair to face Sandy. "Nobody does nothing for me. They wish I was dead." His head swung uncontrollably in an arc along his chest before he was able to bounce it back up to stare challenging at her.

Sandy had grown up watching the Parkinson's disease gradually claim more and more of the old man's body. As a teenager, she'd performed a great imitation of his walk: hands straight at his side, head and torso in a straight line that leaned toward the ground, feet managing only short shuffling steps as they tried desperately to catch up with the rest of his body. He was like a penguin with a pole stuck up its back, and 'Sandy's imitation had sent her friends into fits of laughter. It wasn't until she was an adult that she became aware of the cruelty of the disease.

"Maybe I'd better lock that brake into place so you won't fall off the porch," she told him as she patted his shoulder and shifted the brake into the lock position. "How's that?"

How's about putting a shot in it?" he answered gruffly, pointing his cup toward her.

Knowing there was no way she could satisfactorily answer that question, she ignored it. She turned her attention, instead, to the street. A group of men had gathered around the Volkswagen entangled by wires. From her vantage point a half block away, it looked as if they were trying to dismantle the car. Catching a glimpse of red hair in the group, she swung down the ramp and walked a few steps toward them.

"Mommy go bye-bye?" Jesse followed after her.

Straining to see, Sandy could barely make out the red-haired cop that had let her cross the bridge three days ago. He seemed to be lifting sheet-covered objects out of the car.

"Go bye-bye?" Jesse asked again as he slid his hand into hers.

"Sure wish we could," Sandy answered him. She glanced back at Mr. Morelli on the porch and saw a look of discomfort on his face.

"I gotta go," he informed her.

"What? Hold on, I'm coming," she yelled as she ran back to the porch. A foul stench greeted her return and a dark stain covered the lap of his baggy. brown pants. A glint of smug satisfaction filled the old man's eyes.

"Gonna put a shot in it?" he asked again, holding out his cup.

Sandy stared down at the wobbly, bald head and gray whisker-stubbled face. She knew she should feel sorry for him. A useless, crumbling body with a mind, despite its repetitive demands, still aware of its own helplessness. But all she could do was say a silent prayer for Mrs. Morelli's swift return. Mr. Morelli bobbed his head up to glare at her as if he could read her mind.

"If you're not going to put a shot in it, I can get it for myself," he spat. He began to lift himself out of his chair.

"But the doctor said—"

"That doctor don't know nothing!"

Mr. Morelli wedged himself between the wheelchair and the porch railing. His body teetered under the strain of lifting himself out of the chair.

"What's one shot gonna hurt?" he asked gruffly.

The foul odor was starting to gag her. "Okay, you win," she sighed. "But just where am I supposed to get this booze? Mrs. Morelli doesn't keep any in the house."

"Doesn't your father have some homemade wine stored in the shed out back?"

"You fox," Sandy teased him. "I think maybe you're not half as sick as everyone thinks."

Sandy helped him lower himself back into his wheelchair. "Now don't move and I'll run to the shed and get it for you."

Jesse was intently lining up stones along the ramp's edge. Sandy patted him on the head. "Be a good boy and stay right here till I come back," she told him.

She hurried down the alley to the shed. The wine was under the stored beach chairs. She hefted the heavy jug under her arm and turned to go. Then she noticed the shower door adjacent to the shed. The block of wood that kept the door closed was horizontal and the door was slightly ajar.

Sandy's nose twitched. There was a stale, rancid odor in the air that reminded her of a dead mouse her mother had once removed from a heating vent. The smell made her feel that hair was growing inside her throat.

Sandy swallowed hard and moved to close the door. She pushed and felt a soft squish. Something was blocking the door!

The hair-inside-her-throat feeling grew stronger. Her mouth was pasty dry. She bit down hard on her lower lip and swung the door open wide.

The three-foot-square shower was empty except for a pile of laundry in the farthest corner. This was no strange sight. Often in the summer, wet bathing suits and towels would be piled in a corner before Sandy's mom could gather them up for the daily wash.

Sandy sighed and turned to go. Then her eyes moved to the object that prevented the door from closing. It was a soggy red shoe.

Sandy's heart nearly leapt out of her chest. The fuzzy ball in her throat refused to be swallowed.

It can't be the same one, her mind screamed.

Almost in slow motion, she leaned against the shower door for support.

Suddenly a hand whipped out and locked itself around Sandy's ankle.

The laundry came to life.

Sandy's screams of surprise escalated to screams of horror.

A crumpled body coiled like a snake. It hissed at her through black tangled hair. It dragged her into the shower.

Screaming, Sandy flung out her arms and fell into the shower. She scratched at the shower walls in a futile effort to pull away from the creature.

The door slammed shut. Eyes of tortured pain stared at her. With her free leg, she thrashed out at the creature; the hold on her ankle tightened.

Someone started knocking on the shower door.

Her screams receded to a whimper.

The knocking grew louder.

Why didn't someone save her?

Another hand flung out from the creature and clawed the air, reaching for her.

The knocking accelerated to a frenzied rhythm.

Sandy looked frantically toward the shower door and realized that no one was outside. The knocking she heard was the pounding of her heart.

The creature's hand entwined itself around her other foot.

Sandy felt the walls of the shower closing in on her. She gasped for air and started hyperventilating. She had forgotten how to breathe.

Her eyes searched frantically for a weapon and landed on the jug of wine. In the course of her struggle, the jug had been dropped to the shower floor. Somehow, it had rolled next to the creature. Sandy took two deep breaths to calm herself, then dived forward toward the creature. Her hands quickly closed around the jug and brought it slamming into the creature's face. The bottle shattered on impact. Splinters of glass sliced into the creature's eyes. Howls of a wounded animal reverberated against the walls of the shower.

The grip on her ankles loosened. Sandy continued her attack. She picked up a piece of broken glass and slashed and cut at the hands that held her. The creature snatched its hands back and recoiled into a ball. It continued to howl. The sound was unholy, deafening.

Sandy was panting heavily. She looked down at her own hands and saw that they were gleaming with blood and wine. The broken piece of glass slipped to the floor. Slowly, she backed out of the shower and started to run.

When Jesse and Mr. Morelli saw Sandy scream down the block past them, they turned to look at each other quizzically.

"Why Mommy crying? What happen?" Jesse asked.

Mr. Morelli smacked his lips, "That wine must be powerful stuff," he explained to Jesse.

7.

Stafford didn't know that Sandy had run toward the beacon of his red hair. He only knew that the beautiful blonde he'd encountered over three days ago was magically in his arms. After the torturous days he had spent in the police station waiting for the rain to stop, he needed a fantasy come true.

Of course, the girl hadn't stopped screaming yet, and her arms were clasped so tightly around his neck that he was nearly suffocating. But, what the hell, he'd never demanded one hundred percent perfection from his fantasies in the past and he saw no reason to start now. He held on and let her cry.

Out of the comer of his eye, he watched his partner, Lenny, place another quivering body on the sidewalk. His pickup team could only manage nine or ten bodies at a time and his group had already amassed close to twenty sheet-covered stiffs. The corpses registered as sacks of potatoes in Stafford's hardened mind; he could no longer acknowledge them as fellow human beings. So, all morning he went about his work like a diligent dockworker unloading a ship. He unloaded the potatoes and set them out for someone else to take them away.

If a few of the potatoes were turning moldy and smelling rancid, he didn't even notice. He could even handle the "last gaspers" they uncovered, though it took a little effort. They gurgled unintelligible sounds, their obvious pain confining them to a primitive level of existence. Some clawed at him when he extracted them from cars, and spit on him when he tried to untangle them from wire mesh fences. Others growled and croaked when he tried to reassure them that they would soon receive medical assistance.

The blond fantasy in his arms sounded strangely unintelligible too as she cried and spoke at the same time. "R-r-red shoes... horrible, horrible," she stammered between heaving sobs.

"Take deep breaths," Stafford told her. He eased her arms from around his neck but kept his face close to hers. "Do you think you can do that?"

She nodded slowly, raising her head to meet the deep gaze of his blue eyes. They sparkled as she filled her lungs and held the air, then exhaled evenly, still pressed into his hard body.

"I kn-know all about deep breaths," she finally whispered. "They help you relax and get in tune with the rest of your body." She swallowed the last of her sobs and looked away. "I'm... I was an actress, once."

"That's wonderful." Stafford liked the smell of her breath on his face. It made him think of freshly washed white sheets that had been hung to dry outside on a warm, spring day.

Sandy's hysteria had disappeared, yet she lingered for a moment in the warmth of their instant intimacy. But she broke away quickly and took two cautious steps away from him. "But what does this have to do with that... thing, in my shower?"

"Guess we found another one," Stafford called over his shoulder to Lenny. "Can you hand me a sheet, Buddy?"

Lenny threw a sheet at him. "Need any help?" Lenny asked with a smirk curling his lips.

"I think I can handle it," Stafford assured him. He led Sandy down the street.

Sandy was surprised when she realized how quickly the cop had calmed her nerves. He had not, however, calmed her enough to heed Mr. Morelli's grumbling demands that she return to the shed and fetch the wine for him. She wouldn't go near that damned shower again if an entire police force accompanied her. But she was calm enough to reflect on that small glow of interest that had unexpectedly flickered for an instant inside of her when the cop held her. It was ridiculous, she chided herself. Nevertheless, when Stafford came out of the alley, she kept her eyes on his face. And it wasn't entirely to keep from looking at the sheeted body he carried in his arms.

He had an incredible face—clear, almost translucent skin, wide-open, innocent blue eyes beneath golden-red eyebrows, and a small upturned nose. His mouth, she suspected, often slipped into easy smiles. But it was his shocking red hair, neatly parted on one side, that perfectly framed his face. It held the innocence of a loving little boy, she decided, or a Moonie selling flowers in a shopping mall.

The face seemed incongruous to the rest of his body, like one of those mix-and-match books kids enjoy. Jesse had a Sesame Street one at home. Flip the pages and you could put Cookie Monster's head on Big Bird's torso and complete the picture with Kermit the Frog's legs.

The policeman's body didn't have the girth of Big Bird's, but he didn't appear to have been raised on a bird seed diet, either. Sandy recalled a line from *The Women*, one of her favorite movie classics: "You got to watch out for those big red-haired men."

"Definitely not my type," Sandy told herself.

Stafford, relieved of his load, walked back toward the porch. He flashed a warm smile at her. Again, Sandy felt a ridiculous interior flickering.

He's not my type, but he's not bad, she thought. Aloud she said, "This is the second time you've come to my rescue. I hope I can count on you for my next two catastrophes."

He glanced at Jesse. "How is your little boy feeling?" *He remembers me*, her mind whispered. "He's fine now," she said.

"And you and your parents?"

Sandy blushed. "Actually, my parents aren't here."

Stafford grinned.

"But I'm fine," she added, "except, of course, for being totally confused about everything that's happening around here."

"You're not the only one." Stafford leaned heavily against the railing of the porch. "I've been picking up bodies all morning. Hundreds of bodies. Some dead. Some worse than dead—they're in so much pain."

"But dead from what?"

Stafford ran his fingers through his thick red hair. "From the damn rain, is the best anyone can figure. Soon as the rain started, the switchboard at the station jammed with calls from people in pain. They all claimed it was the rain on their skin."

"The telephones were working?"

"At first. About an hour later, when the lines went down, the calls stopped, and so did everything else. Police cars and anything with an engine broke down. Couple of cops had walkie talkies that worked for a while. They called in to report that hundreds of people were hysterical in the streets with no shelter and no place to go. Captain had us barricade the doors at the station till we could figure out what to do. The Sea Breeze Bridge caught fire, stuck in the raised position, but there was no way to get the fire trucks to the bridge. We were all so helpless."

"That's horrible." Sandy felt too stunned to ask any more questions. She and Stafford lapsed into a conscious silence. Only then did she notice the elderly lady running frantically toward them. Mrs. Morelli stopped a few feet from the porch. Her eyes darted from Sandy's face to Stafford's.

"My Danny," she said. "He's here to tell me my Danny's dead."

"No," Sandy reassured her. "He's here visiting me. We don't know anything at all about Danny. Couldn't you find him?"

Mrs. Morelli sighed with relief as well as exhaustion. "Sandy, I've searched everywhere for him. Nobody's seen him since he was at the armory fixing the roof."

"Did you go to the armory?"

"Yes. It's in ruins," she cried, "destroyed by the storm."

Sandy looked to Stafford for an explanation, but the cop kept his eyes to the ground. She turned back to Mrs. Morelli. "But what about all the people sheltered there?"

"I don't know. Maybe they're all over on Ocean Boulevard," Mrs. Morelli answered, referring to the main street that stretched across the island. "There are mobs of people blocking the entrances to restaurants and stores. Some are screaming for them to open. Some are fighting for a better position. And some are like me." She brought her rumpled handkerchief to her eyes. "Looking for family."

Sandy glanced anxiously at Jesse, still playing contentedly with his sea shell and rock constructions. In that instant, she knew the anguish she'd feel if her son were missing.

"Did you try the police station? Don't they know anything?" Sandy asked.

Mrs. Morelli shook her head and faced Stafford accusingly. "The police station is barricaded, and the mobs outside the station are as confused as I am. The police are only interested in volunteers. They refuse to give anyone any information."

"I'm sorry, ma'am," Stafford finally spoke. He shuffled his feet uncomfortably. "We haven't had time to compile a list of names."

"What names? I don't want names. I want to know where I can find my boy."

"Was he outside after it started raining?" Stafford asked.

"Yes, I think so."

Stafford and Sandy exchanged looks.

"Anyone touched by the rain is being given medical attention for injuries," he said gently.

"Injuries from the rain?"

Sandy went to Mrs. Morelli and put her arm around her shoulders. "Where are they being treated?" she asked Stafford.

"Doctor Jenkins has temporarily set up on the beach," he answered.

"Outside? I don't believe it," Mrs. Morelli cried. She began to walk toward the beach.

"Wait." Sandy ran after her. "I know how worried you arc, but you're in no condition to walk anymore today."

"But Danny might need help."

"He doesn't need you to kill yourself. Now you stay here, catch your breath, and I'll go take a look for you."

"Sandy, I've imposed on you too much already today."

"So now I'll impose on you," Sandy assured her. "Jesse needs his diaper changed, and so does his buddy on the porch." She gestured in Mr. Morelli's direction. "Meanwhile, I promise you, I'll do my best to find Danny."

Before Mrs. Morelli could object, she turned to Stafford and said, "What do you say, Red? Would you care for a stroll on the beach?"

"Well, I'm supposed to..." Stafford began. "Oh, what the hell, let's go."

After Mrs. Morelli's description of the main street on the island, Sandy was surprised to find the boardwalk relatively quiet. Broken benches jutted awkwardly through collapsed portions of wooden planks. The wire mesh fencing that prevented scoffers from gaining free access to the beach was twisted out of place in many sections. High mounds of sand, blown against amusement stands, turned them into eerie sand dunes. Each street opening onto the boardwalk also led to an opening to the beach three feet below the boardwalk. These openings were now blocked by armed guards. Sandy stopped in her tracks and stared at the guards in amazement.

"Now I know why there weren't any cops controlling the mobs Mrs. Morelli mentioned. Is this why you need volunteers?"

"This is just standard procedure."

"Standard procedure for what?"

"I didn't want to say anything in front of your friend back there, but these guards are here for our protection."

"I don't understand."

Stafford waved a greeting to two guards he called Mario and Donaldson, who carried a quivering, sheeted body toward the opening to the beach. Then he turned back to Sandy.

"Look, we don't know what was in the rain that made people as sick as they are. It could be highly contagious. In which case, the safest thing for everyone concerned is to keep the sick quarantined."

Sandy remembered the horror of those clawlike hands clasped around her ankle. She shivered.

"But it... she touched me," she whispered. "So what you're saying is I'll probably get sick, too."

Stafford pulled her over to one of the few remaining unbroken benches. He took both of her tiny hands and held them in his own rough ones.

"I doubt it," he assured her. "Captain Cruthers is a stickler for going by the book. Unfortunately, there's no book written for this kind of situation, so the captain is trying to establish some order, some priorities. And the first priority is to quarantine victims of an unknown disease and provide medical care."

Sandy stood up and for the first time peered through the wire mesh fence to the beach. She gasped at what she saw.

The beach was alive with worms—writhing, slithering human worms. They twisted and coiled in agony on makeshift beds of blankets and sheets tossed on the beach. As Sandy watched, Mario and Donaldson dumped their sheeted bundle into the sand. They didn't bother to unwrap the squirming person inside, before they tramped back to the boardwalk.

"This is what you call medical treatment?" Somehow the grotesqueness of the scene was overshadowed by the inhumane treatment of the victims.

Sandy stared openmouthed at the spectacle, silent for a few minutes before she added, "But who am I to talk? I wasn't exactly overflowing with sympathy earlier today. I'm ashamed of myself."

"You were frightened?"

"Yes, I was, but it's still no excuse. Thank God Mrs. Morelli didn't come up here."

Sandy headed for the nearest opening to the beach. A guard quickly barred her way.

"Let me through," she said.

Stafford came from behind, took her arm, and signaled the guard to let her pass.

"This is crazy. Two minutes ago, you were scared to death of catching something," he told her as they went down the ramp to the beach.

Sandy's steps were slowed by the heaviness of the sand beneath her shoes but she didn't pause until she approached the first "patient."

"It's too late now," she told Stafford, "I've already been contaminated, remember?"

She stooped down and looked into an aching face with brown pools of pain for eyes staring back at her.

Spittle drooled from the corners of a cracked mouth. Hands, clenched in agony, pounded the sand.

It wasn't Danny. Sandy brushed her hand against a forehead in a gesture of comfort before rising to go.

Stafford tried to stop her. "You can't look at everyone. There are thousands of people here."

"Yeah, all receiving medical treatment. Where are the doctors? Taking a coffee break?" She stepped carefully around the twisted bodies and fought the rise of bile in her throat as she examined each contorted face. Refusing to let Stafford see her fear and distaste, she straightened a blanket or smoothed tangled hair. She was constantly on the alert for any sign of Danny.

Stafford struggled to keep up with her. A hooked finger attached itself like a tick, to the cuff of his pants. "It's dangerous out here," he told her after he smacked the fingers away. "Remember what happened to you in that shower?"

Sandy turned over the face of a husky brown-haired man. He felt snakeskin cold. "I think this one's dead." Stafford bent down and felt for a pulse in the man's neck. Then he covered the corpse's face with the sheet that had been beneath him.

"Are you through now?" he asked her.

Sandy felt close to fainting but refused to show it. "No. I made a promise to Mrs. Morelli."

"And you'll keep it. You can come back tomorrow. Lord knows, they need volunteers to help out."

"And I've seen them at work," she told him. A mewling at her feet made her move quickly to the left, only to step accidentally on a partially concealed arm. Howls of torment nearly sent her falling to the ground.

Stafford moved quickly to help her but Sandy waved him back. She righted herself and continued to wade through the sea of sufferers.

"You know, I've never met a woman quite like you. You sure must be a handful to your husband."

"I've been a widow for over a year now."

"That's great." Stafford smiled and then paled when he realized how that must have sounded. "I mean, I'm sorry to hear that. Oh, hell, you know what I mean."

"Do I?" Sandy continued ahead of him.

"I thought... I mean," he stammered. "Well, it could have been under a hell of a lot better circumstances, but maybe it's a good thing we met. Of course, we haven't really met," he continued to babble. "I mean, do you realize I don't even know your name?"

Sandy wiped sand off another face in agony. "That is amazing," she told him offhandedly. There was still no sign of Danny. She had to continue searching.

"Well, mine is Jeremiah Stafford, but everyone just calls me Stafford or Red." He reached out and shook her hand. "And what's yours?"

"Cassandra Galotti," she said feeling foolish, "but everybody calls me Sandy or Cassie. So now that we've formally introduced ourselves, shall we press on?"

The face of anguish Sandy had examined suddenly reared upright with a spasm of pain. Sandy jumped back in shock and caught her foot on a jagged sea shell. She went reeling to the ground, landing face-to-face on top of a mass of squirming flesh. A fetid stench filled her nostrils. Before she could move, legs and arms whipped a bear hug hold on her body.

Stafford reacted instantly. Unable to pry the arms and legs from their death grip around her body, he slammed his fist hard into a forehead. The creature went limp.

Once free, Sandy scrambled into Stafford's arms and it was a replay of their earlier meeting. Stafford carried her across the beach and set her down on the ramp to the boardwalk.

"Now, Sandy or Cassie, I hope you understand why the guards are necessary and why you should forget the whole thing. Mrs. Morelli will understand."

Sandy stood there shaking. Her eyes were wide, startled.

"I-I'm okay," she stammered. "I d-didn't scream this time. I could have handled it."

Stafford walked her back to her beach house. "If that means you're going back tomorrow, you're insane. Come to think of it, maybe I'm the crazy one. After all... His voice trailed on.

Sandy didn't know why she felt so comforted by the down home quality of his speech, or why she felt so compelled to prove something to him. Maybe it was that tingling, that spark of interest, that had so unexpectedly flared inside her after lying dormant for many years. Was that why she'd told him about her other nickname? Why had she mentioned it? It had been a very long time since anyone had called her Cassie.

8.

assie, help me! Mason's mind screamed the words his mouth and lips couldn't form.

He attempted to raise himself up, but his legs buckled and his head jerked spastically when he moved it. His body refused to follow his brain's instructions.

Cassie, I'm over here!

He ordered his mind to concentrate, directing all his energy on gaining control of his movements.

Finally, his arm lifted and waved limply in the air.

It was too late. She didn't see the wave. She didn't rush to his side.

Mason's arm collapsed. Pain washed over him. He opened his mouth to call her name, but only a high-pitched moan came out.

Cassie, don't leave me!

Mason beat the sand in frustration. Why hadn't she noticed him? She should have felt his presence, sensed his need for her.

Maybe it wasn't her. Maybe—a hollowness he couldn't fathom opened inside him—maybe he was hallucinating again.

Right after it stopped raining, he'd been positive he'd seen the worn handles of the medical bag sticking out of the sand. After painstaking minutes twisting his body closer to them, they'd vanished, only to reappear again in the opposite direction. Mason had inched his way toward them once more. Again, they'd disappeared. Now they were less than two yards from his feet, laughing at him, taunting him to jerk himself around and try to catch them.

He salivated at the thought of those pills. Valium, codeine, meptazinal, methadone, morphine — who knew what delicious things old Nurse Dawkins had thrown into the bag. Mason only knew he'd never needed them more.

As if to verify this, the pain flashed through his body, sending tendrils of flame from the tips of his hair to the pit of his stomach. Mason jackknifed in response. He was going to lose control again. His legs kicked out and hit something hard.

Son of a bitch. His toe felt like it had shattered into a million pieces. Then the thing he kicked flopped over and kicked back at him. It was a huge hulk of a man, black crew-cut hair, mean, squinty black eyes, and a faded dragon tattooed on a beefy arm.

Mason met the attack. He kicked back savagely and made direct contact to the groin. The man bellowed.

Mason felt power surge through him. He was going to be okay. With deep satisfaction, he watched the beaten man flip-flop back, away from him. The sand settled.

Pain still flowed in rivers over him. But he was wading through it now, dog-paddling, so to speak, on top of it. He arched his neck to look for the handles of the medicine bag. They were still there, two black arches, beckoning him to try his luck for the pot of gold beneath them.

Mason took a deep breath and began to slide his way toward them. He refused to hurry. His hands and feet obeyed his directions and pushed his body closer and closer.

The pain caused by his movements was dizzying.

For a moment, his eyesight blurred. The handles disappeared again, and then something clicked in his head and his hands closed around the smooth, well-worn leather. With a convulsive jerk, he pulled his body to them. After a short rest to catch his breath, he began digging.

Later Mason unscrewed a pill bottle. He put a handful of pills in his mouth and hid a soggy doctor's bag under his body. Soon sweet daydreams played on his mind.

Cassie, my love.

Next time she came to the beach looking for him, he'd be ready for her. And nothing, no power in heaven or earth, would keep them apart again.

9.

"Is that Doctor Jenkins?"

Sandy posed the question to Sal, a pug-nosed guard who was leaning on his rifle while he munched an apple. Sal followed her pointing finger and looked at the tall, hunch-shouldered man standing a block down the boardwalk. The man wore a white smock and was intently writing on a clipboard.

"Yup, that's him," Sal answered, "but what you asking for?" He wiped dripping apple juice from his mouth onto the sleeve of his defeated-looking uniform.

"Volunteer work," Sandy stated, somewhat timidly. It had taken two days for Sandy to work up her courage to come back to the beach area. Even now, she resisted looking at the victims on the beach. Like a first time sky diver refusing to look down, she restricted her field of vision to eye level or higher. Soon, she knew, she'd have to jump, and then it would be too late to change her mind and run back home.

The guard noticed her nervousness and smirked. "Hey, Missy, you sure you gonna be able to handle volunteer work?"

Sandy treated him to a long, if-looks-could-kill, Bette Davis stare. "I beg your pardon."

The guard stopped wiping and chewing and blasted out a laugh. "Honey, you may feel like Florence Nightingale, but you're not dealing with human beings down there."

"What are you talking about?"

"I mean" — he leaned closer to her — "these things are turning uglier every day."

"Uglier?"

"Shoo. It was bad enough yesterday when they was wiggling around like snakes in acid."

"Did it ever occur to you that they were probably in a great deal of pain?"

"No shit." He removed a piece of apple core caught in his teeth. "But now they look eaten-up, chewed-on. Hell, lady, take a look for yourself."

He stepped out of the way and shoved her against the boardwalk railing. Sandy had no choice but to look down at the beach.

Her first impression was of stillness. The bodies were no longer jerking or writhing. Most victims lay flat on the sand, but a few were sitting, heads hung low, on blankets and sheets.

Sandy realized she had been holding her breath, and let out the air in a great sigh of relief. It's not so horrible, she told herself. It certainly was a big improvement from the last time she'd seen them.

Then the patient nearest the boardwalk turned slowly, almost in slow motion, to look up at her. Sandy froze. Her hand flew involuntarily to her throat. The face was crawling with sores—yellow pus sores, sores on top of sores, sores that distorted and ballooned different parts of his face. They covered every inch of skin, except for patches around the slits of eyes, nostrils, and mouth.

Sandy's mouth formed a wide "O" of astonishment. For several seconds, she remained paralyzed, unable to turn away from the creature facing her. Then she watched it open one of its slits and spew vomit in long, yellow streams up toward her. Sandy jumped back and collided with the apple-munching guard.

"Whoa there, little lady," he said, laughing. "There's no way that old boy can reach you up here."

"You mean he was aiming for me?" Sandy asked, trembling but attempting to regain her composure.

"Beats me." He shrugged, and taking aim, he pitched the apple core at the vomiter. "Bull's eye!" he yelled gleefully.

Sandy watched in horror and then with pity as the creature wailed softly before it crawled slowly, farther down the beach. Other heads turned toward her, faces also covered with sores. Pustule-covered hands stretched out to her for help.

"So, whatta ya say, lady, still want to play Florence Nightingale?" The guard leaned back against his rifle, enjoying Sandy's obvious struggle to stay or run.

"You're all heart," Sandy told him as she started walking toward Dr. Jenkins.

"Shit. They're dropping like flies, anyway," he yelled back to her. Reaching into his pocket, he pulled out another apple and bit into it.

Five minutes later, Sandy knew her role would be nothing like Florence Nightingale's.

"...and you'll find the water and cups in the supply area set up in the lifeguard station," Dr. Jenkins explained.

"In other words," Sandy said, "you want me to be a water girl, like in a football game."

Dr. Jenkins looked at her thoughtfully. "I guess you could look at it like that," he said.

"But, Doctor Jenkins," Sandy said, "I thought I could hand out some pills or distribute ointments."

"I'm sorry," the weary Dr. Jenkins interrupted, "I wish I had time to explain the situation more thoroughly to you. At present, our drug supply is extremely limited. Until help reaches us from the outside, we're helpless to do more than provide the barest necessities."

"When is this help coming?" Sandy asked.

Dr. Jenkins tapped a pencil on his clipboard. "That's up to the authorities," he told her. "Last I heard, a medical ship was on its way here before the storm hit. Now, if you have any other questions, please ask one of the other volunteers." He motioned for a longhaired volunteer on the beach to join them.

"But you still haven't told me what this disease is, or how the rain caused it, or… or if it's contagious… or anything."

Sandy felt an elbow in her side. "Come on," the volunteer with Lady Godiva hair told her. "You won't get any information out of him."

Sandy followed the girl's lead to the supply area. The girl seemed to be caught in a late '60s time warp with her long hair, Indian beaded blouse, and worn jeans.

"Hey, were you ever in the Peace Corps?" Sandy asked.

"No," the girl said as she turned around and smiled, "and I didn't go to Woodstock either."

Sandy laughed and the girl waited for her. "I'm Beth," she told her.

Sandy introduced herself and then asked, "Do you think Doctor Jenkins knows something he's not telling?"

Beth shook her long hair out of her eyes. "Listen, that old quack has problems treating sunburn. He hasn't the foggiest idea what's wrong with these people, and he's shaking in his sandals someone will find out."

"How do you know?"

"I've lived here on the island all my life. My old man was out making deliveries when the storm hit, which is why I volunteered."

They had reached the lifeguard supply station. Sandy opened the door for her. "Are you looking for him?" she asked.

"No, he's lying out on the sand about a block from here," Beth told her, "but they won't let me stay near him unless I volunteer."

Inside, other volunteers handed out supplies of food and water and assigned areas for distribution.

"What do you think it is?" Sandy asked Beth as they were ready to leave. "What's wrong with the people on the beach?"

Beth shrugged. "Could be an allergic reaction," she suggested, "or radiation poisoning, or maybe a new strain of leprosy."

"It's so creepy," said Sandy. "All these horrible sores. I've never seen anything like it, except maybe in a B horror movie."

"I'll tell you something that's even more creepy," Beth confided.

Sandy waited for her to continue.

"My old man swears the only ones dying are the ones with the mildest cases. The ones who look the worst are getting stronger and healthier every day."

While the guard continued to gnaw his apple, the man with the green-tattooed dragon, which now sprouted green scaly pus sores, slowly regained consciousness for the third time.

Mongril shook his head to dispel the drowsiness and tried to get up. Dizziness immediately overwhelmed him and he fell back hard on the sand. "Holy shit!" he said. "Where's the doctor? I don't feel so good." Mason eyed the big man contemptuously. "You don't look too good, either," he quipped.

Mongril's eyes slid sideways to look at Mason before his head followed suit. He scratched furiously at the caked sores on his elbow. His low IQ brain tried to place the stranger. "Hey," he asked groggily, "ain't you the fuckin' dude who kicked me?"

"That's me." Mason glared at him. "So what?" Mongril tried to stare Mason down, but was the first to turn and look away. "Well, why you want to do that to Mongril?" he asked in a hurt tone. "I'm fucking sick. I need a doctor."

"Quit your moaning about a doctor. Do you think anyone cares?"

"But I feel sick, man."

"So do the rest of the slobs on the beach. Look around you. So far we've been lucky to get a drink of water and some crackers to eat."

"I don't think I could eat anything, anyway," Mongril said, holding his stomach.

"Well, if you're gonna puke, could you at least not do it in my direction?"

"No problem," Mongril promised, but before he could bring his hand to his mouth, vomit erupted out of him like lava out of a volcano.

"Jesus Christ," Mason screamed.

Mongril wiped his mouth with the sheet under him. He offered it to Mason. Mason waved it away, disgusted.

Another bout of nausea overtook Mongril. "Oh, shit, I need some drugs. Call the doctor, man."

"I already told you. The only time the doctor comes over is when you're dead. Then they stack up the bodies like dead roaches in a whorehouse hallway." Mason pointed to an area about a quarter-mile down the beach. Mongril looked and saw stacks of white-covered objects piled high.

"Oh, shit," Mongril said, trembling. "I need a doctor, I need—"

"Okay," Mason yelled, crawling over to him. "Calm down. Maybe I can help you."

Mason glanced nervously from side to side before slipping two black capsules into Mongril's hand. "Swallow these and keep it quiet."

"But—"

"They're painkillers," Mason explained in a hushed voice. "In a few minutes you'll feel a hundred percent better."

Mongril gulped down the pills. "Hey, man, I don't hold no grudge about you kicking me. You're an okay dude."

"Right. Now shut your ugly face and let me get some rest."

"Ugly?" Mongril giggled. "Hey, buddy, you ain't no Mr. America yourself."

Mason's hands flew to his face. Bumps and crevices, met his touch. A sticky wetness rubbed off on his fingers. He looked at his hands and saw that they were covered with tumors.

It's not real, his mind whispered. *None of this is real.* Quickly he downed a handful of pills from the medical bag. He squeezed his eyes shut and lay back in the sand, wishing fervently for sleep. The nightmare would be gone when he awoke, and Cassie would be holding him in her arms.

Concentrating on his fantasy, he failed to see the blond volunteer that walked toward him. She carried a large thermos of water and bags of cups.

"Oh, wow, man," Mongril exclaimed, "I hope that's beer you're giving out."

"Just water," Sandy said softly. "Would you like some?"

"What the fuck," he told her, already beginning to feel the effects of the pills. "Give me a cup for my best friend here, too."

"Sure," she said. She glanced at his sleeping friend and paused. There was something familiar about him, Sandy thought. Could it be Danny? She tried to picture him without the sores. No, not Danny, she realized, but still, someone very, very familiar.

She was leaning over for a better look when someone called her name. Sandy turned and saw Stafford across the beach waving his arms. She shoved the cups and thermos at Mongril and ran.

"It's Danny. I found Danny and he's alive," Stafford yelled as soon as she reached the top of the boardwalk.

"You did? That's fantastic," Sandy yelled back. She ran into his arms and kissed him exuberantly.

Stafford returned the kiss more passionately. After a few minutes, he let her go.

"Hey," he said, eyeing her seductively, "do you think I'll get this reaction from Mrs. Morelli?"

Sandy laughed. "Let's go tell her and see."

"In a minute," he told her huskily. He pulled her back into his arms and kissed her again.

"Hey, man, what're ya staring at?" Mongril asked his friend. Even though the sores covering Mason's face made it impossible to read facial expressions, Mongril could tell that Mason was extremely upset. He was sitting rigid as a board. He had clenched his fists until his nails had torn open the pulp of his palms, and his eyes were tiny beads of blue steel.

"You checking out the chick with the water?" Mongril asked. "Sure is some piece of ass."

"Shut the fuck up," Mason hissed.

"No offense, man," Mongril apologized, hurt and confusion edging his voice. "Hey, where ya going?"

Mason stood, wobbling slightly, and watched the redheaded beast walking down the boardwalk with Cassie. "Watch my pills," he spat, turning slightly toward Mongril, "and I got every one of them counted, so if more than two or three are missing, I'll kick the holy shit out of you, understand?"

"No problem," Mongril promised. "But where you going?"

Mason ignored him and continued making his way across the sand.

"Hey!" Mongril called out after him. Then he dragged the black hag to his side and unzipped it. He selected one pill bottle, bit off the top, and dumped the contents into his mouth.

10.

"**G**od bless you," Mrs. Morelli cried when Stafford told her he'd located her son. She hugged him heartily and then embraced Sandy before the questions began.

"How is he? Is he all right? When can I see him? Why didn't he get in touch with—"

"How about you and I going over to see him right now?" Stafford interrupted.

"Could we?" She quickly untied her apron and looked around for her pocketbook. "Does he need anything? What can I bring him? Oh, dear," she exclaimed. She turned and looked at Sandy. "I forgot all about Mr. Morelli."

"I'll stay," Sandy assured her. Before Mrs. Morelli could protest, she continued, "and it's no imposition. When I need a baby sitter for Jesse, you'll more than pay me back." Sandy looked around the room. "By the way, where is my little monster?"

Mrs. Morelli smiled. "He and Mr. Morelli are both asleep in the back bedroom. Jesse was pretending to read a story from an old Reader's Digest and they both conked out on the bed. As a matter of fact," she added, "they're in the bedroom directly across the alley from yours, so if you leave your window open, you could hear Mr. Morelli from your own house."

"Are you sure?" Sandy asked. "I wouldn't mind staying here in the kitchen."

"Not necessary." She looked at her black-strapped wristwatch. "It's seven o'clock. It'll be dark soon and I know you and Jesse will be more comfortable in your own beds."

Mrs. Morelli clicked her pocketbook closed and walked to the front door.

Stafford put a gentle hand on Sandy's back as he moved closer to her. She felt the thread of excitement pulled taught inside her as she put her hand against his hard chest. He leaned down and whispered, "I'll stop over to see you on my way back."

"I'll be here," Sandy whispered back.

Stafford leaned forward to kiss her, and Sandy glanced around his shoulder at Mrs. Morelli patiently waiting half-in and half-out the front door.

"Shouldn't you hurry before it's too dark to spot him?" Sandy asked Stafford loudly.

"Oh, right." Stafford cleared his throat and hurried out with Mrs. Morelli.

Sandy watched them walk up the street. Mrs. Morelli's five foot frame was dwarfed by the burly redheaded cop. She had to take three steps for every one long stride of Stafford's. Slowing his gait to a crawl, Stafford bent down and hooked his arm with Mrs. Morelli's and gently led her toward the boardwalk.

Two hours later, Mason snapped awake. He had dragged himself to the top of the beach before pills and exhaustion precipitated a need for sleep. Now he was alert. His senses were aroused.

He eyed the guard on the boardwalk leaning on his rifle. "Hey, you," Mason called to him.

Sal squinted in the gathering dusk to make out the figure on the beach below him.

"You calling me?" he asked Mason.

"Yeah." Mason answered, "I'm thirsty. I need some water." He lifted himself to a standing position and began dragging his feet slowly forward.

"Whoa, boy." Sal lifted up his rifle and pointed it at him. "Now just you back up and settle down. There's no friggin' maid service around here. If you want something, you just wait till morning and them pretty little volunteers'll be passing out what you need."

Mason heard mumbling around him.

"We need to get off the goddamn beach," someone behind him shouted. "We ain't no sand crabs."

Other complaints followed. "I'm so hungry I could eat a sand crab," called yet another, and soon the entire beach echoed with shouts from the creatures.

A corroded apple core whizzed by Sal's left ear. He ducked and the beach erupted into laughter. "How about shutting the hell up?" he screamed. He cocked the hammer of his rifle and waved it toward various individuals on the beach.

The laughter died.

"Fuckin' freaks," Sal mumbled before lowering his rifle. He wiped his sweaty forehead with his sleeve and wondered how much longer it would be before he was finally relieved. It was getting so dark he could barely see his own hand.

The enveloping blackness, however, was no hindrance to Mason. His eyesight sharpened and he watched the beach coming alive, flowering, in the descending darkness.

Mason realized that he felt different. The pain had eased to a dull throb. Although his stiffened fingers and toes cracked loudly with every move he made, his head felt light and his mind was crystal clear. Thoughts drifted like helium balloons in the confines of his skull, attuned but detached from the rest of his body.

The guard on the boardwalk sensed the surge of power in the air. He reached for the homemade torch he'd been supplied with and lit a match to its gasoline-soaked rag top.

. While the guard's attention was diverted to lighting the torch, Mason saw his chance and dived under the boardwalk. Cement barriers and packed sand prevented an exit underneath the structure, but there was enough room for Mason to creep unnoticed directly under the berm. He looked through the cracks between wooden planks and positioned himself directly under the guard's feet.

Sal held his rifle in one hand, waved the lighted torch in the other, and leaned over the railing to check on the beach dwellers. Then he paced up and down.

He's keeping the monsters at bay, Mason thought. His mind drifted back to the red monster with Cassie. He suppressed a cry of despair that constricted his throat. Soon, he told himself, soothingly. He tensed his ragged body and waited for the guard to settle down.

Minutes that felt like hours later, Mason heard him angle the gun on the boards and lean heavily against it. Mason moved slowly, silently, under him. He shoved his fingers between a crack in the boards and pushed hard against the gun muzzle. The guard lost his balance and fell with a loud crash. The torch flew to the boardwalk.

Mason quickly scrambled up the ramp. He ignored the guard's surprised protests and went for the gun. So did the guard. Unable to wrestle it from him, Mason went for the torch and flung it high over the boardwalk railing. Then he scurried across the boardwalk, down the street to Cassie's house.

He heard shots behind him. The boardwalk creaked with the sounds of running feet. More shots sounded, but Mason ignored them. They couldn't touch him. He knew he was safe in the folds of darkness. He was camouflaged, as invisible as a panther against the night.

Soon he crouched under Cassie's window.

The panther was ready to pounce.

———

Sandy snipped an inch-long piece of string and centered it in a small bowl of olive oil. Deftly lighting the string with a match, she placed the homemade lamp on the table and stood back to admire her handiwork.

The tiny glow flickered, casting warm shadows on the walls. Sandy watched the reflected light dance on the bungalow windows. She peered outside and was surprised by the reflection of her own anxious expression.

I'm acting like a love-starved teenager from an Andy Hardy movie, she realized. *Forget about waiting for Stafford to come back. I couldn't care less why he's been gone for five hours*, she decided. To prove it to herself, she yanked down the shades and signed off for the evening.

Bowl of lighted oil in hand, she crept upstairs to check on Jesse, and found him sleeping like a curled-up puppy. She kissed his cheek and tucked the covers around him, and a tear rolled down her cheek. Every time she touched her child she realized how lucky she was to have him safe with her. Two years of her mother's blanderings paled against her overwhelming love for Jesse. With a last loving look, she turned away.

Back downstairs, she resisted looking out the window again. Instead, she quickly threw on one of her mother's white cotton shifts and went to the back bedroom.

Mr. Morelli's rhythmic snoring was audible through her open window. She yawned. Carefully, she blew out the oil and laid her head on her pillow.

Sleep wouldn't come. She rolled over, punched the pillow, and willed herself to sleep. Nothing. *Think about something calm and pleasant*, she told herself, *like waves breaking gently on the shore*. Then she remembered the sore-encrusted creatures on the beach, and her stomach turned.

No, no, she scolded herself, something soothing, like clouds floating lazily in a summer sky. But the clouds she imagined soon burst into rain and thunder, and she recalled the hellish storm that had split this nightmare from the sky.

Damn, I'll never get to sleep, she thought. She tried to steer her mind to memories of happier days.

She took a deep breath and was struck by a slightly mildewed scent that reminded her of a beautiful, battered old theater she'd performed in years ago. A flood of peaceful images washed over her—the feel of a crisp new script, the thrill of seeing her name on a cast list—and she smiled as she settled back into her bed of memory. She breathed in deeply again, then let it out in a slow sigh.

Suddenly she bolted upright. This was no memory. A foul, rancid smell engulfed her senses, and the smell was nothing at all like a theater. She sniffed the air again. It was the blast of smelly rotten meat when a neglected refrigerator is first opened.

Sandy moved to the window and thrust her head outside. The air in the alley was worse. Vile, gut-wrenching odors assaulted her. Hand over mouth and nostrils, she looked up and down the alley.

She saw the blackness. The slightest sliver of a moon had just disappeared behind the starless, cloudy curtain. She pulled her head back inside and dropped back on the bed. The smell was nauseating, sickening. She stared at the window, tempted to close it, but she hated to break her promise to Mrs. Morelli. What if Mr. Morelli called out? What if he needed help?

With a martyr's sigh, she pulled the sheet over her head and tried to block out the stench. I hate this room, she told herself. I hate this room, I hate this house, I hate the whole goddamned island. What can the smell be?

The putrid stench crept right through the sheet, up her nose, and down her tightening throat. It was worse than bad meat, or the dead mouse that had been trapped in the pipes. Worse than the smell in the shower...

Her body stiffened. Was it worse than the smell of the creature in the shower, she asked herself, or was it the same smell greatly intensified?

She strained her senses, alert for any movement, any sound. She could detect nothing but the raspy, snoring monotone of Mr. Morelli. She heard nothing else, except... She just barely caught a shuddering, a vague sighing, or shift in position from something outside the window. Then again she heard nothing.

Still under the sheet, her face dripped with perspiration and her hands were clammy. This can't be happening to me again, she told herself. I refuse to let myself be frightened again.

It was almost a relief when it finally came. Suddenly a door banged open. She heard footsteps inside the house.

"Who is it?" she yelled.

No one answered.

She threw the sheet off and stumbled to the dresser for the matches. In her haste, she knocked the bowl of oil to the floor.

The footsteps came closer to her bedroom door.

"Who's there?" she screamed.

She found the matches. Her hands trembled and she fumbled the first match she tried to light. She pulled out a second one.

Her bedroom door swung open.

Sandy's shaking hand finally lit the second match. She raised the small flame toward the open door—and Jesse stared back at her in the doorway.

"Jesse," she sighed, "why didn't you answer me?"

"Me wanna drink, Mommy," he told her, rubbing his eyes with his fists.

Sandy lit a candle and plopped down on the bed.

"What matter, Mommy?" Jesse asked. "What you doing?"

Sandy shook her head and laughed softly. "Nothing. Let's get that drink and put you back in bed."

After tucking him in, Sandy walked down the stairs and heard a soft knock at the door. She opened the door without hesitation.

It was Stafford.

"Well, you don't seem surprised to see me," he said.

"Believe me, your entrance is anticlimactic." She let him in and explained her earlier scare.

"You know, I don't like you living all alone here. And that's not just because it smells here. The whole island stinks of garbage and it can only get worse," he told her. "It's just not safe for a woman to live here alone." He looked down at his hands. "And not necessary," he continued. "I have a small place over the hoagie shop on

Ocean Boulevard. It's not much, but you and Jesse are more than welcome to move in with me."

"Is that a proposal or a proposition?"

Stafford looked up and stared blankly at her.

"Kidding, only kidding," she told him. She lit two more bowls of oil and sat down at the kitchen table.

"How is Mrs. Morelli?" she asked, changing the subject.

Stafford pointed emphatically as he joined her at the table. "That broad is one tough fucking cookie."

Sandy grinned. "What happened?"

"Danny didn't look too good," he explained. "He's lost hair and the sores cover most of his body."

"Was he conscious?"

"Oh, sure. He pleaded with his mother not to fret over him. He said he was feeling fantastic and his only complaint was that he was hungry. Mrs. Morelli insisted she was bringing him home with her."

"And?"

"Well, I tried my best, but they're not letting any of the sick leave the beach."

"So what did Mrs. Morelli do?" Sandy asked.

Stafford grinned. "She said if they wouldn't let him come home, she would camp out with him on the beach. And damned if she didn't."

Sandy shook her head in disbelief. "So she's staying on the beach?"

"Tonight, anyway. She told me to tell you that she'll be back to take care of Mr. Morelli in the morning. Just keep him in bed till she gets home."

"I'll try. Thanks for the message. But tell me..." She paused. "What took you so long to deliver it?"

Stafford looked at her seriously, and she sensed a strange coldness in his words. "Had a few beers with my buddies after a little target practice."

"Target practice?"

"Someone jumped Sal up on Kearney Avenue and we tried to catch the fella."

"You shot him?"

"Naw. I got a few shots off but it was too dark to see clearly."

Sandy looked aghast.

"You don't understand," Stafford said, "this is no weekend vacation crowd out there. People are starting to get ugly. The police have had to consolidate food supplies from the supermarket and local stores and post guards to protect them. Guns are at a premium. We haven't gotten motors or engines running yet. Radios and telephones aren't working, and people are getting itchy. Worst of all, there's no source of drinking water on the island. If we don't get help from the outside soon, there may be riots over canned tomato juice and Diet Coke."

"But when is help coming?" she asked softly.

Stafford heard the fear in her voice. He saw the tension in her eyes. "Soon," he told her, "but don't worry. Till then I want to make sure you're safe and have everything you need. Cops get special rations."

"I have enough. My mother always kept the cupboards fully stocked."

"Then maybe I could just make you feel safer." "How?"

Stafford leaned over and kissed her.

Sandy tasted the bitter beer on his lips and realized the meaning of his words. She pulled away from him. "Are you trying to bribe me into going to bed with you, Stafford?"

"What? You're not that kind of girl? Or is this a game of playing hard to get?"

Sandy stared at him, still smiling, but a look of disbelief crossed her face. "Don't you think your line is a little heavy-handed? If you want to go to bed with me, say so. You don't have to buy me. Besides, if I was for sale, I'd be worth a lot more than tomato juice and a can of Diet Coke."

Stafford's stoniness disappeared as he stammered, "I... I... didn't mean..."

Sandy smiled at his embarrassment. "What did you mean?" She stood up from the table, walked over to him, and ran her fingers playfully through his hair. "Why don't you come upstairs with me? I'll show you what I'll do for V-8 juice and a whole case of Diet Coke."

Stafford pushed her hands out of his hair. "Sandy, I'm concerned about your safety." He reached down, under his pants leg, and pulled out a small pug-nosed gun. He handled it like a precious sculpture. "This baby's a Colt .38." He swung out the cylinder barrel and showed it to her. "It's fully loaded, as you can see, and easy for a woman to handle."

Sandy pushed the gun away in horror. "Please, put it away. If I'd had a gun tonight, I might have killed my son."

Stafford looked hurt. He turned to go. "Fine. Okay. Forget I mentioned it."

"Now don't get mad," Sandy said. "It's nothing personal."

"Nothing personal just about sums up our entire relationship." He slipped the gun back neatly into his ankle holster.

Sandy yawned. "Well, that's not my fault."

Stafford walked to the door. "Since I'm obviously boring you, I guess it's time for me to leave. Maybe I still have time to shoot a few people on my way home." He slammed the door behind him.

"What happened?" Sandy asked the closed door. She'd wanted to sleep with him. He'd acted like he'd wanted to sleep with her. So what went wrong? Another loud yawn and she decided she was too tired to figure it out. Then she blew out the candle and groped her way back to bed.

There would be no problem getting to sleep now. Her eyelids were extremely heavy. The moment her head touched the pillow, her eyes closed, and she started to drift...

Hazily, she realized the stench in the room had gotten worse. The air hung heavily with its rankness. The floorboards under her bed reeked of it.

Tomorrow, gotta clean up the garbage, she thought fleetingly before sleep overcame her.

But the garbage had already climbed in from outside. And he was feeling quite happy beneath her bed.

11.

Lenny was slouched in the worn brown Lazy Boy recliner when Stafford entered his apartment. Candles were lit on the coffee table in front of him.

"Hey, Buddy, it's about time you showed up," Lenny greeted him.

Stafford stood in the doorway and watched his partner slurp Budweiser from the can. "Didn't know I was expecting company," he told him. "Why don't you help yourself to a beer?"

"Now why didn't I think of that?" He threw a can to Stafford.

Stafford caught the beer with one hand, yanked off the tab, and started guzzling. After dousing the can, he sat down heavily on the sofa bed.

"Nothing tastes worse than warm beer." Stafford grimaced. "Throw me another one."

Lenny pulled another can from the case of six-packs at his feet and flung it at Stafford. "Bad night?" he asked as he watched Stafford attack a second can.

Stafford swallowed hard. "I've had better," he answered.

"The blonde?" Lenny guessed.

"None of your goddamn business."

Lenny laughed. "Buddy, when are you going to learn? You've got to play the game. Don't come on straight. Keep the broads guessing."

"You don't know what the hell you're talking about."

"Shit I don't. You're always too serious when it comes to chicks—too direct. You've got to learn how to use a little hearts-and-flowers repartee or you'll keep getting shot down."

"Shut up and hand me another beer."

Lenny obliged and opened a can for himself. "Just giving you a little friendly advice."

"Thank you, Doctor Ruth. But tell me, since you're the expert, why is it you've been divorced three times?"

"That's experience."

Stafford leaned over to look his friend in the eye. "That's bullshit," he told him.

They both started laughing.

Stafford pushed his shoes off with help from the edge of the coffee table. He leaned back against the sofa bed and took a sip of beer. Gradually he felt the tension slip away and he relaxed.

Lenny always made him feel better. They'd been friends from day one of working together at the Sea Breeze Police Department. This was surprising only because their personalities were diametrically opposed. Stafford had traveled extensively through the Midwest with his widowed trucker father. He grew up without roots, easygoing, even-tempered, if occasionally slow to react. Lenny, on the other hand, came from a huge family planted in Queens. He was volatile, quick to jump, a screamer, and a self-proclaimed lady killer. Stafford's open face was in direct contrast to Lenny's sharp-featured, long and narrow one.

For similarities, both had a religious devotion to drinking beer, both were divorced, both were thirty-three years old, and most important, both had a restlessness, an outlook on life that kept them in their present jobs. It was a desire for non-responsibility, a marked absence of drive toward accumulating socially demanded goals like two-story houses and two-kid families.

"Any word from the mainland?" Stafford asked.

"Nope. Can't even get the ham radios to work."

"How about the boats? Captain said he was gonna send a few men across the bay."

"He did."

Stafford sat up. "He got the motors running?"

"No. The batteries are all dead, even the brand new ones at Al's Exxon. And nobody can figure that one out. Captain had Joe and Charlie row over this morning."

"What'd they find?"

Lenny took a long time to answer. "They never came back."

"What? It's only a mile away."

"He sent three more boats over there, volunteers—nobody we know—and gave them strict instructions to stay in the boats, look around, and row back."

"And?"

"Waited all day and nobody showed."

"It's impossible. Why didn't you use binoculars to keep them in sight?"

"We have binoculars, but the bay's covered with fog. Captain says he'll wait till it clears before he wastes any more boats."

"That sounds just like him, the bastard."

Lenny helped himself to another one of the beers. "But I got a better idea," Lenny told him.

Stafford waited.

"What I need is a rope, about a mile long. Then I'll tie it to one of those small rowboats, and presto! If the boat doesn't come back in an hour, we pull it back to the island and find out why."

"You're crazy. Who'd be dumb enough to go?"

"Me," Lenny answered.

He lay under her bed on his back, arms stretched out in an embrace, and closed his eyes. This was fulfillment. This was the pinnacle of his desires, his dreams, his quest, his being. Cassie was in his arms.

The slightest shift in her sleeping posture and Mason felt a corresponding pressure from the mattress on his body. If she turned her head, he could hear its rustle. She sighed, and he could hug the sigh to his breast. She slept, and her fragrance swirled in the air, intoxicating him.

He was separated from her by mattress and box spring, but what was a barrier of bedding compared to all that had kept them apart before?

Cassic rolled over and Mason raised himself up to meet the pressing of the bed. It was like making love to her. For a moment, they swayed together in rhythm. He was in ecstasy. The old linoleum beneath him disappeared. The bed evaporated. There were no red monsters, no parents, no police, no doctors to keep them apart. He closed his eyes and there was Cassie and there was he and there were their bodies becoming one, again.

Like the first time...

Mason and his parents had stood outside the Sea Breeze Island Theater handing out leaflets denouncing the current production of Jesus Christ Superstar.

His father delivered a searing sermon on the blasphemy of the play. When he was ignored, he stood in front of the ticket window refusing to allow patrons to purchase tickets. Soon the police arrived. In the scuffle that ensued, Mason ran into the theater, opened the first door he saw, and came face-to-face with Cassie.

She was playing Mary Magdalene, the female star of the show, and was not the least bit perturbed that he had stormed into her dressing room. Stuttering, he began his sermon. She listened. He raved. She smiled. He sputtered, forgetting what he was trying to say. She gently suggested he stay and watch the play.

Hours later, still mesmerized by her performance, he walked her home along the beach. They'd paused, staring out at the ocean, letting the waves tickle their toes. Then without words or awkwardness, they made love in the sand. And the hard shell that protected him cracked open.

———

The bed creaked above him and an arm dropped over the side. Mason moved to touch it, but stopped. He caressed the air around it, remembering how the hand had caressed him. He shivered with delight.

The room was silent, devoid of all sound but Cassie's soft breathing. Mason slithered his way out from under the bed and stood in the dark, bending over her.

Cassie's eyes were closed. Her brow wrinkled. Evil, evil, his mind had screamed. He was evil. He was forever damned. But he was loved. He would love her forever. She murmured something too low for Mason to decipher and rolled over on her back.

Mason gasped. Her body was luminous in the dark, so smooth, so pure. The sheets were hiked up and the cotton nightgown she wore was twisted around her hips. His Mary Magdalene was aglow on the cross, offering herself to him.

Mason felt himself grow hard. Soundlessly, he removed his clothes.

This is how it was meant to be, he told himself. *She'll awaken in my embrace. The years we've been apart will* be forgotten.

He moved to the foot of the bed and lowered himself down on her.

Sandy felt the touch of cold, clammy flesh, and her eyes shot open. She screamed—howled in protest. Leaden, noxious lips covered her mouth, sucking in her screams.

She pushed and clawed at a slimy head, tearing out skin and hair, but she couldn't get the thing off her. She kicked her feet. The abomination seemed to possess superhuman strength. She tried to twist her body free. It jammed her legs wide apart and slammed against her. With a guttural growl, it tore into her, between her legs, and began pumping and pumping.

She cried, tears of rage more than fear. It had happened too fast for her to be truly afraid. With all her strength, she tore at her attacker's face, feeling for the eyes. More skin came off in her hands. And still it continued pumping itself deeper and deeper inside of her. She gagged. Bile caught in her throat.

The creature's mouth remained glued over hers. She couldn't breathe. The smell of rotting corpses tilled her nostrils. The room was spinning. Her body was being ripped apart, but she couldn't feel the pain anymore. She could only hear the bed rocking and creaking.

On the edge of unconsciousness, her arms flailing hopelessly at him, it was suddenly over. The creature heaved with relief and was still. He lifted his bleeding mouth off hers and she tried to scream. Nothing came out but a hoarse shriek. Her flailing arms continued to pummel him. When his eyes made contact with her eyes, she stopped, and a new, totally alert fear filled her. She recognized him.

"Cassie, I'm back," he whispered to her.

12.

Stafford stood in the dark, holding a candle like Wee Willie Winkie, and watched Lenny tie the rope to the wooden pilings at the end of the pier.

"I really don't think this is a good idea," Stafford informed Lenny for the fifth time.

"Nothing to worry about," Lenny assured him. He yanked the rope, testing its strength. "These knots will hold. I wasn't a Boy Scout for nothing."

"You were never a Boy Scout," Stafford told him.

Lenny smiled. "Would I kid you?"

Stafford smirked.

"Hey, maybe I didn't help old ladies across the street, but I did earn a merit badge in knot-tying," Lenny said. "Almost made Beaver Patrol too, till I got kicked out. for stealing a Girl Scout's cookies." He winked.

Stafford sighed deeply. His free hand plowed nervously through his red hair, pushing it back, away from his face. "This is no time for jokes. We're talking life and death here. You told me yourself—nobody had come back."

Lenny lowered himself into the rowboat and tied the rope to one of the wooden planks that served as a seat. Carefully, he placed two lit candles near his feet. The dull glow reflected eerily in the foggy night, giving Lenny the look of a shadowy ghost out on a haunt.

Stafford heard the slap of the oars into the water.

"Lenny, listen to me! What if the tide changes and I'm not strong enough to pull you back?" he asked. "At least wait until morning till I get a couple of the boys together."

"Easy, Buddy. The water's so still you could pull an ocean liner across it single-handedly. Besides, I'm only going a short distance. If I get into any trouble, I'll have you to pull me back here."

"I shouldn't be letting you do this," Stafford said. He watched, frustrated, as Lenny braced his feet on the bottom of the boat, gripped the oars, and took a deep breath.

"Catch you later," Lenny said. He began to row.

Within seconds, the fog and darkness enveloped the boat and its passenger. Eventually, even the dim glow of the candles disappeared.

"Why?" Stafford, alone on the pier, yelled into the fog.

"Somebody's got to play hero," Lenny finally answered. His voice sounded faint and seemed to come from far away.

"Bullshit," Stafford yelled. "Don't you know there are no heroes. There's only jerks with a death wish that happen to be in the wrong place at the wrong time." Stafford paused. "Are you listening to me, Lenny?" He waited for an answer. "Lenny, answer me," he yelled.

The only sound he heard was the lapping of the water on the dock. He concentrated harder, trying to pick up the slap of the oars in the water, but there was only silence.

"Lenny! For God's sake, keep talking to me so I'll know you're okay."

No answer came.

"Lenny," he screamed, "if this is some kind of joke, I swear I'll kill you soon as I lay my hands on you."

Stafford walked quickly to the wooden pilings and held his candle down for a closer look at the rope. It was completely uncoiled, strung out across the water into the fog as far as he could see.

Stafford slammed his candle on the pier and grabbed hold of the rope. It resisted his efforts to pull on it, as if a giant force held it tight. Maybe he should jump in the water and follow the rope to where Lenny was stuck or maybe he should run back to the station for help.

He paced up and down the pier for several minutes trying to decide what to do.

"Lenny, you crazy son of a bitch, you moron," he cried. He yanked the rope hard again, felt it give a little, and continued to pull. Inch by inch, he gathered enough slack to wrap the rope around his waist and brace himself to the pilings.

"Easy as pulling a goddamned ocean liner, isn't that what you said, Lenny?" he cried out.

Sweat poured down his forehead. He spit into his hand, rubbed his palms together, and continued pulling in the boat.

———

Sandy squeezed her eyes tightly shut. She prayed that when she opened them, the nightmare would be over, her room empty.

Slowly, she raised her eyelids. She blinked. Her eyes adjusted gradually to the first hint of morning light filtering through the dark outside her window. She turned her head.

He was still lying beside her on the bed, staring at her, propped up on one elbow.

Sandy's stomach turned over.

Now that the room was growing lighter, the full impact of his grotesque condition hit her. Blood and pus dribbled down the sides of his head. Part of his earlobe hung raggedly by a thread. Crevices in his face where skin had been gorged out, and a swollen ulcer sore, where a cheekbone should have been, nearly disfigured him beyond human recognition. But Sandy knew him. One look into his eyes, and she remembered.

The name hissed in her mind: *Mason*. He had come back to plague her, only now his appearance matched the horror of the evil inside him.

Sandy's mouth opened to scream, but the scream remained choked inside her throat.

Mason moved toward her. "My Cassie," he said. With a blood-caked hand, he stroked her face.

Sandy cringed at the touch and shifted away from him, crowding the wall on her side of the bed.

"Cassie," he murmured. He pushed closer to her, bringing his face next to hers.

Sandy smelled his odious breath on her. She shuddered, and the shudder turned into uncontrollable shaking. *No more*, her mind screamed. *Please God, no more!*

"We've waited so long," he whispered. The dripping head bent to kiss her.

"No," she screamed. Finally able to break her paralysis, she shoved him away and scrambled over him. She hit the floor and crawled toward the door.

He lunged and was on top of her again. Her head was slammed into the floor.

Sandy cried. She knew from experience how easily he became violent. Violence was his whim, his pleasure, his addiction, and the enforcer of his reality. Ten years ago, he'd created a fantasy relationship between them. The wild, crazed eyes told her he still believed in it.

"Please, Mason, please let me go," she begged.

Daylight streamed in through the window, completely lighting the room.

Mason blinked. He turned his head toward the window, confusion evident in his contorted features. The pressure on Sandy lessened.

Sandy moved quickly. She untangled herself from his grasp and slid backward, toward the door.

Mason shook his head as if to clear it. He turned away from looking at the window and seemed surprised to find that she had moved. He made a swipe for her, and missed. "Wait, Cassie," he stammered.

Sandy backed into the door, turned, and clasped the doorknob. She pulled the door open. One step past the doorway, and she felt his fingers clutching her ankle.

"Cassie, wait," he stammered weakly.

Sandy yanked hard and kicked her ankle free. She raced through the bungalow to the front door and ran outside. Half a block down the deserted street, she stopped. A new panic consumed her.

"Oh, my God," she screamed out loud, "I left Jesse in there."

Mason dragged himself up, using the door for support. He wondered what was happening to him. Where was the strength he'd felt all night? His head throbbed with pain. His arms and legs felt rubbery and weak.

Where was Cassie?

He had to search the house for her.

Sandy looked frantically at the houses on the street. Mr. Morelli couldn't help her. Stafford lived too far away. There was no one else she could think of and no one in sight. She raced to the house closest to her and pounded on the door.

"Please hurry," she cried.

The door opened a crack.

"Help me," she begged, "I've—"

Eyes took in her torn bloodstained nightgown, her bruised face, and matted hair, and the door slammed shut in her face.

"No, you don't understand," she cried. She pounded on the door again and again.

It was no use, she realized, and she had no time.

Even now, Mason could be upstairs, his hands squeezing Jesse's neck.

With a scream of anguish, she ran back to the cottage.

Mason stumbled up the stairs, almost knocking the Budweiser mirrors off their hooks.

Why had she run from him? Why was she doing this to him?

At the top of the stairs, he opened a bedroom door. Inside, a sleeping boy lay in his crib, but Mason didn't even see him. He was drawn only to the *Jesus Christ Superstar* poster hanging on the wall. Cassie was nowhere in sight.

Mason clenched his fists. His eyes narrowed to slits. She had no right to do this to him, no right at all. After all he suffered for her, he'd have to make her realize she shouldn't tease him this way.

He would have to punish her.

With a piece of driftwood clutched in one hand, Sandy crouched in the alley and watched Mason limp down the street. When he was a safe distance away, she hurried into the cottage.

Her heart beat wildly. Her lips quivered as she picked her way past the mirrors on the stairway, which were now lying shattered and bloody on the floor. Sandy prayed the blood was Mason's.

She swooped into Jesse's room and pulled back the covers. Jesse was fine, breathing normally, oblivious to the horrors that had occurred so close to him. Trembling with relief, Sandy covered him again. It was then she noticed the shredded pieces of paper scattered on the blanket and the floor. She gathered a few pieces and examined them, turning them over and over in her hands.

Sandy started to laugh. They were the torn fragments of the *Jesus Christ Superstar* poster that had hung on the wall. One piece of paper was sticky with blood. She laughed harder and slumped to the floor. Tears ran down her cheeks as she laughed.

Jesse stirred in his sleep.

Sandy covered her mouth with her hands to muffle the noise she was making, and the laughter changed to sobs— deep, gulping sobs.

She crept to the farthest corner of the attic room and drew her legs up to her chest. She wrapped her arms around her legs, curled up in fetal position, and rocked back and forth as she continued to sob.

13.

Mrs. Morelli leaned wearily against the handrail as she climbed the ramp to her porch. A bone cracked. Her hand flew to her back, and she paused, puffing, before resuming her ascent.

"I'm home," she called out as she opened the front door. Uneasiness strained her welcoming smile.

Mr. Morelli struggled to raise his head, flushing crimson from the strain. His head bobbed up and down in her direction.

"Get me out of this bed," he said gruffly.

She moved to the bed and untangled the blanket twisted around him. His sheets and pajamas were drenched with urine.

"Oh, dear." Mrs. Morelli sighed. "Guess we'll have to change you first. Can you lift off these wet things?"

"Go to hell," he spat. "You never do nothing for me." He held his body stiff, resisting her efforts to move him. "I been in this bed for hours."

"I know and I'm so sorry, dear. But I've been with Danny. You remember how I told you I was going to see Danny. I stayed with him all night."

Mr. Morelli fish-eyed his wife suspiciously. While his attention was diverted, Mrs. Morelli yanked off his soiled clothes. Another bone in her back cracked. She winced, then resumed her morning ritual. She pulled out the extra-large Wipe 'Ems, talcum powder, and clean, blue-striped shorts.

"Tell Danny to get me out of this bed."

"I told you, dear," she explained as she changed him, "He's on the beach. Had some kind of reaction to the rain. Nothing for you to worry about. He was in great spirits last night. Said he never felt better. I had quite a time keeping him still, God bless him."

"Get me out of this bed," he ordered.

"I don't know why they won't let him off the beach," she continued as she bent down and struggled to pull her husband up to a standing position. "Danny should be home with us, where he belongs."

"Danny never did nothing for me." Mr. Morelli leaned heavily on her shoulders. She guided his shuffling feet to the wheelchair. "Nobody'd care if I dropped dead."

"Now I know you don't believe that, dear. You're just upset." She pushed his wheelchair into the kitchen and locked the brake into place. "Danny will come home soon. I'm sure of it."

"Laid in that bed for hours. Couldn't get up," he mumbled, "and couldn't sleep with all that goddamned noise."

"What noise?" Mrs. Morelli asked.

"That blond one..." He tried to gesture toward next door, but his arm slapped limply against the wheelchair. He smacked his lips. "The blonde next door with the wine."

"Sandy?" Mrs. Morelli asked.

"She wouldn't do nothing for me." His head nodded affirmatively up and down, rhythmically, as he spoke.

"That doesn't sound like Sandy. Maybe I should go over and see if something's wrong."

"Fry me a potato first. I'm hungry."

Mrs. Morelli dragged the camp stove to the window and lit a match. She looked outside at Sandy's house.

"Nobody does nothing for me," Mr. Morelli continued. "Where's Danny?"

———

"Mommy, what's matter?" Eyes still half-glazed from sleep, Jesse climbed out of his crib and waddled toward Sandy. He cupped his small hands under his mother's chin and tried to raise her head. "Why you crying, Mommy?"

Sandy uncurled herself and pulled her son close to her. She held him tight as she continued to cry.

"You scared, Mommy? You crying 'cause you scared? Me look out window for you. Okay?" Jesse scrambled out of her arms and pulled at the window shades. Hard as he tugged, the shade would only go down, until it hung a foot below the sill.

"Me fix," he informed her. He lifted the shade and ducked his head under it. Suddenly, with a snap, the shade whipped past his head, clanging loudly around its rollers.

Jesse jumped back, frightened by the noise. He scurried back to his mother, into the safety of her arms. Sandy smiled. "There now," she cooed. "My brave little man. What would I do without you?"

"No more crying? Right, Mommy?"

"Right," she answered. Then a new wave of tears overwhelmed her.

Jesse stroked her face, worry filling his pale blue eyes.

Sandy took his hand in hers and kissed it. "Mommy's a little crazy today. But don't worry," she explained, "Fearless Mom is here and everything will be all right soon. I promise."

Jesse looked unconvinced.

Sandy dabbed at her eyes. "Come on, let's go downstairs and have breakfast. Okay?"

"Yeah," Jesse answered. He bounded out of her arms and headed for the staircase.

With great effort, Sandy pulled herself up. Tears once again streamed down her face.

Her body felt cracked open, like a ripe melon. She half-expected to see her insides dumped on the floor—a glob of gelatinous fruit. But she looked down and saw nothing. Where was the blood? Where were the broken bones? She hobbled to the staircase. Glass from the mirrors littered the stairs, and she picked her way carefully through it.

"Jesse," she called, "stay away from the glass."

"Okay, Mommy."

She heard him rummaging in the cupboard for the cereal. In the refrigerator, still utilized for storage out of habit, she removed the jug of bottled water, poured some into a bowl for Jesse, added cereal, and carried the jug into the bathroom. After the door slammed shut behind her, her hands grasped hold of the sink for support.

She looked into the mirror and saw bruises—black and yellow-blue marks, some the size of thumb prints, some larger. The bruises were scattered up and down her arms and neck and on one side to her face. Her lips were cracked and swollen. Sandy surveyed, finally, the physical proof of her attack, and started shaking. She put her hands over her mouth, but the cries were impossible to muffle. *Dear God*, she wondered, *what am I going to do*?

"Mommy?" she heard from the other side of the bathroom door.

"Be... right there," she said between sobs. She poured water on a wash rag and scrubbed herself. Each new bruise threatened to bring on a fresh spasm of tears.

"Mommy, what you doing?"

Sandy swallowed hard. What was she doing? She stared at her reflection, at the bruised swollen lips, matted hair, blotchy skin, and very red eyes, and saw herself as the victim. Her stomach turned over. Very likely, it was a role she'd be forced to play again. Unless...

Sandy opened the mirrored medicine chest door and took out her makeup. The makeup covered all the bruises but the ones on her lips. It would have to do. One sure way to prevent a repeat performance was to change the script, add a new character. Sandy knew a redheaded cop who would suit the part perfectly.

The streets outside were entrenched with garbage. Fog and thick gray clouds blocked out the sun and held the vapors of raw sewage and decomposed food close to the ground.

Sandy wrinkled her nose as she and Jesse reached Ocean Boulevard. The main thoroughfare of the island was like a walk through a town dump. Broken furniture and half-burned cars smoldered in heaps at various intersections. Ripped-open trash bags spilled tin cans and fly-encrusted carcasses onto the sidewalks and streets. Paper was everywhere. Newspapers, toilet paper, even old insurance policies and canceled checks were strewn about. Jesse waded through the mounds of litter like a puppy in newly fallen snow.

"Jesse, please hurry. We've got to go see Stafford." Stafford, the name had such a calm, warming effect on her. Soon she'd be with Stafford, blissfully safe and secure in his powerful arms. She'd been a fool to turn him down. If she'd listened to him, Mason could never have hurt her.

On the next block, she saw a mob of people outside the Surf Side Bar and Grill. Determined, angry faces eyed her as she approached. She clutched Jesse's hand tightly as she passed them, and then barely moved to the side as a sun-bleached lifeguard type nearly collided with her.

"Hey," she called after him. "Can you tell me how far it is to the hoagie shop?"

The lifeguard type came to an abrupt stop and whirled around to face her.

"Are they opening for trade?" he asked expectantly.

"What?"

"Do you have any food or water for barter?"

"I don't know. I'm looking for a friend of mine. He has an apartment over the Hoagie Shop."

Disappointment swept across his sunburned face. He turned to go. "Three blocks down, on the corner," he yelled over his shoulder. He was already running to join the mob at the Surf Side.

Sandy pulled Jesse closer and continued walking. Exactly three blocks later, she saw the sign: *The Hungry Hoagie*. It was the only thing left intact. Shelves inside were empty. Glass panes, display cases, soda machines, counters—all were shattered beyond repair. *The Hungry Hoagie* didn't look hungry. It looked emaciated.

"What's matter, Mommy?"

Sandy smiled down at her son. "Just going a little crazy again." Around the comer, she spotted a side door. J. Stafford was engraved on a green metal strip beneath a rusted mailbox.

"Stafford?"

No answer. Up a narrow dull staircase and down a small stuffy hallway she found a door to knock on.

"Stafford, it's me, Sandy."

She tried the doorknob. It turned easily, but the door wouldn't budge.

"Nobody home, Mommy?"

"What are you talking about? Now who's crazy? Of course he's home." Sandy looked at her solemn-faced son outlined in the dim light, and struggled to keep her growing hysteria under control. She pounded on the door. "Stafford, please, please open the door." There was a grumbling sound in reply.

Sandy froze. "Did you hear something, Jesse?" Without waiting for an answer, she pounded on the door again. "Stafford, are you in there? I need your help."

She turned the doorknob and this time put her weight behind a determined push. The door flung open.

"Stafford?"

The room was darker than the hallway. It took seconds for Sandy's eyes to adjust. The first thing she focused on was a coat rack, sagging with jackets and sweaters, standing sentry near the door. Boots and shoes were clustered on a yellowed piece of newspaper.

Sandy's eyes gradually grew accustomed to the dim light and she could make out beer cans, overflowing ashtrays, and familiar-looking gun holster littering a coffee table. Then she espied two stockinged feet propped up in the middle of the mess.

"Stafford?" she asked tentatively.

"Over here."

Confused, Sandy walked the rest of the way into the room, Jesse trailing behind her. Finally, she stood before him as he sat slumped in the recliner.

She felt a lump as big as a boulder in her throat.

"Stafford. Thank God," she began. Then she was in his arms. The lump inside her throat melted. The dam holding back her tears finally burst. Several seconds later she realized Stafford was crying too.

"I didn't want anyone to see me like this," he cried, "especially you."

Sandy jerked her head from against his shoulder, his warm and comforting shoulder. "What are you talking about?"

"I'm no good," he sobbed, "never been any good. Nothing but a coward."

"Stafford, I don't understand."

"He was the best friend I ever had and I let him go. I didn't do a thing to save him." His voice cracked on the last words.

Sandy blinked her eyes. She felt dazed. "Who are you talking about?"

Stafford mopped his face with his sleeve and stared, blurry-eyed, past her. "He wouldn't listen to me. I told him not to go across the bay. Warned him it was an idiotic idea, but he wouldn't listen. I stood in the dark and let him go." He reached over the side of the chair for a can of beer and popped it open.

Jesse, crouched beside her, sucked his thumb, and looked up quizzically at her.

This was all wrong. She felt like she'd just stepped from one Twilight Zone episode into another. There had to be some way to make him understand how much she needed him.

"Stafford, pull yourself together. I have to talk to you. Something terrible happened to me last night."

"You know what the really terrible part was?" he asked. "The terrible part was the silence. I kept calling his name and he wouldn't answer. Never had time to answer me. Never even had time to scream." Stafford took another long gulp of beer and, choking on it, started crying again. "When I finally got the goddamned boat pulled in, I still didn't realize what had happened. I saw the water inside, figured the boat had sprung a leak and maybe he'd fallen overboard. I was just going to jump into the bay, clothes and all, I swear I was, when I spotted what was in the bottom of the boat."

Jesse started whimpering at her side.

"Stafford, please. I don't want to hear any more. You're scaring Jesse and you're scaring me."

"At first, all I saw was something black and gooey, then I saw the bones sticking out. Bones molted with wet tar paper. It still didn't dawn on me what it was. Finally, I saw his skull. It was stuck in the corner of what was left of the boat, wedged in the corner as if he'd flung back his head when he'd died." Stafford gulped the rest of his beer. "I don't know how long I stood there. I kept watching the boat take in more and more water, until Lenny's corpse disappeared into the bay. And then I figured it out—it must have been the fog. Just like the rain had something in it that changed everyone. Only this happened faster. Too fast."

He bowed his head and heaved huge, gasping sobs. "Why did I let him go? Why was I such a coward?"

Head still bowed, he held out his arms to Sandy and she gathered him to her, letting him weep on her shoulder.

"There now," she said.

Jesse inched his way into her embrace, and soon she found herself rocking and stroking both of them until they fell asleep in her arms.

Later, Sandy lowered Jesse to the floor. She propped the sleeping Stafford into his recliner, stared at him, and sighed. Her face was stiff from dried tears, but she didn't feel like crying at all now. Slowly, she moved to the coffee table and picked up Stafford's gun. It was heavier than it looked. She felt calm now, strangely at peace. Her mouth set in a tight, determined line, she strapped the gun to her leg.

After a short practice walk to make sure it wouldn't fall off, she lifted Jesse into her arms and walked out the door.

14.

Well, look-ee, look-ee what we have here."

Mason felt himself jostled. He struggled to open his eyes.

"Hey, freak, I'm talking to you. Crawl out of there where I can see you."

Mason's eyes flicked open a sliver, discerning a flat nose saddled between slabs of meaty jowls. His eyes opened the rest of the way, and he took in the thick, sweaty neck anchored to the cop-uniformed body—a very familiar cop-uniformed body. Mason's stomach felt like he had a belly full of week-old sausage grease inside him. Garbage he had used as camouflage fell away from him. Slowly he unraveled himself from his hiding place under the street side of the boardwalk and stared at Sal, the apple-munching guard.

"Move it, boy."

Sausage-grease bile rose in his throat, but he swallowed it back down. He reached out to the guard for support.

Sal jumped back in shock. "Keep your friggin' hands off me," he screamed. Using his rifle as a pitchfork, he caught Mason under the back of his shirt and dragged him into the street.

The glare of murky daylight caused Mason to squint. All the powers and strengths from the previous night had vanished. He coughed. Spittle drooled out of the comer of his mouth.

"Sweet Jesus, if you ain't a disgusting sight."

Mason got his bearings and attempted to stand. His legs buckled under him and he fell. A warm, soft breeze was blowing in from the ocean. Sand and paper debris whirled gently down the boardwalk ramp. The beach was so close. Up the ramp, across the boardwalk and over the fence— fifteen to twenty feet total between him and the pills Mongril was holding. Last night he could have jumped that far. On hands and knees he started for the ramp.

"Whoa there, old buddy," the guard called. "Where you going?"

"The... beach," Mason said between gasps. The crawl was hard going. His arms had to do most of the work, dragging his weak, almost useless legs behind him.

"The beach, you say? Hey, you wouldn't by chance be the son of a bitch that jumped me last night, would you?" He delivered a savage kick into Mason's side, sending him rolling over on his back and over again on his stomach.

Mason landed at the foot of the ramp on the street. One hand briefly held his side. His other hand clutched a wooden plank, then both hands grasped the plank, and he pulled his body forward, inching his way slowly up the ramp.

"Naw, it couldn't have been you. You're just a yellow-bellied snake, ain't that right? 'Course I never seen a snake quite as ugly as you, but I could be wrong. What do you say, freak?"

This time the kick caught him in the ass, sending him facedown and scraping on the splintered boardwalk access.

"Bull's eye," the guard yelled.

Mason raised his head and tried talking to the guard.

"Look, I don't want any trouble," he said. He was halfway up the ramp now. His body sprouted splinters like a porcupine, but he continued to creep forward as he talked. "Let me go back to the beach and I...

He sensed another kick coming. His body stiffened to receive it. But he was wrong.

This time the cop used his rifle and whacked the butt of the handle into the small of his back.

Mason yowled. He curled into a ball and rocked back and forth with the pain.

Sal chuckled and took time out to unwrap a pink wad of bubble gum. He popped it in his mouth, chomping on it loudly as. his pig eyes watched Mason unfurl and move forward again. Then he walked to him, positioning himself over him like he intended to play a fast game of leap frog.

"Let me go to the beach," Sal mimicked in a high shrill voice. "You looking to go back to the beach after all the trouble you took to leave it? Huh, freak?" He kicked Mason with the inside of his foot. First one foot, then another, alternating feet like a soccer player teasing a ball across a playing field.

Mason grunted with each blow, but restrained himself from yelling out again. He wouldn't give the pig the added satisfaction.

"What's the matter? You missing your freak friends? Or maybe you're looking for another opportunity to go for my gun. That it, freak?"

Mason reached the top of the ramp. Moisture dripped from his forehead, blurring his eyesight. It could have been sweat from the exertion or mucus from newly opened sores, he couldn't tell which. He raised a hand to wipe his eyes, and the guard mistook the action as an attempt at defense. A resounding kick caught him under the chin, knocking him. over on his back.

The guard dug a heel in his chest. Flabby jowls jiggled obscenely as he chewed on his gum. His teeth were yellow and crooked when he smiled.

Mason had met the type before. Liver-lipped sadists that worked as orderlies in the mental institution often abused helpless patients to make up for the endless hours they spent washing bedpans and urine-stained walls.

Mason returned the smile, flashing one of his own. Then he whipped his hands around the guard's leg and bit down hard.

The guard screamed in protest, tried to kick free, and fell down in the process.

The scream was reveille to Mason's ears. He let go of the leg and strained to cross the boardwalk. His elbows dug into the wooden planks, giving him more leverage, and he reached the railing.

"Fuckin' freak," the guard screamed behind him.

Mason grasped the railing, pulled himself up, and felt the gun muzzle jabbed into the back of his head. He didn't turn around.

"I'm a snake, not a freak, remember?" Mason asked evenly. "And maybe the snake's poisonous. Maybe the snake left poison in your leg that's working its way into your blood right now." Mason paused, giving his words a chance to sink in.

The guard cocked the hammer, but the gun in Mason's back wavered slightly.

"What the hell you talking about?"

"You said it yourself. We look like snakes, squirm like snakes, now we even bite like snakes. Just remember, the longer you give the poison to work, the sooner you're gonna end up dead. Or maybe you'll just end up like me."

Mason felt the gun shake uncontrollably. There was a cry of anguish, the gun was lowered, and Mason heard the guard take off down the boardwalk.

"Don't worry, I'll save a place for you next to me on the beach," Mason called after him. Then he dived to the sand.

22 boxes Hefty Lawn Bags
125 rolls toilet paper
1 case Beech Nut Jr. baby food

So much for the attic storage area behind the bureau in the upstairs bedroom. Sandy took a new sheet of paper and began a list of the downstairs pantry.

Peppermint Schnapps
Cherry Kiafa
Chocolate Vandermint
3 masking taped boxes Frankenberry Cereal
23 boxes spaghetti, shells, noodles, etc.
6 gal. olive oil
28 cans assorted tomatoes

The list went on for a page and a half. The only disappointment was the lone can of fruit juice and the total absence of bottled water.

Sandy put down her pen and tried to think of the alternatives to water. Fruit juice, soda, juice from canned goods, what else was there? How about syrup or vinegar? In a pinch, could maple syrup keep you from dying of thirst? The thought made her cringe.

She picked up her pen to begin a new list of "barter" items when she heard a soft knock at the front door. Suddenly she was very much aware of the gun still strapped to her leg.

"Who is it?" she called.

"Mrs. Morelli."

Sandy unlocked the door and her neighbor rushed in, looking flushed and out of breath. "Sandy, I've been worried sick. I came over before but you weren't home ..." Mrs. Morelli saw the bruises on her lips. "Oh, my dear, Mr. Morelli was right. You were in trouble last night."

"I'm fine now," Sandy said.

"But what happened?"

"Someone tried to break in," Sandy explained casually. She moved to the table, sat down, and doodled in the right-hand corner of her list. "We struggled. I fought him off. No big deal."

"And Jesse?"

"He's fine, sleeping upstairs, just like last night."

Mrs. Morelli placed her hands on Sandy's shoulders. "I'm so sorry. I should have never stayed so long on the beach."

Sandy held herself rigid and continued doodling. If she turned around and looked at Mrs. Morelli, she'd start crying again. Crying would accomplish nothing.

"Don't blame yourself. I'm a big girl, Mrs. Morelli, I'm perfectly able to take care of myself." She gestured toward the toolbox leaning against the bathroom door.

"Of course there are precautions that must be taken, and I'm making a list of all the food in the house. Thank God Mom and Dad are such pack rats." She laughed a short, forced little laugh, then bit down on her lower lip— and winced.

Mrs. Morelli sat next to her. "Why don't you and Jesse move in next door? We can all protect one another. I'm sure it's what your folks would want." Sandy's eyes darted up to Mrs. Morelli's face, then back down to her doodling. A circle of winding O's bordered her list. She began placing dots in the O's.

"Thank you. I really appreciate your concern, but no. This is something I have to deal with myself. Please understand."

Mrs. Morelli remained silent for a moment before she gently covered Sandy's hand with her own. "Just remember, if you decide to change your mind, the offer holds. Danny'd love having another woman in the house. And you know how we all feel about Jesse."

"How is Danny? Is he home?"

"No. But I'm sure he will be soon."

"He's feeling well, then?"

Mrs. Morelli's face sagged. "I didn't say anything to Mr. Morelli," she confided, "but his skin is pretty bad — all swollen and broken out in sores. In all my years, I've never seen anything like it."

"Is he in a lot of pain?"

Mrs. Morelli brightened. "Why, no. It's the most amazing thing. Danny's always had a low pain threshold. I had to drag him to the dentist when he was little. But last night, with his face all puffy and tender looking, he said he felt great. I had a job keeping him still, let me tell you. And what an appetite." Mrs. Morelli's blue eyes twinkled. "Tonight I have a feast planned for him. All his favorite foods — that come in a can."

"I can still mind Mr. Morelli," Sandy began. "I'm nailing all the windows shut, but if you bring him over here, he can sleep in my back bedroom."

"Bless you, Sandy, but it won't be necessary. He insists on visiting Danny. We'll have a picnic with him on the beach. Danny will be so surprised."

Sandy hesitated. She hated to dampen her kindly neighbor's enthusiasm, but quickly decided she had no choice.

"Are you sure that's wise? I was on the boulevard today and I couldn't believe my eyes. Empty stores and hungry people—it's a dangerous combination. That picnic lunch could be an open invitation."

"Really, Sandy! You make it sound like Little Red Riding Hood and the Big Bad Wolf."

"I didn't mean to. I could handle fairy tale monsters. But the people on the beach are not all like Danny." She swallowed hard. "If they attacked you, how could you and Mr. Morelli protect yourselves?"

"That would never happen. They're ordinary people like you and me. Besides, they're much too weak to do anyone any harm. When I left Danny this morning he barely had strength to kiss me good bye."

"I'm sorry," Sandy said, "I thought you said he was doing well."

"Yes, he was. The relapse this morning was probably from overexcitement, nothing to worry about." She flicked her wrist as if pushing the unpleasant thought away from her. Then she brightened. "I forgot to tell you the good news. I had a talk with Doctor Jenkins after I left Danny, and he told me that nobody on the beach died last night."

Sandy stared at her blankly.

"Don't you see, Sandy? No more casualties means the disease has run its course. Doctor Jenkins said he was most optimistic that an easing of the symptoms and increased activity will soon follow. Isn't that marvelous?"

"Yes, marvelous," Sandy answered.

Mrs. Morelli didn't notice the deadpan quality in her reply. She rose to leave. "Well, dear, have to run. Mr. Morelli will be calling for me. Kiss Jesse for me and I'll check on you tomorrow."

Ten minutes later, Sandy was still sitting quietly at the table while Mrs. Morelli's words screamed inside her head. *"Increased activity would soon follow."* Well, wasn't that swell. But what kind of activity, and to whom?

"Nobody on the beach died last night... Nobody on the beach died... Nobody died... Nobody..."

Sandy rose from her chair and walked over to the hammer and nails. She hoisted up a piece of wood and angled it against the first window.

———

He vomited up chunky black pools of liquid, raised his head, and patted his face. The lumps and boils had grown monstrous; they were swollen and moist. Some were crusted with flaky brown scabs that peeled off and crumbled in his hands. Gnat-like insects buzzed around him, angling for an open pus sore in which to nest. He made no attempt to brush them away. Hours had passed—he was sure it had to be late afternoon.

He turned his head and peered at the creatures nearest him Dazed and half-conscious, they looked as weak as he was. None was familiar. He espied movement near the water's edge, then recognized Mongril waving at him. Crawling, for some reason, was easier now. Maybe it was because he knew the pills were soon at hand. Pills would ease the pain and clear his mind. First he'd swallow the pills, then he'd think about Cassie. He wiped his mouth and continued to crawl toward Mongril.

"Hey, man, what's happening?" Mongril said in greeting.

Mason didn't answer. The thirty-minute crawl had exhausted him. He took a few minutes to catch his breath, regarding Mongril suspiciously. Eyes, squinty and slanted to begin with, had sunk deep into mounds of fleshy cysts on Mongril's face, leaving small dark tunnels in their wake. His crew cut had dwindled to sparsely spaced tufts of black hair. The dragon tattoo was no longer visible. There were only sores on top of sores, blisters inside blisters, torn open and gangrenous, covering his arms and hands.

"You missed a hell of a party last night—had these guards running crazy." The stoned, happy smile on Mongril's face was totally incongruous to the rest of him. His lips were unblemished, normal looking.

"Oh, wow, I just remembered. It was you that knocked the pig on his ass. Fucking okay, man."

"Glad you enjoyed it," Mason said, barely holding in his rage. The geek was flying high, wasted on his junk. "I hope the refreshments I supplied were equally as enjoyable?"

"Huh?"

"My pills, you bastard! There better be plenty left in that bag or I'll slit your stomach open and salvage the ten or twenty you probably stuffed down your throat when you saw me crawling here."

Mongril's smile drooped to a hurtful pout. "That hurts, man. Is that the thanks I get after the way I guarded your shit, man? Guarded it like it was my very own."

"I'm sure you did. Now hand it over."

Mongril hesitated half a second, long enough for one animal to assess another animal's strength or weakness. Then he pulled the bag from under the sand.

"No problem," he said as he pushed the bag to Mason. He held up his hand, palms out, in a *no contest* gesture.

Mason snatched the bag open. Maybe two hundred, maybe three hundred pill bottles were inside. It didn't look much less than the previous day. Hungrily, he grabbed one, unscrewed it, and swallowed half the contents.

"Ah, that's better," he said immediately. His brain was so conditioned to the taste of the capsules, the slick feel of them sliding down his throat, that he already felt eased. A fuzzy-edged euphoria becalmed him. All was right in the world again.

"Mongril, you did good." He rummaged in the black bag. "Think you could stand a few more pops?"

The shit-eating dopey grin reappeared and Mongril shifted closer to Mason. "Far out," he replied. He cupped his bloated hands to receive the pills.

15.

Between the time Mason reached the beach at midday and four-thirty that afternoon, when Mongril guzzled his fistful of pills, Sandy had slammed the hammer three times on her unsuspecting fingers. Nevertheless, all but the front door and the picture window on the porch were nailed drum-tight.

She positioned a large flat piece of paneling against the picture window and felt around for the hammer. "Jesse, bring that hammer back."

"Okay Mommy," he called from the back of the kitchen.

"Now."

"Okay."

She heard the faint tapping of the hammer against the sink. "Jesse, I'm counting to three."

"Coming."

"One." The paneling slipped out of her grip. It started sliding down the wall. "Two."

"Coming."

"Two and a half. Jesse, I'm warning you." The paneling crashed to the floor, narrowly missing her toes

"That's it! Now you're in for it." When she shifted the paneling against the wall, her attention was diverted by a familiar face outside the window.

Stafford glanced nervously at the cottage and paused at the foot of her steps.

Inside, Sandy also hesitated. Something seemed to stop her from going to the front door. She couldn't decide if it was pride or disappointment. Maybe it was both, maybe neither.

Unaware of her presence at the window, Stafford seemed to come to a decision. Shoulders hunched, he passed by the cottage steps and walked toward the boardwalk.

Suddenly Sandy felt very tired and alone. The man had done nothing to her except make a clumsy pass and break down over the death of his best friend. Why should that make her feel so bad about him? Unconsciously she brought her fingers to her swollen lips, patting them, touching them, exploring the boundaries of the tiny blisters that had formed on them. Then she moved swiftly to the front door and pulled it open.

"Stafford!"

He turned around, saw her standing in the doorway, and his slow easy grin slid into place. "Wasn't sure you'd want to see me after the way I acted this morning," he said. He joined her on the porch.

"Of course I want to see you," she said, "and you did nothing you should regret. I'm sorry about Lenny."

"It's just a crazy situation," he mumbled more to himself than to her.

"I know." She rubbed her nose, shielding her bruised mouth from his eyes. "But how are you feeling?"

"Well, besides the fact my eyeballs hurt so bad — they feel like they're bleeding — I'm just fine."

Sandy laughed. "Come on in. I've got a great remedy for hangovers."

Jesse had moved from the sink to the stove, hammering to beat the band. "Good Lord," Stafford yelled as he followed Sandy into the kitchen, "if this is a cure for a hangover, I know I'm in trouble."

"Jesse, that's enough now," she yelled.

The hammering subsided long enough for Sandy to pour Tabasco sauce into a glass of tomato juice and hand it to Stafford.

"Try this," she said before the hammering resumed to its original earsplitting volume. Too late she realized her injured lip was exposed, and her hand flew to cover them.

"Hey." Stafford caught her hand as she tried to turn away. "What happened to you?"

"Nothing," Sandy answered.

Stafford forced her to look at him. "Oh, Jesus, does this have something to do with why you came to see me this morning?"

"No. Jesse, put that hammer down."

"Okay, Mommy," he said, still ignoring her.

"Of course it does. What a moron I am. What happened, Sandy?"

"Nothing! Jesse! Stop it! You're driving me crazy!"

"Tell me."

"Jesse!" She pulled away from Stafford, quickly crossed the room, and yanked the hammer out of Jesse's hands. The butt of the handle brushed against Jesse's chin. He wailed, more in protest than from actual pain.

"Tell me."

Sandy bent down and drew Jesse close to her. He resisted, refusing to cry against her shoulder. Instead, he grabbed for the hammer in her hand. Angrily, she flung it across the floor, out of his reach.

"Tell me!"

Sandy exploded. "I got raped. Okay?" she screamed over Jesse's wailing. Before Stafford could say a word, she carried Jesse, still wailing, into his room for a bottle and a nap.

When she returned downstairs, Stafford was sitting in the same position. Hand curved around the untouched glass of tomato juice, he looked straight ahead, unblinking, staring sadly into the now quiet room.

Sandy bit down on her lower lip and winced from the pain. "Look. I should have listened to you. I didn't. It happened. It's over with. And now I'm making goddamn sure it doesn't happen again."

Stafford broke free of his reverie to turn slowly toward her. He held out his arms and she rushed into them. His arms were strong and warm and so comfortably safe. She let herself be rocked. She tried to let herself go. This was what she'd wanted, wasn't it? But why, then, she asked herself, why did her body feel so stiff? Why was her mind still racing?

"Relax," Stafford soothed, "you're safe now."

"But I'm not," she whispered, still holding back her tears. "Mason'll come back."

"Who?"

"Mason. Doctor Jenkins said they were getting better. He's predicting increased activity. Isn't that a joke?"

"Hold on a minute. You're not making sense. Start at the beginning and tell me what happened."

Sandy leaned heavily against him. She took a deep breath and began.

———

Still groggy with dope dreams. Mason lifted his head off the sand. Mongril sat close by, black tunnel eyes gawking at him.

"You okay, man?" Mongril asked.

Mason's hand flew to his pill stash. The black bag was there, zippered shut and safe beneath him. "I'm fine. Why shouldn't I be?"

"No sweat. Only... you was screaming in your sleep, screaming after some Cassie bitch."

Cassie. What had happened last night?

Mason hurried open the zippered bag and popped three black capsules into his mouth. He pitched a couple more in Mongril's direction.

"Hey, thanks."

"Don't mention it," he muttered before turning on his side, away from Mongril.

Cassie... Oh, yes, now he remembered. They had shared a night of love together. He'd left briefly to get some more pills, then that pig attacked him. Mason slammed his clenched fist into the sand. The guard would pay, he promised himself that. His fist was sticky from the opened boils, and coated with sand like a veal cutlet coated with bread crumbs. It looked swollen and raw and felt ice cold when he touched it with the other hand.

Funny, he thought, *it should hurt like hell, but it doesn't. It doesn't even feel sore.* He pinched his hand, then the skin on his leg, and finally the skin between his toes. He pinched as hard as he could. He felt absolutely no pain. There was only the sensation of slight pressure, a feeling of being touched, as if someone had pinched a strand of hair. *Weird,* he mused, *decidedly weird.* It had to be the combination of pills he'd taken.

Mason felt his face, the oozing pustules on his cheeks, the earlobe flapping on a thread of skin at the side of his neck—all painless. But then why shouldn't they be? Hallucinations couldn't cause real pain.

He looked up and scrutinized the people nearest him. Mongril was peacefully leaning back on his elbows, mouth open, head tilted skyward, lost in a junkie land of Nod. Past Mongril were blankets, empty defeated blankets, half-submerged in sand. Similar rough army blankets were scattered all over the beach. Past the blankets, a group of "patients" were talking together quietly. Faces were hideous, clay caricatures dripping with red and black colors, or so it seemed to Mason. Were these real or also hallucinations?

Now and then several members of the group would make angry gestures toward the boardwalk, but otherwise, he noticed no signs of agony or distress.

It was the same everywhere he looked. Clumps of people sat around talking, laughing occasionally, and no one appeared to be suffering any great pain. There was even one group playing touch football in some unoccupied space near the stacked sheet-covered corpses that had remained unburied from day one of the disaster.

Mason shook his head and wondered where they'd found a football. He doubted the guards had supplied it.

Mason looked up at the boardwalk and spotted the apple-munching guard that had kicked the shit out of him that morning. The bastard seemed to be staring at him, too, and Mason felt the outside of his body freeze, while his insides boiled with rage. He'd annihilate him, make him scream in repentance for what he'd done to him.

Poker-hot hatred surged through his mind and body like adrenaline. He'd make the bastard pay. Then he'd return to Cassie and make love to her. They'd revel in each other's arms again.

But first he had to figure a way to squash the guard—squash all the fucking guards—so he could make his way back to her.

—————

Less than half an hour later the sky had turned to dusk. A gray stillness settled over the beach.

Mason pounced to his feet. He was so agile that for a moment he could have sworn that his feet had paused, suspended in midair, before planting themselves firmly on the ground. He felt alive, and slick. His head was cocked. Sounds and smells of the beach rushed over him, making him tingle with excitement. He sized up the guards on the boardwalk, then sauntered across the beach to a group of fellow patients and stretched out casually at the edge of the group's circle.

Mason's body slumped over in imitation of the group's posture. He kept his head down and nodded in sympathy as experiences were shared. Gradually, he was able to sort out names and personalities as he listened quietly to their rage and tales of woe.

"... and after my Volkswagen smashed into the telephone pole, pinning me under the steering wheel, I screamed and screamed for someone to help me. My kids were knocked out, unconscious in the back seat, but I couldn't reach them. Guess I must have blacked out too, for a while. Later, when I woke up, I started screaming again. Screamed for hours, begging for help.

I wouldn't leave a dog to suffer like that. Would you?"

The speaker was Vicky. She brushed clumps of her dry black hair forward, over her face. It concealed all but the clotted scar tissue that snaked red and black across her nose and between her eyes.

Mason took an immediate dislike to the man next to Vicky. He was a shirtless, barrel-chested guy with short arms and short legs, like Humpty Dumpty. Lou had an annoying habit of constantly picking at a tumor on his neck.

"I know just what you mean," Lou told the group. "I felt like someone had a potato peeler and was slicing my skin off piece by piece, and it took the volunteers three days to find me."

He paused to let the cross-legged group digest this injustice.

"Their inadequate response time and utter lack of concern will be reported. Captain Cruthers happens to be a personal friend of mine. Heads will roll!" he promised.

What an asshole, Mason thought. From the expressions on other faces, he knew he wasn't alone in his opinion. Two men yawned loudly. Vicky twisted a strand of hair savagely around one of her fingers. Only the girl called Carla registered no emotion.

She's a strange one, Mason decided. Other than her name, he couldn't get a handle on her. She seemed to be part of the group. Now and then, someone would direct a remark to her. They didn't ask her questions, though, and she made no effort to communicate with them or contribute to their conversations. Neither did she attempt to conceal her disfigurements as Vicky did. She seemed oblivious to the watery pustules covering her body. She sat motionless, eyes fixated on the sea.

Vicky resumed her tale. "But the best part," she said. "After I finally squeezed out of my car two nights later and dragged my broken bones out in that rain to find help for my kids, some food, and a warm place — the best part was the bitch in the first house I went to."

"Wouldn't open the door," Lou cut in. "Nobody opened for me either, the bastards."

"Not only wouldn't she open the door," Vicky continued, "but the next day she smashes glass into my face, tries to blind me, 'cause I have the audacity to pass out in her outdoor shower. Look at the scars I got from her."

She held back her hair for a second. The jagged scars across her nose and eyes led to mounds of scar tissue, sores, and slivers of glass that had congealed into hideously gnarled masses. There was a quick intake of breath from Lou, before Vicky spread her hair back over her face.

"Oh God," Vicky sighed, "I could kill for a cigarette right now."

"What happened to your kids?" Mason asked, speaking for the first time.

Her yellowed eyes burned up at him from between the black curtains of hair. She shook her head. "My Jenny was only three years old. She used to make up little songs, crazy little songs about what happened at nursery school and what wonderful things would happen to her the next day. She was always singing," Vicky said softly.

"And my beautiful Melissa, six years old and so proud of all the S-pluses she got on her first-grade report card. I'd promised her a treat for that, a day at the beach... Vicky's voice broke. She cleared her throat before continuing.

"The guards threw my babies over there the first day, dumped their bodies over the railing like yesterday's garbage."

She pointed toward the sheeted graveyard. The football game was still taking place several feet in from it.

"Jesus," Mason sympathized.

"Vicky, I promise you," Lou said, "tomorrow I will personally speak to Captain Cruthers. He'll surely want to comply with a simple request for a decent, civilized burial for your children."

"Captain Cruthers," Vicky spat, "doesn't want to do anything but keep us quarantined on the beach."

"But, the volunteers promised—" Lou insisted.

"Lou," Vicky screamed, "the volunteers are guards without guns. Haven't you realized it yet? The same people who let us crawl in the rain are not going to give two shits if we rot on this beach."

"That's not true," Lou said.

Carla turned away from the ocean to stare at Lou. Her face twisted into a grimace. Dry heaves shook her body. Finally, her mouth yawned open and she emitted a stream of squealing laughter. It was a sound only the utterly insane could make.

Before anyone could move toward her, Carla clamped her hand over her mouth, stifling the sound, until she was once more quietly, catatonically, staring at the ocean.

"Why doesn't anyone do something about it?" Mason broke the silence.

All eyes fixed on him.

"Carla's okay," Vicky said. "She goes off like that every now and then. It's nothing to worry about."

"I don't mean Carla," Mason explained. "I'm talking about the deplorable conditions we're forced to endure here. It's so unjust, so inhuman! I think we should get together and do something about it."

"What do you suggest?" she asked sarcastically. "Shall we sign petitions or organize a hunger strike?" Several members of the group burst out laughing, but saw the fury seething in Mason's eyes and quickly contained themselves.

When they looked sufficiently chastised, Mason resumed his preacher pose and turned to Vicky. "What you jokers don't understand is that right now, this minute, we're in a war. There's no medical ship coming here to pick us up, no supply ship bringing food and cigarettes. I don't think there is any way on or off the island. Otherwise we wouldn't still be here." Mason moved closer into the circle. He sat up on his haunches as he spoke. "But the answer isn't tired old nonviolent actions." He eyed Lou. "And it ain't begging favors from Captain Cruthers and his guards."

Vicky waited. Mason knew she was the one he had to convince. The rest would follow her lead.

"It's almost dark. What do you say we talk to some of the others on the beach. I've listened to a lot of misery the past few days. And I'm sure there are plenty of us who are ready to do more than sit around and complain."

"Ready for what?" Vicky asked.

"Ready to act."

"And do what?" she insisted.

Mason looked around and then answered in a hushed voice, "Ready to rush the fucking guards and take what we want, go where we want, when we want."

"That's crazy," Lou said, "We're patients. Whoever heard of patients overthrowing a hospital."

"Shut up, Lou," Vicky told him. "What about all the guns and ammunition the guards have?" she asked Mason. "We'd be slaughtered before we hit the boardwalk."

"Not if we worked together and surprised them. We outnumber the guards a hundred to one."

"Still," Vicky reasoned, "some of us are bound to be shot."

"Sure," Mason conceded, "but let me ask you this." He leaned over and gently brushed the hair back from her decaying cheeks. "How much worse off could we be?"

16.

Sandy moved to the kitchen counter and poured more tomato juice. Lighted oil cast warm shadows on the eagle-papered room, but did not reflect on the window panes. It couldn't. The glass was entirely covered by the rough, wooden planks and teak-colored paneling. She pressed her hand against the wood. *I'll be safe here*, she thought.

"Sandy, you're not listening to me," Stafford said. Lines creased his forehead. He had been raking his hands through his hair for so long that it was standing straight up.

"I am listening," Sandy said. "But you keep asking me the same questions. We've been at it for hours." She slumped into a chair next to him at the table. "I'm starting to feel like a suspect you're interrogating."

"That's crazy. I'm just trying to get all the facts together so I can make some sense out of this and arrest the man who's responsible."

"What's to make sense? Mason broke into the house and attacked me. He looked like the creatures on the beach, but I know it was Mason."

"And Mason is this old boyfriend of yours?"

Sandy shrugged. "Yes, I guess you could say that. He was someone I dated a few times. When I realized how weird he was, I ditched him or at least I tried to. Mason refused to be ditched."

"How do you mean weird?"

"I mean *weird!*" Sandy slumped further down in her chair.

"Mason's parents were religious fanatics, real screwballs. They preached up and down the boardwalk about hellfire and Armageddon—you know the routine. Mason grew up tagging behind them, their faithful little clone. The family was harmless. Everyone on the island considered them the island's resident kooks."

"But you went out with him?" Stafford asked.

"I was eighteen years old, for God's sake, playing Mary Magdalene, my first semiprofessional role, when one night Mason walked into my dressing room, and there was something about him... I don't know how to explain it, but he was so intense, so different from any other guy I'd ever met."

"And good looking, I suppose."

"Yes," Sandy retorted. "Even with his short-cropped hair and hand-me-down suit, he was handsome in a blonde-sensitive-poet-type way. But it was something more than that."

Sandy thought for a moment before she continued. "Maybe it was the part I was playing. Maybe that's why his religious activities didn't seem so crazy. Or maybe I saw him as a challenge, a diamond in the rough, so to speak, a blank canvas that I could bring to life. You see, he'd never had a date before, never so much as held a girl's hand."

"In other words, you were his first lay?"

Sandy jerked up from the table and walked across the room. "Forget it. I'm not answering any more questions. Why don't you go join your chauvinistic buddies and leave the wanton woman alone? I'd appreciate it if you'd let me keep the gun I borrowed from your apartment. Otherwise, I'll do fine without your help."

Stafford worked the fingers of both his hands through his hair. "I don't know why I said that." He turned and found her facing away from him. "I had no right to say that. Whether you slept with him or not has no bearing on what happened yesterday."

"Doesn't it?" Sandy asked, still refusing to look at him. "Because I did sleep with him — the first day we met, in fact, and maybe four or five times after that." She waited for Stafford to comment. He didn't, and she started pacing the kitchen floor.

"It was no big deal," she finally said. "At least for me. Mason, of course, thought that the heavens had opened up and Jesus, Mary, and Joseph had come down in the flesh all wrapped up into one neat little bundle."

"He was in love with you?"

"In love? No. It was more like he was obsessed... or possessed — yes, that's it — he was like a man possessed. He attached himself to me like a third arm. Morning, noon, and night he wanted to be with me to know minute by minute what I thought, what I felt, what I dreamed, what I was going to dream. I tried to end it. He refused to accept it, refused even to acknowledge that I wanted to end it."

Stafford looked at her skeptically. "How hard did you try?"

Sandy stopped pacing. "I screamed at him. I ignored him. I tried to reason with him. I had him barred from the theater. I refused to talk to him or look at him. Nothing worked. The harder I tried to dump him, the crazier he became. He concocted these crazy fantasies about our 'upcoming marriage' and invited all my friends. The worst part was he believed it."

"What did your parents think of him?"

"Let me put it to you this way. How would you feel about some guy camping out on the curb in front of your house every night, staring at your daughter's window?"

"Didn't you call the police?"

"Of course we did," she said evenly, "along with everyone else we could think of. No one could get through to him."

"Not even his parents?"

Sandy shook her head. "Not that they didn't try. Their methods were firmly rooted to their religious beliefs. Exorcise the demons with pain and prayers. Insanity is not an illness, according to the Bible. Did you know that? Naturally I was the she devil who had corrupted him. His mother actually called me the Whore of Babylon. I was sure his father would whip out a crucifix when I'd pass him on the boardwalk."

"His parents sound like full-fledged shits. They still live on the island?"

Sandy sat down near him. "They don't live anywhere. Mason murdered them."

"Murdered?" Stafford's bloodshot eyes looked ready to pop out. "Why didn't you tell me we were dealing with a murderer?"

"Didn't I mention it?"

"Hell no, you didn't mention it," Stafford complained. "Go on now and tell me the rest of it."

"Well, according to newspaper accounts and the letters he sent me, Mason thought he'd devised the perfect punishment for his parents. After a particularly gruesome night of beatings, he awakened the next morning with new resolve. He fixed a breakfast tray for his parents: Eggs Benedict, orange juice, bacon, bran muffins. I remember him writing me how buttery and moist the muffins were."

Stafford blew out a long stream of air in exasperation. "Gee, maybe we can ask for his recipe. Please get on with the story."

But Sandy was not to be rushed. She was like someone roused from a bad dream. She struggled to grasp each detail, each remembered item, in order to bring it out in the open to be examined and rationalized and eventually diminished by the telling.

"The orange juice contained the ground up sleeping pills — not enough to kill them, just enough to give Mason time to drag them to the cellar."

Sandy paused, relieving her dry, parched mouth with the rest of the tomato juice in her glass before she continued. "Then he fashioned two wooden stakes and attached them to the cellar beams. I don't know how — he didn't say how — but somehow he got his parents tied to the stakes. He called them crosses. He waited until they both woke up before he started with the first nail."

"I get the picture," Stafford said hoarsely.

"The newspapers reported how neatly he'd managed it, how he'd first dig out a small hole, no bigger than a baby's pinky ring, before inserting a long ten penny steel nail. Carefully, he hammered clear of bones, or vital organs, at least on the first day."

"Nobody heard the screaming?"

Sandy broke her reverie long enough to stare blankly at Stafford. "No one ever went near the house, and Mason only left them alone twice, both times to rush over to Bay Hardware for fresh supplies of nails."

"He didn't try to see you?"

"No. Not until it was over and he'd set a fire in the basement to eliminate the remains. What he hadn't counted on, was the unusually quick response of the Sea

Breeze Volunteer Fire Department. They'd had the engine out, sirens full blast, speeding to pick up a keg of beer at the Surf Side Bar and Grill when someone spotted the smoke.

"An hour later the police arrested him outside my house. He'd been standing at the curb calling out my name."

"And that was the last you heard of him?"

"Except for the letters. He wrote me once or twice a day while he was awaiting trial." She was drained now and barely able to drag the words out. "Some I read. Most went into the garbage."

"How long did this go on?"

"I don't remember. After he was committed to the asylum they stopped altogether, and that was the last I heard from him. Until yesterday."

Stafford and Sandy sat together in silence, lost in their own thoughts.

"Jesus," Stafford murmured, "the crazy bastard crucified his own parents."

Sandy sat slumped, leaning heavily on her elbows.

Stafford glanced at her dejected pose with a sly sideways look. "Can I ask you just one more question?"

Sandy sighed. "Go ahead."

"Was it just Mason or does this kind of thing happen to all the men who make love to you?"

———

On the beach that night, Mason suddenly realized that he was assembling an army. He'd talked war, spewed a little jive about equal rights, cooperation, and strength in numbers—all bullshit, naturally. It was all a scam to (A) kick the shit out of the flabby-jowled guard that had abused him, and (B) make it back to Cassie.

Somehow the idea had snowballed. The pitch-black beach was buzzing with plans for the upcoming attack. He was the assumed general, the king of kings, the lord of lords gathering his armies to do battle. It was like the prophecies in Revelations that his parents drilled into him.

Even Mongril was pumped up with enthusiasm after Mason had jostled him out of his nodding stupor.

"All right, let's party," he kept whooping at Mason's side.

Mason gestured him toward the beached lifeguard boat that he'd decided to use as a makeshift command center.

"Mongril, try to understand," he explained patiently. "I'm making you second-in-command. You played straight with me and I think I can trust you."

"Damn straight," Mongril replied.

"Good, but you have to understand; we've got to plan some strategy here. Figure a way to overpower the guards without too many people getting shot. Especially without the general and his second-in-command getting shot, if you catch my drift."

Mongril scratched feverishly at the mound of sores that had once been his dragon tattoo. Mason waited patiently for him to finish.

"So I'd appreciate it," Mason finally continued, "if you'd quit referring to our upcoming campaign as a 'party.' Okay?"

"No problem," Mongril assured him.

"We're not brawlers."

"I hear you."

"We're officers maneuvering our soldiers for the first skirmish."

"No problem."

"Good. Any questions?"

"Just one."

"Shoot," Mason said.

"How long do you figure it'll be before we start bashing heads and partying?"

Mason shook his head in disbelief. "I'll let you know," he sighed. He resigned himself to the inevitable. Turning away from Mongril, he diverted his attention to the small group still playing touch football across the beach.

"Who ever heard of playing ball in the dark?" he asked aloud, but to himself.

"Twi-Night doubleheader, man," Mongril quipped.

"That's baseball. Besides, I'm wondering how the hell they can see the ball, or one another, for that matter?"

Then Mason realized the foolishness of the question. If he could see them, obviously they would also be able to see one another. But how was it possible?

"Night vision," he muttered. His vision was as acute now as it had been last night. And the guard hadn't been able to see two feet in front of him after the torch went down. Mason watched a player miss a deep pass that was thrown to him. He could easily make out the outline of the fumbled ball bouncing across the sand.

Smiling broadly, he gestured to Mongril. "Come on, let's take a walk and talk to these Joe Namaths. I got a feeling they're our kind of people."

Mongril shrugged and followed Mason across the beach. Three quarters of the way there, a long pass, way off side, sent the ball flying high in the air toward them. Mason zeroed in on it and easily caught it on the fly. It was a very odd ball—too round for a football, too small for a medicine ball, too lumpy for a basketball. Actually, it was way past its prime for use as any type of ball at all. Sticky and mushy, it kept coming apart, disintegrating in Mason's fingers.

"Here, catch," he called to Mongril, throwing it at him.

Mongril felt it leaking on his hands before he realized what it was. Then he quickly let it drop to the sand, backed away from it, and gagged from the feel and the sight and the smell of small fragments of it still festering on his hands.

"What's wrong?" Mason asked him. "I thought you liked bashing heads?"

"Yeah," Mongril choked, "but I like the heads to be attached to something breathing."

Mason laughed and picked up the severed human head from the sand. "I knew that goon squad was our kind of people."

He continued walking toward them, lazily bouncing their ball up and down in his hands. Outlines for the upcoming attack danced in his head.

17.

Danny twitched nervously as he sat waiting for his mother. He was positive she'd said she'd be coming back tonight. At least, he was almost positive. A few hours ago, he'd felt so weak and disoriented that he wasn't absolutely positive about anything. Maybe he'd dreamed she'd been there the previous night.

No... Impossible, he reassured himself.

His thinking was clearer now that it was getting dark, and the wrappings and containers from last night's meal were scattered near his feet. They were proof that his mother had been there last night, and proof that she'd bring more food tonight. She wouldn't let him go hungry.

Of course, he didn't really have much of an appetite. There was only a need, an ache inside, that he should be eating.

It was crazy; the whole situation was insane! At this time of the day he should be home, watching Family Feud or playing cards with the guys at the firehouse.

He looked up wistfully at the armed guards standing sentry near the burning torches that lined the boardwalk. A few of his buddies were playing soldier up there. They had spoken to him once or twice, but no one lingered for long and no one offered to help him move off the beach. Less than two blocks from his home, he was forced to remain on the damp sand, alone among strangers.

Where was his mother?

Along the darkened beach, many of the patients seemed to be placing themselves in small groups that were directly in line with the guards above them.

Danny had listened to some half-baked plans of attacks that were to take place. He'd waved the idiots away, refusing to take them seriously. Now it looked like the crazy bastards were actually going to try a surprise attack. Didn't they realize they'd all be shot?

Maybe he should try talking some sense into them. Or maybe he should reveal their plans to the guards, who seemed totally oblivious to the beach activity. But something held him back. *Fuck 'em*, he decided. *It's no skin off my back*.

His hand flew to his face and he ran his fingers over his encrusted skin. He hadn't looked in a mirror, but there was no fooling himself. The feel of the sores, the appearance of the other beach freaks, had etched a vivid picture in his mind. The shock and pain in his mother's eyes when she'd first recognized him confirmed it. Once again he had to ask himself if this could really be happening.

Mongril was primed for action. He paced up and down near the lifeboat as the last of the volunteers carted rocks from the jagged cliffs that dissected the beach area.

"Ah-RIGHT!" he simply couldn't contain himself from crying out.

Mongril felt like he was in school again. He would have gladly stayed in high school forever, and in truth, he nearly did. He had never passed tenth grade, but he had spent the best six years of his life trying. Riotous football games, food fights in the cafeteria, sneaking reefers in the toilet, burning rubber out of the school parking lot, and mooning out of a car speeding eighty miles per hour to the next party — that was the life!

"Par-ty!" he screamed out, forgetting himself again.

Mason turned and glared at him from across the beach.

"Sorry, man," Mongril called back. Sheepishly, he focused his attention to the work at hand. His job was to divide the large clay and sandstone chunks among his runners who, in turn, would cart them to the squads Mason had strategically placed for the attack.

Easily accomplished, he turned to stare menacingly at each runner. "Okay, we're set," he spat. "Whatever squad you deliver to last becomes the squad you join for the attack. And don't none of you fuck up. Understand?"

Mumbling assent, the group was soon dispatched. Mongril waited until they were a safe distance away before heading for the bag of pills newly concealed under the lifeboat. A couple of pops, he decided, would be just enough to get the party rolling.

"That looks like a doctor's bag," said a voice behind him. Mongril whirled around and stared down at a short, barrel-chested man.

"What the fuck is your problem?" Mongril asked Lou, who was calmly picking at the tumor on his neck.

"Nothing a few of those pills couldn't cure," Lou answered.

Mongril smirked. "That tumor's gone to your brain, man, so get the fuck out of my face and get to your squad."

Lou's hand quickly dropped to his side. It was his turn to smile. "I have no intention of being part of these childish war games. Rock throwing! Rushing the guards with blankets and sand to extinguish their torches. Really? The best you can hope for is that the guards will laugh themselves silly and forget to use their guns."

Mongril casually bent down and slid the pills back under the boat.

"I only hope," Lou continued, "that Captain Cruthers believes me when I explain to him how I so strenuously tried to dissuade you people from this lunacy."

Mongril rose slowly before he whipped around and smashed his fist into Lou's mouth.

Lou's head cracked against the side of the lifeboat. He gagged, his mouth filling with blood, yet he continued to speak.

"Asshole," Mongril mused out loud. He grabbed hold of Lou's belt and effortlessly dragged him toward Mason.

———

"Listen, lady. I don't care if you're almighty God's mother. Nobody ain't going on the beach or anywheres near it tonight."

Mrs. Morelli looked down at her husband asleep in his wheelchair. It had taken an hour to dress him suitably, an hour to arrange him comfortably in his chair, and another hour to push his chair down the porch ramp, up and down two curbs, around a fallen telephone pole, in and out of a giant pothole, and up and around the steep ramp to the boardwalk. Somewhere in between all that activity, darkness had descended and Mr. Morelli had dozed off. She'd become exhausted, on the verge of falling asleep herself. But Danny expected her. She had to see him.

"But you don't understand," Mrs. Morelli implored. "I have his dinner all prepared. It won't take more than a few minutes to bring it to him."

"Lady," the guard said in his best straining-to-be-patient voice, "do you see these torches?"

Mrs. Morelli stared at the flaming sticks along the boardwalk and nodded.

"They ain't good for lighting more than a two-foot area, but it's the best we got. Unfortunately, we spend half our time tripping over one another to keep the flames going. You see these guns?" He didn't wait for an answer, but swung the rifle off his shoulder and held it up for her inspection. "The other half of our time we spend trying to cool down trigger-happy cowboys that are itching to shoot these at anything that moves."

"I understand that." Mrs. Morelli bit down hard on her lower lip. "But last night I visited him and—"

The guard reached the end of his patience. "Look, lady," he exploded. "Last night, one of them freaks attacked us — tried to grab a gun. Tonight, we're more than ready for them. Now you and the old man go on home before you get hurt."

Mrs. Morelli opened her mouth to protest, but closed it again. She remembered the assault on Sandy. Maybe such measures were necessary to guard against additional attacks. But why did Danny have to suffer? The guard continued to glare at her, his mouth set in a tight, straight line. She knew it was useless to argue further. Sighing deeply, she removed a shopping bag of food from the handles of the wheelchair and held it out to him.

"Please," she said in a trembling voice, "could you see to it that my Danny has his supper?"

"Yeah, sure," the guard promised. With eyes averted, he took the bag from her hands.

Shoulders hunched, Mrs. Morelli gripped the handles of the wheelchair and released the brake. Mr. Morelli had never awakened. He continued to sleep on the long, arduous, half-block trek home.

"Any apples left?"

"Christ, Sal, you already ate all the sandwiches. The old lady gave the bag to me."

The pig-faced guard snatched the shopping bag out of the other guard's hands and reached inside. He smiled broadly. "One little sucker left," he said. Saliva glistening from the corners of his mouth, he opened wide. Suddenly the apple was knocked from his hand.

"What the hell—" he began, but before he could finish the question, he was bombarded with stones. Shots rang out in the distance. Dimly he realized he should drop to his stomach and position his rifle, but it was already too late. Within minutes, his torch was out and the freaks were on him.

The screams of the battle echoed across the island, more piercing and with more volume than the combined screams of a summer's worth of roller-coaster riders.

Sandy listened through the barred windows and doors of the bungalow and shuddered. She looked up at Stafford, who stared back at her imploringly.

"I know," she said softly, "you have to go."

"I'll be back," he promised. "I'll be back in an hour."

She remained silent.

"Sandy, it's my job. I have to go."

She held herself rigid when he moved to embrace her.

"My friends are out there. I can't let them down."

"I know," she said, breaking away from him and heading for the door. "I'll be fine. Just... go." Her voice threatened to break and she leaned against the door for support.

"Everything's locked up," Stafford said. "And you've got the gun. I'll be back in less than an hour. Less than fifteen minutes, I promise."

After he left and the door had been securely locked behind him, Sandy struggled to remain calm.

"I'm not going to cry," she told herself, "and I'm not going to fall apart. I knew it all along — knew it was me that I had to depend on — me and nobody else!"

Sandy walked to the kitchen table and sat down.

The noise outside came in waves, rising and falling like the roar of a huge audience. Gunfire crackled like the grand finale of a fireworks display. But the most terrifying sound — the sound that chilled her inside and out — was the sound of laughter — high-pitched, insane laughter.

Sandy picked up Stafford's gun from the table. She pointed it toward the front door... and waited.

18.

"**P**lease let me go." Sal whined. "'You can have my gun. You can have drugs or food or anything you want. I'll get it for you, only please, you gotta let me go."

The guard's voice was deeply blurred with fear. Tears etched dirty streams down his checks and flabby jowls. His pug nose was running. Pinned to the railing of the boardwalk by two members of the Goon Squad, he had long given up struggling in the dark to free himself.

Mason moved closer to him until their faces were inches apart. "We already have your gun," he informed him, "and we already have everything in the supply station. Freaks like us don't need very much."

Mason stroked the tearstained face and watched in fascination as the guard cringed from his touch.

"What are you going to do to me?" His voice was barely above a whisper.

Mason grinned broadly and stopped stroking. He motioned for the Goon Squad members to drag the prisoner to the flagpole near the supply station. They quickly complied, moving swiftly through the night.

The first skirmish had been a cinch. Most of the volunteer guards, out of condition and slow to act, had been overpowered. With the torches extinguished, any attempt to defend themselves was impossible.

Blocks away, Mason saw specks of light, torches that were still unreachable at the top of pavilions on the amusement pier. There was also the constant clatter of gunshots coming from the same direction. Mason hesitated, unsure whether he should continue with the job at hand or send his squad to reinforce Mongril's troop on the pier.

He turned back to the profusely sweating guard, the one who only hours ago had brutalized and humiliated him, the pig who had forced him to crawl snakelike on his belly. He gritted his teeth.

No, he decided as he joined his squad. This was too good to hurry. Slowly, almost seductively, he took hold of the cord on the flagpole and began snaking it gently around the guard's neck. Goon Squad members snickered their approval. Once the neck was securely wrapped, Mason ran the cord down the back and began tying the hands. A crowd of creatures gathered nearby on the beach and Mason paused to wave at them. From the looks of entrancement on their faces, he knew it wouldn't be long before many others joined him. Feelings of power and immense pleasure rushed through him.

When the slow trussing was completed, he stepped back to admire his handiwork.

"Something's missing," he mused. A quick search produced the apple he'd knocked out of the guard's hand. He held it up for his troop and the audience on the beach to see.

Then he jammed the apple into the guard's mouth.

"Tie it so he can't spit it out," he ordered one of his goons. "We wouldn't want to deprive a dying man of his favorite food, now, would we?"

Mason couldn't resist humming a few bars of his favorite song, Cassie's favorite song, as the flag of his new regime was raised.

———

Danny stood numb with horror. The guard hanging from the flagpole had finally stopped writhing. The grotesque gurgling had ceased. Even the thumping sound of the deadweight against the metal flagpole had stopped. Yet he remained transfixed, unable to turn his head away from the lazily twisting body and the contorted purple-black face with the apple obscenely stuffed in its mouth.

Finally, Danny clenched his eyes tightly closed. His head was pounding. *What's wrong with me?* he asked himself. He'd seen death before. As a volunteer fireman, he'd viewed bodies dredged out of the bay. The first few times he'd upchucked immediately. Eventually he learned to steel himself against their putrescence. But never had he been fascinated or entranced by them. Watching the guard tortured had almost been exciting.

Danny shook his head violently. He had to get away from this place, away from the creatures who were acting so crazy and making him crazy. Without another glance at the swinging corpse, Danny took off across the beach toward the lights on the amusement pier. Running in the sand relieved the pounding in his head. His thinking cleared. He belonged with his buddies, the guards. They'd need his help against the crazies on the beach. No way would they ignore him now, when a war was being fought.

He approached the ramp to the pier. Creatures were huddled in small groups, cursing at the torch-lighted areas on the pavilion roofs, but unable to figure out how to attack them. Many creatures lay dead. Their bodies formed a circle around the lighted areas. Danny soon discovered why. One step into the light and the guards opened fire. From their vantage points atop the one-story pavilions, it was like shooting the proverbial fish in a barrel.

Danny pondered how he could signal the guards that he'd decided to join their ranks. He shouted at them from the darkness. The only answer he received was an eruption of gunfire. If only he could spot someone he knew, one of his poker buddies, then maybe they'd all realize who he was.

He walked around the pier, ignoring the other creatures, always careful to stay clear of the lighted areas, until he came to the Paul Bunyan Arcade. A miniature golf course was on the roof. Danny had kicked many a golf ball through its windmills and logging streams, up and around the green asphalt hills, and most fun of all, over the inadequate fence that allowed a well-aimed stray ball to hit a sunbather on the beach below. Yes, he knew the place well. There was a stairway inside the arcade that lead to the golf course; and an outside wooden ramp that hugged one side of the building.

He considered this latter entrance first, but it appeared to be too well-lighted by the torches on the roof. Again, he tried calling out to the guards, and for a moment he thought he'd succeeded. A big, red-haired man stood up and seemed to look out in his direction. Danny moved closer to the ramp, but before he could make contact, a creature near him took aim and fired. The red-haired man dived for cover and soon the area exploded with bullets.

Danny decided he had to try for the inside stairway although it would mean crossing into the light. And then he remembered another entrance: the trapdoor under the pier. It had been installed for the sole purpose of retrieving all those run-afoul golf balls that he and others had enjoyed shooting over the fence.

It took no time at all to find his way back to the beach and under the pier. The trapdoor opened easily after one strong tug, and soon he was maneuvering soundlessly through the dark, musty arcade, past pinball machines and Skee-Ball, up the center stairway, and through the legs of the fifteen-foot plaster statue of Paul Bunyan that formed the archway of the golf course.

He heard voices. Stepping quickly into the shadows, he squinted from the glaring fight of the torches.

The redheaded man he'd spotted earlier took a step back and turned to peer into the darkness where Danny stood.

Danny knew the man. It was the cop who'd befriended his mother and gone out of his way to help him when he'd been sick and helpless on the beach. He moved closer to the man and tried to remember his name.

"Who's there?" Stafford shouted tersely. Conversation on the roof abruptly halted.

Guns appeared from all directions.

"Hey, don't shoot," Danny called out, "I've come to join you, to help you fight the monsters on the boardwalk."

He heard footsteps running over the green asphalt turf. More torches were lit. The guards had him surrounded.

"Wait," he shouted again, "you know me."

Stafford conferred with another guard before yelling back, "Yeah, we know you, but show yourself so we'll be sure it's you."

Danny took a step into the light. "Jesus, you guys sure are paranoid."

Stafford's face suddenly registered alarm. "Danny, I didn't know—"

Then Danny felt arms crushing him from behind. There was a flash and a sweep of a knife. His eyes caught a glint of steel. Then his hair was yanked hard, his head snapped backward, and a silent blade sheared a deep gorge across his neck.

Danny shrieked in protest but felt no pain. He watched, stunned, suspended in time for one frozen moment, as blood sprayed out of him, like water from a shower head. Then his knees buckled. His body went limp. Slowly, he collapsed into the pool of blood and the darkness.

— ——

The bungalow was alive with grisly shapes. Every flutter of the tablecloth, each ball of dust adrift in a darkened corner, became a monster ready to devour her.

Sandy waited, rooted to the chair that was directly opposite her front door. Her ears registered each nuance of sound, from an explosion of gunfire outside to the vaguest creaking of a floorboard inside her barricaded home.

Another shadow crawled up the wall. Sandy knew it was a reflection from the makeshift oil lamp on the table beside her, but it still frightened her.

Upstairs, Jesse slept fitfully. Once or twice he had called out for her, obviously in the throes of nightmares of his own. She ached to go to him, to brush back the hair from his forehead and lie next to him until the bad dreams passed. Yet she forced herself to maintain her sentry position, gun riveted to her hands, waiting for the inevitable — the sound of Mason coming back for her.

Time expanded, every second leaden and inert. Then she heard it.

Footsteps tip-tapped up the stairs to her porch. Labored, heavy panting echoed in the room, and Sandy realized it was coming from her.

Click! The doorknob turned.

Mouth dry and hands trembling, she cocked the gun.

A stench filled the air. Was it her imagination, or did the room reek of the same putrid odor she'd smelled in her bedroom the night she was raped?

Remembrance of that horror steadied her hands.

Click! Click! Click! The doorknob rattled loudly.

Sandy was positive it was the same odor. Waves of nausea washed over her body as she imagined the vaporous rot seeping through the barred door, sending tentacles of foul air around her.

Whack! Something slammed hard against the door. Sandy rose to her feet. *Well, all right*, she decided. *Why don't you just come in. Mason? Let's finish this*. The nausea passed. Her hands steadied and she parted her legs slightly, like a TV cop.

Whack! Whack! The door bulged farther and farther from its frame. Nails twisted loose. A board began to crack from the strain. Suddenly the light blinked. Rapidly changing shadow patterns flickered briefly across the walls and then died.

Sandy whipped around and saw a puff of smoke coming from the oil lamp. The flame was out and the air in the room quickly changed to black soup.

Crash! She heard the sound of splintering wood. He was almost through!

Sandy hesitated, but only for a split second. Gun or no gun, she knew she'd be at his mercy in the dark. A cry, half of frustration, half of terror, echoed in the room as she fumbled over the table for the matches and salad oil. The gun, still cocked, slipped gently from her grip and banged on the table.

Crash! Cru-n-n-ch! The door exploded off its hinges.

Sandy finished pouring the oil as the intruder stumbled over the debris of the shattered door.

"Cassie."

Miraculously, the first match lit the string wick. The warm glow soon spread over the room. Sandy let out a sigh and then spotted Mason's silhouette illuminated in her doorway. She scrambled for the gun.

"Cassie," he whispered again.

The gun was in her hands. Quickly she assumed her firing position.

"Get out of here. Mason," she said evenly. "This gun is loaded, and believe me, I'll use it on you."

"Cassie," he repeated. He took a step forward.

"Mason," she screamed, "I'm warning you!"

He took another step forward. "Cassie," he whispered mildly, "you know you could never hurt me."

Two steps closer and there was only the length of the table between them.

"Stay back," Sandy shrieked. Tears of hysteria formed in her eyes and she let out an involuntary sob.

Mason's eyes flicked to the lighted oil on the table.

Sandy went blank and then found herself slammed against the wall of the cottage. Her cries and screams were almost as loud as the gun she was firing at Mason. She fired until it was empty. She screamed until she was sure his body, slumped over the table, wouldn't move.

Minutes passed. Mason's body remained motionless and Sandy's cries subsided. There was a lump on her head where the force of the firing gun had sent her reeling against the wall. Her hands were sore from gripping the gun so tightly. Had she really killed him?

She crept over to the body and examined it. The blood and sores covering his body made it impossible to tell where he'd been wounded. Sandy hated to touch him but forced herself to feel for a pulse on his neck. There was none. She tried his wrist. Nothing.

She turned him over to check his breathing and saw that his chest was split open, ripped apart from the blasts. Gagging, she backed away from his remains. She knew she should feel remorse, or at least pity, for this man she had once known. But she felt only horror and numbing relief. The sick bastard was finally dead. He deserved to be killed. She'd been forced to do the job because no one had been there to help, but it was finally over.

The gun dropped from her hands and clanged loudly to the floor. She climbed the stairs slowly and crawled in bed with Jesse. Minutes later, she was asleep.

19.

Death descends upon the body in the following manner.

Immediately: Muscles relax. The brain begins to liquefy. Body temperature drops.

10 minutes: Eyes fly open, pupils dilate widely, and corneas cloud over.

3-5 hours: Blood drains to the lowest areas of the body as dictated by gravity. These areas turn a reddish or reddish-blue color.

6 hours: Rigor mortis has set in. The face stiffens. If not composed, legs and arms assume contorted positions.

First day: Body tissues are attacked by bacteria and begin to decompose. It is a process very similar to that which occurs in moist gangrene. Foul smelling gases are released. Tissues start to soften and liquefy. The skin starts to shrink and gradually decays.

All the corpses on Sea Breeze Island followed this natural order of death. But there was one difference: those consecrated by the toxic fallout continued to live.

THREE

THE RISE AND THE RISE OF THE BEACHERS

20.

Stafford stood shoulder-to-shoulder with the guards on the roof and watched another corpse shudder to life.

None of the guards gasped. None of them moaned. None of them, including Mario, continued to say, "Holy shit."

Stafford decided that if he suddenly took a flying leap off the building or if he began barking like a dog while he ran around on all fours, no one would blink.

Below, on the boardwalk, the corpse raised himself to a teetering, standing position. A tumor-ridden, disfigured head moved slowly side to side. Torn remnants of a mauve-colored leisure suit, pink shirt, and white tie hung loosely on the body. Like the resurrected corpses before him, he moved sluggishly, hesitantly, making several false starts before dragging himself, finally, in the direction of the beach.

"Somebody give me a gun," Mario said.

Mario was the youngest cop on the force and, like Lenny, had grown up in Queens, New York.

"What do you want it for?" asked Stafford.

Mario wet his lips nervously and smiled. "I'm out of bullets and he's too far away for me to use... this."

A ten-inch switchblade snapped open in his hand. It was a gesture Mario performed habitually, one from which he derived immense pleasure.

Stafford looked at the blade and remembered the last time Mario used it — on Danny Morelli's neck. He also remembered the look on Danny's face, and his stomach turned over.

"Haven't we done enough?" he asked in a quiet, strained voice.

"Just give me the goddamned gun." Mario yanked the rifle out of Stafford's hands, took aim, and fired.

The corpse had reached the entrance to the beach when the shot rang out. There was a vibration and a small dark stain on the back of the mauve-colored jacket, but otherwise there was no indication that the corpse had been hit.

"Shit. I hit the bastard dead on, I know I did," Mario said after the corpse had moved down the ramp and out of sight.

Stafford waited until he could swallow again. "We hit the other ones too. So, what does it prove?"

"Maybe our bullets are no good," Mario said.

"Yeah and maybe them corpses all turned into Supermen," said Donaldson, an old-timer from the Sea Breeze Fire Department.

Several men chuckled and the tension lessened by a few degrees. Shoulders relaxed. Fingers unclasped and flexed. Mario stuck a cigarette in his mouth and lit a match, but he had to use one hand to keep the other steady. Donaldson took out a blue-and-white bandana and wiped his forehead.

Stafford realized the other men were as terrified as he was. "Anybody else got any ideas?" he asked.

A few men mumbled. Most shook their heads no.

"Look," said Stafford, "if we don't know what we're dealing with here, maybe it's time we retreat to the station house and try to find out."

"You turning into chicken shit, Stafford?" Mario asked, a smirk curling his lips. "The captain told us to stay until relieved. So, who are you to change the orders?"

"I'm not changing a thing," said Stafford. "You guys do what you please. All I'm saying is that it's time we stopped shooting people — forcing them to stay isolated on the beach — when our main concern should be finding a way to get all of us off the island."

Donaldson was the first to agree. "Stafford's right. What we need is a town meeting. Get the doctor to speak his mind. Maybe find out what that asshole mayor's been doing to contact inland authorities."

"Hell, I'm for it," someone else added. "We can go on home, check on our families, and report to the town hall this afternoon."

Stafford thought of Sandy and Jesse, alone in the bungalow. He sighed. Then suddenly, his attention was riveted to the boardwalk. A corpse had just emerged from the arcade below them.

The other guards saw his expression, and all discussion ceased. Tension resumed. Rifles were hefted into position. Shoulders tightened. There was no sound at all but the snapping of Mario's switchblade. The corpse paused and turned... very slowly ... to look up at the roof. Then, even the switchblade quieted and Mario whispered, "Ho-ly shit." There was a deep red gash slashed across the corpse's neck.

Stafford tore his eyes away and scanned the roof near the plaster statue of Paul Bunyan. There was no trace of the body they'd left there — no trace but a puddle of blood where it had fallen.

A shiver started in the small of his back and crawled up his spine. Stafford knew he was on the brink of hysteria. He forced himself to look back at the corpse on the boardwalk. But Danny Morelli had turned away and was headed home.

———

"Sandy."

She floated on a blue-green ocean. The water was deep and blissfully warm.

"Sandy."

She turned her head and saw Mason, on the shore, calling her name, but Mason looked different. His hair grew thick and wavy; it was sun-bleached blond. His smooth, copper-tanned skin glistened in the hot noon sun. It was Mason as she had known him ten years ago. Mason had become young and handsome and normal again... except for his eyes. His eyes were balls of gray flesh without pupils, eyes without life or expression, and yet Sandy knew they were seeing her and hungering for her.

"Sandy."

She swam furiously out to sea — away from Mason, away from his eyes — but the current was too strong. No matter how hard she struggled, the ocean waves pulled her closer to the shore, until she knew he was standing over her. His hands touched her shoulder, and she went rigid. Instantly she was jerked from the waters of sleep into wakefulness.

"Sandy," Stafford whispered.

Her eyes flew open and she saw that she was in the upstairs bedroom. Jesse lay beside her, sleeping like a kitten. Stafford was leaning over her.

"Sandy," he said. He held her face between his hands. "I came as soon as I could. When I saw that door ripped apart, I-I didn't know what I'd find. Was it Mason? Did he hurt you again?"

Sandy lowered her eyes. "Mason's dead," she said. "I killed him."

Stafford looked at her silently for a moment and then held her close. "I wish it were true," he said softly.

"But it is true, Stafford," she said, pulling back to look up quizzically at him. "He's dead and his body's downstairs, unless somebody moved it."

"No one moved it. Mason isn't dead. Look, maybe I should explain what happened —"

"No, wait a minute. You don't have to explain anything. I know exactly what happened. Last night, while you were off playing policeman, Mason broke into the house and I shot him. He's dead, finished, over with, ka-put, end of problem."

"Yes, but —"

"There was a hole as big as a bowling ball in his chest and his guts were spread out all over the table. So, don't tell me he's not dead!"

"Sh-sh... Stop screaming. Do you want to wake Jesse up?" He put his arm around her shoulder, but she shrugged it off. "I know it sounds unbelievable," he said. "I can't quite believe it myself, but Mason isn't dead. None of the creatures is dead."

"You're crazy," she hissed. She jumped off the bed and rushed out of the bedroom.

Stafford made no attempt to stop her. Head in his hands, he listened to the sound of her bare feet on the stairs. There was a pause, time enough for him to regret the way he'd shocked her with the truth, and then the screaming started.

Later, after her screams subsided, he scooped Jesse into his arms and carried him downstairs to find Sandy standing quietly in the center of the room. Her arms hung limply at her side. She stared at the empty table.

"Look... some of us are organizing a town meeting," Stafford said. "You can come with me if you like." He shook his head sadly. "After what you've been through, you have the right to be there."

He waited several moments and then, receiving no response from her, he added, "Sandy, have you been listening to me? Are you okay?"

"There's a lot of blood on the tablecloth," she said finally. Her voice was hoarse and strained, yet resigned. "But there are only a few drops leading to the front door. Where is Mason now?"

Stafford walked over and transferred Jesse into her arms. "I don't know."

Sandy clutched her child to her chest and closed her eyes. "Before I get dressed for the meeting, tell me what you do know."

———

Like Sandy, Mason also dreamed he was swimming, and it was some time before he could ride the waves of his semiconscious state and open his eyes.

Cassie? Where are you, Cassie? Why am I on the beach?

He blinked several times, but the beach and the creatures around him looked blurred at the fringes. He tried lifting himself, but his arms and legs refused to follow his mind's commands. Images of Cassie filled his mind: Cassie holding the gun, Cassie shooting him, Cassie killing him.

No, it's impossible. Cassie loves me.

With intense effort, he forced his back up, feeling the strain in his neck, while his arms flailed helplessly at his sides. As he struggled to maintain a teetering, sitting position, he heard a familiar voice behind him.

"Don't fight it, just go with the flow," said Mongril.

Mason lost control and began to crumble. In the midst of falling backward, he was charged with the voltage of a new sensation. Suddenly, he felt weightless, ethereal, disencumbered. His vision cleared. He sat upright with perfect control. At first he thought he'd been lifted a few inches above the sand, but then he realized that it was not his body but his mind that was adrift. Unbounded by laws of gravity or reason, his mind floated, detached from the rest of his anatomy.

Mason stared at his tunnel-eyed, dopey-smiling second-in-command. "What makes you the expert?"

The words felt funny coming out of his mouth, as if they didn't rely on the movement of tongue or the inhaling and exhaling of breath.

"While you took your time coming back to the beach this morning, I been practicing," Mongril answered. "Shit, that was some beautiful party we had ourselves last night. I almost pissed my pants when I seen old Apple Jaws strung up. Everybody's been talking about it. You were beautiful, man, beautiful. But then you disappeared. I looked everywhere for you. Where'd you go?"

Mason looked upward, across the beach to the swinging corpse hanging from the flagpole. He remembered the intense feelings of the previous night, the thrill of revenge, the power of watching the guard's pain, and the desire to share it all with Cassie.

But Cassie wasn't home. I never saw her, did I?

"No place," Mason told Mongril. "I didn't go no place."

Mongril snorted with disbelief. "Right. No problem. You don't want to share information with Mongril, Mongril will still share information with you. Wait till you see this."

Out of the remnants of his tattered blue jeans, Mongril pulled out a thin, sharp object and held it up in the air.

Mason recognized it immediately as the hemostat he'd taken from the clinic. "That's mine," he said.

"For sure, man. I only like borrowed it from your black bag. Now, watch this."

Before Mason could protest, Mongril made a big show of holding the hemostat in the air, swinging it around and around, like some sort of dramatic baseball windup, before jamming the instrument deep into his own chest.

Mason's mouth dropped open.

Mongril's face showed no pain, no sign of discomfort. He screwed the hemostat in deep until it almost disappeared completely into his flesh. Then, gauging Mason's every reaction, he pressed two fingers on either side of the instrument while his other hand jerked and pulled it out again.

"Ain't that something?" Mongril asked.

"You're crazy."

"Yeah, ain't I?" Mongril basked in the compliment. "Watch this one."

This time he stabbed the hemostat into the huge tumor on his forehead. He dug it in deep, securing it in a mound of bulging tissue, so that when he let go of it and shook his head, it wiggled in the tumor like a spoon in Jell-O.

"Ain't it something?" he again asked Mason. "And it don't hurt a bit, not one bit. Hey. Why don't you try it?"

The hemostat made a loud sucking noise before it popped out of his forehead. He held it out to Mason.

"I'll... pass," Mason said.

"Go ahead. Try putting it in one of the holes you got in your chest. See if you can get it to come out the other side. It won't hurt. I tried sticking it in my eye and I didn't feel a thing. Nothing. I could even see out of the eye while it was stuck in there. Then I tried jabbing it..."

Mongril droned on and on, but Mason no longer heard him. He no longer saw him. His fingers traced the outlines of his wounds and Mason saw only the image of Cassie, thrown against the bungalow wall, as she fired bullet after bullet into his body.

Why, Cassie? Why don't you love me?

21.

After Stafford finished telling of the night's events, Sandy got dressed and took Jesse with them to the town hall. They walked in silence: Jesse holding tightly to his mother with one hand while his other clutched his half-filled Fred Flintstone bottle; Stafford, head down, completely engrossed in his private hell of guilt and fear; and Sandy, numb and unable to shake off the feeling that she was dreaming.

Streets that had recently resembled garbage dumps now looked like bombed-out war zones. Parked cars were demolished. Windows, everywhere, were smashed. Doors were twisted off hinges. A sallow-faced adolescent urinated against an uprooted tree. A knot of people slept near a barrel of burning trash. Children, glassy-eyed and shell-shocked, wandered aimlessly through charred bricks.

The town hall was one of the few buildings untouched by vandalism. Rifled guards were posted around its white-columned, stately exterior and along the thirty steps that led to two ornate doors. The meeting was being held in a court room on the main floor.

There were approximately a hundred people, standing and talking in small groups dispersed throughout the room. Stafford joined a group of guards near the windows, while Sandy sat with Jesse on the nearest bench. On her right, a girl with long, straight hair looked up and saw her, then slid next to her.

"Hi. Remember me?" she asked.

Confusion flickered briefly across Sandy's face. Then she broke into a smile. "Sure, you're the volunteer Doctor Jenkins introduced to me. You're... Beth, right?"

"Right, and you're the volunteer with all the questions. Tell me, did you get any answers yet?"

Sandy shrugged. "No. That's why I'm here. How about you?"

"I'm here for questions, not answers," she said. Her mouth was set in a thin, straight line.

A side door opened and Dr. Jenkins entered the room accompanied by two other men. One man wore glasses and was about fifty-five, short, chunky, and jovial-looking with a flushed complexion and thinning gray hair. The other man was taller, younger, with an athletic build and a military posture.

"Who are those men with Doctor Jenkins?" Sandy asked Beth.

"The one in uniform is Cruthers," Beth answered, spitting out his name like it tasted bad. "He's our illustrious police captain. The other one is Mayor Raposo, aptly nicknamed *Rabozo*."

Mayor Raposo stepped up to the judge's bench and tapped a heavy gavel on an ebony block. "Please, everyone be seated," he said. "There's so much to be done, I'd like to start this meeting as soon as possible."

Stafford and the other guards shuffled down the center aisle to sit together in the second row. The clamor of voices died down.

"Thank you," Mayor Raposo said. He assumed an attitude of solemn concern. "Many of you thought it would be a good idea to have this town meeting in order to ask questions. I understand your concern, believe me. We've had a rough night. The lives of a lot of good men have been lost and there's so much more to do. But let's try to hold off questions until —"

Beth sprang to her feet. "If this is a town meeting, why wasn't the rest of the town notified about it? How come most of the people in this room are policemen, firemen, politicians, and their friends and families?"

Mayor Raposo squinted until he recognized the speaker. "Ah, Miss Beth Simpson, isn't it? As you well know. Miss Simpson, all our communication systems are out. But anyone in town who wished was free to join us for this meeting. We didn't turn you away now, did we?"

Abruptly he dismissed her with a turn of his head. "We'll begin with a report from Captain Cruthers," he said. "And please, everyone, hold off all questions until the end."

Cruthers walked to the side of the judge's bench and faced his audience. "Most units have reported in or been relieved, except for the men on duty outside and at the A and P supermarket," he said. "Clean-up crews went out this morning, and the casualties and the wounded were brought to the station house next door. Families have been notified. Doctor Jenkins will be posting a list for the general public soon."

His voice was calm, even, controlled, and very matter-of-fact. Except for the tension lines creased around his eyes, his face was emotionless.

"I would be lying if 1 said last night's attacks came as a surprise," he continued. "It's exactly what I've been expecting and preparing for all along. Unfortunately, we weren't as prepared as we should have been. According to the reports I've received, the lifeguard station was looted and demolished. That's one third of our food, water, weapons, and medical supplies... gone. More rifles were seized during attacks on guards. Therefore, as I see it, we have no alternatives. We must consolidate all remaining supplies. Enlist more guards from the best of the riffraff roaming the streets and — I think this is something you women can do for us — move ahead with our rationing program. Most important of all, we must immediately begin to prepare ourselves for the next attack."

Cruthers finished his speech. There was a beat of absolute silence, and then the room exploded into pandemonium. Twenty people jumped up screaming questions. A baby started crying. An elderly couple began to moan. Almost everyone in the room had something important to say to somebody else. Beth, sitting next to Sandy, shook her head, saying over and over again, "I can't believe it. I just can't believe it."

Sandy looked at the uproar around her. She held Jesse a little closer, bouncing him nervously on her knee, and remained silent.

Raposo banged his gavel five or six times before the commotion subsided. Thirty hands waved in the air with questions. "Stafford," he said, "you were one of those who wanted this meeting, so why don't you go first."

Stafford stood up, looking nervous and uncomfortable. "You mentioned one of my concerns a second ago — namely, our communication systems. What some of the fellas and I wondered was... well, what exactly is being done to regain contact with the mainland?"

The mayor took a deep breath before he answered. "Of course, that's the question that's uppermost in all our minds." He leaned farther forward on the judge's bench and folded his hands. "Most of you are aware that everything — water, gas, electricity, telephone — is run in or piped in from the mainland. We have no power source of our own. The Sea Breeze Island Bridge was destroyed by fire the first day of the storm. Naturally we have boats, but so far our expeditions across the bay have been unsuccessful. Now that some of the fog has cleared, however, we'll be making further expeditions. Another idea that's been suggested is to send a sailboat down the Jersey shore and contact authorities."

A voice in the back of the room yelled out, "How about trying a ham radio?"

"Yeah," said a senior citizen. "There's a family on my block that's got one. Only thing it was ever good for before was messing up my television picture. Maybe now you can put it to some real use."

"There's a family in my block that keeps throwing their garbage in my driveway," said a plump woman in a flowered smock. "It stinks to high heaven and I want to know what can be done about it."

A babbling of voices erupted again, but it quickly quieted with a few taps of the mayor's gavel. "There are several battery-powered ham radios on the island," he said. "When the storm hit, it was one of the first things we tried. But maybe I ought to let Al Granger explain it to you."

Al Granger from Al's Bayside Exxon stood up. He was tall and thin, but muscular, with big, competent hands and a mild disposition. "Soon as the storm let up, believe it or not, first thing on a lot of folks' minds was getting their car started. The bridge was burned out, there was no place to go, but I can't tell you how many people came to see me insisting that I fix their cars." He shook his head. "Trouble is, there ain't a workable battery anywhere on the whole damn island. I've tried dozens of 'em, including brand new ones out of my storeroom, but I can't get enough juice out of any of them to light a flashlight."

"How is that possible?" someone asked.

Al shook his head. "Don't know. It's the damnedest thing I ever seen. No kind of batteries will work. I could understand it happening temporarily during the storm but —"

"It's just like in that movie, Close Encounters of the Third Kind," Mario said. "Remember when the spaceship flew overhead and the car engines stalled out?"

"Hey, Mario," teased Donaldson. "Maybe we're all prisoners in a Steven Spielberg movie."

"And maybe you're an asshole," Mario shot back.

Several people laughed. Donaldson started humming the theme song of *The Twilight Zone*.

Sandy decided she couldn't take much more. She rose slowly to her feet, holding Jesse protectively against her shoulder. "Is it true they can't be killed?" she asked.

Mayor Raposo squinted to get a good look at her. "What did she say?" he asked.

"Is it true the people on the beach can't be killed?" she repeated, louder this time.

The rest of the room quieted. Stafford looked anxiously in her direction, but she didn't acknowledge his stare.

Finally, Raposo broke the silence that had settled like a shroud over the room. "I'd say the little lady has a question you can best answer, Doctor Jenkins." He gestured for Dr. Jenkins to take the floor.

Sandy lifted Jesse higher against her shoulder and sat down, while Dr. Jenkins flipped several pages on his clipboard, and began, "Okay. As most of you know, we have no hospital on the island. Medical supplies are limited. Laboratory equipment is nonexistent. Despite these limitations, I've spent considerable time treating victims of the recent disaster and I've made extensive notes on my observations. The first stage was a severe reaction to the unusual toxicity of the rain. Death occurred immediately or within a few days. My rough estimate would be fifty percent fatality rate during this first stage. Second stage of the illness produced intense pain, seizures, high fever, disorientation, low blood pressure, hysteria, and in some cases, partial paralysis. Third stage — and again, these are my observations, not proven scientific fact — third stage produced the disfiguring skin lesions, tumors, ulcerations, et cetera, that we've come to know so well."

"But, Doc," said a guard named Ernie, who sat behind Stafford, "we want to know if it's possible for them to be killed and then come back to life."

Dr. Jenkins smiled. "I've heard the rumor," he said patiently, "and I assure you, it's ridiculous. It's medically impossible."

"But last night I seen people shot and —"

"Look," the doctor said, cutting him off. "Right now we have enough real problems without worrying about any *walking dead*, so let's get serious, okay?"

Donaldson called out, "I seen a man with his neck sliced open lose more'n two quarts of blood. And this morning he got up for a morning stroll on the boardwalk. That sound serious to you, Doc?"

Dr. Jenkins looked at the mayor for an answer, received none, and turned back to the audience. "How can I answer that?" he asked, irritation clearly evident in his voice. "I wasn't there. I didn't see it."

"You calling us liars?" Mario asked.

"No," he answered. "Of course not. But the island was very dark last night. None of you is used to seeing by torch light. It would be very easy for your eyes to play tricks on you. And perhaps the rain has one or two beneficial side effects. It's not impossible. After the atomic blast in

Hiroshima, for example, it was observed that victims who suffered flash burns were protected from radiation sickness. Maybe the same principle applies here. This is all pure speculation, of course, but maybe the rain deadens pain centers in the brain. Or —"

"You're damn right it's pure speculation," yelled a guard who was wearing a T-shirt with a picture of a dog squirting a fire hydrant. "You weren't out there this morning watching corpses drag themselves to the beach. No, sir! And you weren't there taking notes when twenty bullets shot through one freak without him so much as flinching."

Beth jumped up again, this time with her fists clenched tightly into hard, round balls. "Do all of you know how you sound?" she asked. "Can you hear yourselves? These 'corpses,' these 'freaks,' as you so callously call them, are human beings. Some of them are your friends and neighbors. All of you talk about them like they're animals or some sort of monsters."

"Hey, lady, we didn't string up one of them on a flagpole," Mario said. "We didn't start the riot last night."

"Didn't you? Then who was it that forced them to remain on the beach against their will? Who was it that denied them the basic necessities of food? Or shelter? Of proper medical care? Of basic human dignity?"

"My dear Miss Simpson," said Mayor Raposo, "we've been all through this. The care of the sick has been a top priority from the beginning. But with limited resources, we can only do so much."

"Your Honor," said Stafford, "some of the things Miss Simpson says are true. Things have gotten out of hand. With all due respect to Captain Cruthers, I think we should make some compromises. Maybe set up a committee. Have them meet with representatives of the people on the beach, work out an agreement. With the fog on the bay clearing, it can't be more than a few days before help arrives. All we have to do is remain calm and wait."

Several people mumbled agreement.

"It's your decision," Cruthers informed the mayor. "But in my opinion, you'd be making a serious mistake. You can't make deals with maniacs, and that's what the disease has reduced them to: irrational maniacs."

An old man in a wrinkled brown suit stood up. "Maniacs?" he yelled. "I'll tell you about maniacs."

Heads jerked in the direction of the speaker.

"Because of maniacs we're surrounded by deadly viruses, nerve gas, and mutant bacteria. We're up to our eyeballs in radwaste."

Mayor Raposo shifted uncomfortably on the judge's bench. "Uh, thank you, Professor. We'll take your thoughts into consideration —"

"Hell, don't you people know what's happened?" He glared at the hushed audience in the courtroom. "By some miracle we've managed to survive fallout that should have razed the island. The winds may have something to do with it. The unusual electric activity is definitely part of it. Whatever the reason, I figure we're in a bubble, an air pocket, so to speak, a clean spot that's floating on top of one humongous toxic dump. You can sit around and wait, make deals or kill one another off. It doesn't matter. But don't expect outside help to come near us. By rights, we should all be dead."

The old wizard-faced man rubbed at his chin thoughtfully. "Maybe we are dead."

The mayor cleared his throat in the silence that followed and looked helplessly at Stafford and Captain Cruthers for guidance.

"Yes... well, that may be — if we don't come to some decisions soon. Therefore, I'd like Captain Cruthers, Doctor Jenkins, Stafford, and the other guards on duty last night to reconvene in the conference room down the hall in five minutes." He banged his gavel once and pronounced, "Meeting adjourned."

Several people protested loudly, but the mayor hurried through the side door, tailed closely by Cruthers and Jenkins. Stafford waved at Sandy from across the room.

"I'll meet you at your place," he yelled out over the rising din of voices in the room. Sucked away by the swell of guards, he quickly disappeared.

The people around Sandy started filing into the aisles, slowly making their way to the back doors.

"Well, that was an abrupt way to end the meeting. Who was the crazy old man?" Sandy asked Beth as they stepped into the aisle.

Beth shook her long hair out of her eyes. "Professor Trifun," she answered. "He's lived on the island for as long as I can remember, but I heard a rumor once that forty years ago he was part of a research team at Los Alamos, you know, the place they built the first atomic bombs."

"You don't really think what he said could be true, do you?"

Beth shook her head. "I have to get back to my father now," she said. She ruffled Jesse's hair affectionately and pushed her way through the crowd. Sandy stared after her with a quizzical expression on her face. Then she lifted Jesse into her arms and slowly headed home.

It was four or five hours later — if she hadn't forgotten to wind her wristwatch she'd have known exactly — when she let Stafford in through her new patchwork door.

"Perfect timing," she said. "I just finished repairing the door. I'm getting so handy with a hammer and nails that maybe after all this is over, I'll hire myself out as a carpenter."

The stricken look on his face registered, and she became serious. "What's wrong? What happened at the meeting?"

"Let's sit down," Stafford said.

Quickly, she led him to the kitchen table and sat down next to him.

"Did they decide to attack or negotiate?"

"Negotiate. Everything's set. Tonight at dusk, we're meeting with the leaders of last night's riots."

"Well, that's what you wanted. It's what you pushed for. So why the long face?"

"Sandy," he said, taking hold of her hands in his, "the leader of the riots, the one we're meeting with tonight, is Mason."

Sandy stiffened at the sound of his name. Suddenly she was intensely focused on everything Stafford was saying.

"And we have no choice but to negotiate with him," he continued, "because there's nothing left on the mainland. Everything's gone. Professor Trifun was right. Everything is burned away. Everything's destroyed. There's no sign of anyone to help us, no sign there ever will be anyone. Everything's bones and liquid soot. Everything's dead."

22.

At six-thirty Mrs. Morelli sat at her kitchen table and listened to the creaking of the rocking chair across the room. The sound made her think of coffin lids and cemetery gates. It was like the beginning of the old radio show, *Inner Sanctum*, which she and Mr. Morelli had listened to long ago, before the Parkinson's.

"Your father was so worried about you," she told Danny. "First thing every morning he asked for you. He stayed awake every night calling and calling your name."

Danny, his back to his mother, continued rocking and made no comment.

"He wouldn't let me shave him," she said, laughing nervously. "He said only Danny knew how to shave him. Only Danny knew how to fix his pillows the way he liked them. He just about drove me crazy, he missed you so much." She shook her head, still smiling.

"Who's crazy?" Mr. Morelli yelled from the back bedroom.

"No one, dear," Mrs. Morelli yelled back.

"What I don't understand," she continued, "is how sometimes he knows everything that goes on around him, and other times he forgets his own name."

"Danny! Get me out of this bed," Mr. Morelli yelled.

"He never forgets your name, God bless him," Mrs. Morelli said.

The rocking chair continued creaking.

Outside the cottage windows, bright sunlight had shifted to gray daylight. The air inside was hot and humid, and a mute gloom settled over the room.

"More coffee?" Mrs. Morelli asked her son. "Or soup? Or some ham? Why don't I make you a nice ham sandwich with some of that canned ham I opened this morning?"

The rocking chair squeaked even faster. Danny said nothing.

"Fry me some ham," Mr. Morelli shouted. "Get me out of this bed and make me a sandwich. I'm starving."

"I'm talking to Danny, dear. You've eaten your supper already and Danny hasn't touched a bite all day.

"Danny, you have to eat," she coaxed her son. "Let me make you half a sandwich."

"I haven't eaten nothing for hours. I might as well starve, for all anybody cares. Might as well be dead. Where is Danny? Tell Danny if he don't get me out of this bed. I'll get myself up and make a sandwich."

The rocking chair picked up speed, groaning furiously, but otherwise there was no indication that Danny had heard his father.

"Do you think maybe he's hungry?" Mrs. Morelli asked anxiously. "Maybe we should —"

A loud thump sounded from the back bedroom, cutting off Mrs. Morelli's words. Then came the distress call.

"Help! I've fallen on the floor. Somebody get me up! Danny, where are you?"

Mrs. Morelli dabbed at her forehead with a handkerchief. "I'll go, dear."

Danny stopped rocking and turned his head to look at his mother. His facial features were blurred beyond recognition — but a look of pure hate was unmistakable in what was left. The lipless mouth opened. "Shut him up, Mother," he said. "Shut him up or I swear I'll kill him."

———

"My mind's made up, Stafford. I'm going to the negotiation meeting with you."

Stafford stared at Sandy incredulously. They were still sitting in her kitchen. The argument had been going on for hours.

"Let me get this straight," he said, running his hands through his hair. "You're terrified of the lion, so you throw yourself into the den. Makes perfect sense to me."

Sandy tried to explain it to him for the tenth time. "I'm not throwing myself into a lion's den alone. You'll be with me. But if we're going to have any success at all dealing with Mason, you have to remember that he's crazy. Your logic won't be his logic. Your reality won't be his reality."

"But if that's true, why do you insist on seeing him?"

Sandy shook her head. "I don't want to see him, but what choice do I have? If Mason's alive and I'm on this island, he'll find me again. I'll have to deal with him eventually. At the meeting tonight, I'll have other people around when I see him. And who knows? Maybe I can convince him to leave me alone."

"And if you don't?"

Sandy looked across the table at her son, at the glaze over his eyes, at his thumb forever plugged into his mouth, and said, "Then at least Jesse won't be there when he kills me."

———

"We got 'em by the balls," said Mongril at eight-forty-five.

The approaching dusk had changed the beach from the aftermath of a battle to a rock-concert warm-up.

Creatures formed in small clusters or moved freely from group to group, laughing, trading stories, relishing their rejuvenation from the day of rest.

Mongril addressed a group of hard core supporters sprawled in the sand around Mason. "We got 'em by the balls, and now it's time for us to squeeze 'em dry." On the word "squeeze," he emphasized his meaning by slowly bringing his hand into a tightly closed fist.

A Goon Squad member agreed. "And when their committee comes here tonight, we tell them to shove their compromises, 'cause the party's just beginning."

Whoops of cheer registered approval for this plan of action. Excitement swelled through the group like the waves on the nearby ocean.

Vicky turned to Mason, her glaring yellow eyes peering out at him from behind black curtains of hair.

"What do you say, Mason? Do you think we should compromise?"

Mason gulped another handful of pills. All afternoon he'd been trying to come to terms with Cassie's baffling behavior. He'd swallowed hundreds of pills to relieve his depression, but it was hopeless. The pills were as effective as single drops of water in a dry riverbed. His thirst for Cassie was unquenchable.

"Mason's got nothing to say about it. Why should we compromise?" the Goon Squad member demanded. His face was a mass of purple blotches and oozing craters. "They can't hurt us. You seen what happened last night. We're invincible."

"Are we?" Mason asked.

Reluctantly, his mind shifted from Cassie to the creatures around him. "Show them," he said to Mongril. "Dig up Lou."

Mongril, giggling, lumbered over to the lifeguard boat, kicked one end of it out of his way, and started digging. Several minutes later he unearthed a sand-covered bundle.

"Don't untie him," Mason commanded. "Just hold him up high so everybody can have a look."

Mongril complied. He wiped the sand from a section of Lou's face, flipped him, and caught hold of him by one foot. Lou dangled in the air like a sand crab.

"Anybody still think they're invincible?" Mason asked.

When no one answered he gestured to Mongril. "Okay, bury him again. But make the hole deeper this time."

"He ain't dead," Purple Blotches muttered.

Mason snapped his head around to face the insurgent. "No, he ain't dead. He's worse than dead, the same as you or anybody else will be if you think you can run things better than me. Understand?"

His eyes passed over the members of his group, watching them as they avoided his glare or nodded humbly in acknowledgment of his authority. Purple Blotches hung his head.

"I say we give them their compromise," Mason told the group. "Let their hopes rise that their sacrifices have assuaged us. Let them feel secure. A compromise will allow us to prolong our pleasures. Instead of killing them all in one night, we can watch them squirm as we annihilate them one by one."

"Ah-right'." Mongril screamed. "Parties every night. That's fuckin' beautiful, man."

The rest of the group agreed. There was no question that Mason was their leader now. Their nodding submissiveness took on a snickering, breathless quality.

Mason finished explaining the conditions of the compromise, then added, "When the committee arrives, let them wait on the boardwalk until I signal to bring them here."

———

At five minutes to nine, Sandy left Stafford hunting for torches while she trudged up the Morelli ramp with Jesse and knocked on the door. Mrs. Morelli opened the door a crack and peered outside.

"Sandy, I didn't expect you tonight." Her voice wavered nervously. "Is anything wrong?"

"No, everything's fine. I was just wondering if Jesse could sleep here with you tonight while I attend a meeting?"

Mrs. Morelli looked confused and didn't answer immediately. She opened the door wider and Sandy saw a candle glowing in the kitchen. A black shape moved across the floor.

"Sandy, I don't think tonight's a good night. I'm a little tired and…"

Suddenly the door swung open all the way and Danny, with his pustule-covered head and moldy-yellow eyes, was standing in the doorway behind his mother. He held a candle in his hand. Across his neck, a blood-clotted slash dripped thick body fluids on his clothes.

Sandy gasped, stepped backward, and almost fell, stumbling over Jesse, before catching herself.

"What my mother is trying to say," Danny said in a low, hoarse voice, "is that she doesn't think you'd want your son left alone in the same house as a dead man. Isn't that right, Mother?"

Sandy felt chills run down her spine.

"How can you say that?" asked Mrs. Morelli, her voice trembling. "You're not dead, Danny. You're just... just..."

Danny let out a shriek of laughter that froze Sandy to the bone. "I'm not dead. I'm just changed a little, is that it? Take another look, Mother. Look at my hands. See how stiff and gray they are? Look at my neck." He stretched his neck and held the candle under his chin, and Sandy watched a gelatinous red substance ooze out of the wound. Danny caught it in his hand and threw it on the floor. He laughed again.

"I'm a walking carcass," he told her. "I'm a piece of spoiled meat that should be buried somewhere out of sight. I'm dead, Mother, admit it."

Suddenly Mr. Morelli called from the back bedroom. "Danny, come in here and fix my pillow. Danny!"

Danny's face contorted with rage. "But you're wrong to say I've changed. I haven't changed at all. I've been dead for forty-five years." He began to laugh again.

"I've spent forty-five years doing nothing but catering to an old man's orders and constant demands. He drained every drop of life out of me. Isn't it hysterical? Now I'm as dead as he is."

He dropped the candle to the floor and shoved past his mother and Sandy, through the front door and down the ramp. Stafford was on the sidewalk, clutching his unlit torches, when Danny made his exit.

Mrs. Morelli started after him. "Danny, where are you going?"

"I'm going to the beach," he said, turning back to answer her, "and don't come after me. One dead man in the house is enough." Laughing wildly, he headed toward the beach.

"He doesn't mean it," Mrs. Morelli said. "He's only tired and a little upset, He'll be better tomorrow. I know he will."

"Where's Danny?" Mr. Morelli yelled from inside the house. "Nobody does nothing for me around here. Danny!"

Sandy and Jesse moved to go.

"Please, Sandy," Mrs. Morelli said, "leave Jesse with me."

"But you have enough problems," Sandy said, gesturing to Mr. Morelli's room.

"Please, Sandy. Danny won't be back tonight and I could use the company."

Sandy hesitated, then looked at Jesse. "What do you say, baby?"

Jesse, pale, listless, his thumb almost motionless in his mouth, made no attempt to answer her, but when Mrs. Morelli held out her arms, he leaned toward her and she lifted him up and pressed his head against her heart. The old woman squeezed her eyes shut, but it was not to stop the blinding flow of tears. Mrs. Morelli had been pained so much all day that she wasn't certain she'd ever have another tear to shed.

———

Outside the cottage, Stafford set the torches flaring.

"It's not too late to change your mind," he told Sandy as he handed her a lighted torch. "You saw how it was with Danny. It'll be a thousand times worse on the beach."

"I can handle it," she said.

"Fine," said Stafford, "only maybe you should think a little more about your son's safety. If Danny comes back home, how safe will Jesse be?"

Sandy's eyes flashed anger. "That's not fair. I am thinking of Jesse's safety. How safe were Jesse and I last night when you left and we stayed home? Tell me that."

Stafford sighed. "Okay, you win. But don't say I didn't warn you, and don't get in the way. Do me a favor and stay to the back of the group and try to keep out of trouble."

"I'll try," Sandy agreed. "And in return you can do me a favor. After your negotiations are finished, let me be the one to approach Mason about my problems with him. Let me handle him. If he thinks you or anyone else is involved, it'll only make things more difficult."

"Fine," he agreed. The sweat was pouring down from Stafford's forehead now.

Sandy watched as he wiped the palms of his hands on his trousers, transferring his torch from one hand to the other before leading the way to the boardwalk.

23.

A small circle of torch lights greeted Stafford and Sandy's arrival on the boardwalk.

Sandy was introduced to the other committee members, Mario and Donaldson. They nodded to her, curiosity evident in their fire-lit eyes, but neither one asked why she'd joined them.

"Heard anything yet?" Stafford asked.

"Nothing," said Donaldson.

"Bet on it, they know we're here," Mario said, taking out his switchblade and flicking it open.

"Put that away," said Stafford. "You know the agreement. No weapons."

Reluctantly Mario complied. "We should at least have backups," he said defiantly.

Stafford sighed and looked around nervously. "Play it cool, Mario. We don't want a replay of last night."

Mario opened his mouth as if to pursue the argument, when a face entered their circle of lights. The face, covered with pustules, was almost featureless except for two things: his eyes were huge cylindric mounds of fleshy cysts, and his mouth was unblemished.

The mouth smiled. "You ready to party?" Mongril asked.

The group was led single file across the sand. Sandy trailed behind. A dull throb in her head made her wonder if she'd made a mistake. There was movement in the dark, movement all around her.

Calm down, she told herself. *Forget about other creatures in the dark. Forget everything but Mason.* Seconds later it was impossible to think of anything else.

The committee stopped. Torches were whisked out of their hands, placed in a wide circle around them, and Mason was suddenly in full view. He was sitting on top of a lifeguard's chair, leering down at the committee like an ancient pagan god.

Mason was numb. He stared at Cassie and it was like the first time he saw her on the stage. She was so beautiful, so full of light, like the pictures of the Blessed Virgin that had hung on the walls of his parents' old house.

He'd never seen her more radiant. Standing at the edge of the group in front of one of the torches, she was bathed in light, shadows flickering behind her golden hair. She was his Madonna, and he forgave her for the pain he'd endured. It had been a test of his worthiness. It proved that he loved her in the most sacred way, in the most everlasting, ever long-suffering, total denial-of-self way.

Mason felt a nudge. "You can start now," Mongril said. "They're all yours."

But he couldn't take his eyes off Cassie. He couldn't take his mind off her. Nothing else mattered. Nothing else was important. "Vicky. Explain our conditions," he said after a long silence. Then he returned his full attention to Cassie.

The words caught Vicky by surprise. She looked up at Mason and was confused to find him staring at the woman committee member. Then she stepped into the center of the lights and the committee men introduced themselves to her. They tried to hide it, but each of them had to suppress the violent and overwhelming sensation of upheaval when they looked at her. She brushed her hair forward to cover her face. But she made no attempt to cover her hatred of them when she spoke.

"Our conditions are simple. The people on the beach only want their fair share. We want half of all food and water, half of all liquor and cigarettes, and one hundred percent of all medicine and pharmaceutical supplies that should have been ours days ago. Delivery must take place tonight, to a place of our choosing."

"Yeah," said Mario, "and what do you beachers agree to do for normal people in exchange?"

"We agree not to take it," spat Mongril. The corpses in attendance snickered.

Vicky looked up at Mason. He shook his head no. His eyes remained glued to the woman.

"We also want access to the island at night—the entire island—without interference from you 'normal' people. In exchange, you can have the island during the day."

"You gotta be kidding," Mario said. "That's ridiculous."

"Hold on, Mario," Stafford interrupted. "I'll handle this. Now let me get this straight. We turn over the supplies and stay out of your hair at night, and you end all violence. Is that correct?"

Another look at Mason, another nod, and she answered. "You stay out of our hair, we stay out of yours."

"Well, it's a starting point," Stafford said to Donaldson and Mario. "Now we can go on from here. Oh, one other thing." He turned back to Vicky. "Any compromise we agree to also has to include a personal guarantee from your leader" — he pointed to Mason — "that the woman known to him as Cassie will be strictly off limits to him and any other beacher."

Stafford and Sandy exchanged looks. Hers said, *Are you crazy? That is exactly what I didn't want you to do*. His said. *Calm down. Take it easy. I've got everything under control.*

Everyone else turned to Mason.

Mason snapped out of his trance with Cassie and focused on the redheaded man.

It was the red devil. Why hadn't he noticed it before? The red devil he'd seen with Cassie days ago had reappeared, enticing him to do battle. Or perhaps he was being tested again, the way Jesus was tested in the wilderness.

"No guarantee is needed," he replied. "Cassie knows that her requests are my commands. For it is written, 'Thou must obey God as ruler, rather than man.'"

Stafford stared at Mason's crazed eyes, at the serious tilt of his tumor-racked face. The man made less sense than a wino on a soapbox. How could he negotiate with him? How could he answer him?

"Please, Mason," Sandy said in a small voice. She pushed past Stafford, stepping to the foot of Mason's chair. "I am making a request. Please... don't hurt me anymore. Don't bother me. Let me be left alone."

Mason felt himself tighten. His mind was reeling. What should he do? Was the test to free her from the devil or do as she asked? "Cassie, is this really what you want?"

"Yes." Her answer was barely above a whisper.

"In other words, Cassie is to be protected from your kind as well as mine. Her house will be strictly off limits to both of us. Isolated from everyone."

"What? That's crazy," Stafford sputtered. "I'm not the one who attacked her. Why should she be isolated from me?"

Mason's anger washed from his mind; he had them.

His mouth twisted into a thin crocodile smile as he watched the red devil squirm. "No agreement, no compromise," he stated casually. "We will attack immediately."

Mongril heard the words as a command. "Yeah! All right let's do it!" he screamed. He aimed his first punch at the redheaded dude, hit him in the jaw, and knocked him unconscious. Then he let out a roar and jerked his head around for his next victim.

His eyes lighted on Donaldson and he pounced.

Donaldson saw him coming. He took a step backward, but it was too late. Two hundred and fifty pounds of decaying flesh landed on top of him.

Mongril pinned Donaldson's arms behind his head and watched him twist helplessly from side to side. He brought his face within inches of Donaldson's face and watched him writhe.

Rancid fluid from Mongril's pus sores dripped onto Donaldson's cheeks and into his mouth.

Donaldson gagged.

Mongril chuckled, enjoying himself immensely. He felt like a cat that had a mouse by the tail. Then he heard a commotion on his right and turned to look.

Mario flashed a switchblade at the beachers nearest him and was screaming for action.

"Come on, freaks," Mario yelled. "Leave the old man alone and try me on for size."

Mongril eyed the blade in Mario's hand and tittered with delight. "Oh, wow, he's got a knife," he exclaimed in mock horror. He leaned his weight on Donaldson's face and stood up to deal with Mario.

"Stay back," Mario screamed.

"Hey, man, I only want to, like, take a closer look at your knife —" Suddenly he sprang at Mario, chest first, his arms flung out at his sides. The knife caught him under his left breast, slicing into his flesh all the way up to its handle.

Mario froze.

Mongril faltered, staggering backward, his hands clutching the handle of the blade. He stumbled forward and backward again, groaning and gasping for air like a bad Shakespearean acting student performing a death scene. Then he straightened, popped the blade out of his chest for Mario's inspection, and grinned. "Gee, that was fun," he said. He took a step closer to Mario. "Now it's your turn."

Mario's mouth gaped open. His eyes bulged, mesmerized by the sight of a piece of moist red tissue hanging from the tip of the knife.

Mongril took another step toward him.

Mario's eyes darted from Mongril to the knife, to an area on Mongril's right.

Mongril glanced sideways too and saw that Stafford had regained consciousness. He looked dazed but he was on his feet.

Mario called out to him. "Stafford, come on, man. Help me take him."

Mongril turned back to Mario. His grin widened. He took another step forward.

Mario slipped and almost stumbled. "Stafford, what the hell's wrong with you?"

Mongril paused. He licked his lips. The game had gone on long enough. He was ready for the kill.

And then something hit him from behind. Something — it didn't hurt but it was annoying — dug its claws into his back.

He reached around, snatched if off, and threw it to the ground. He made a swipe at it. And suddenly Mason was there, blocking him from hitting the blond broad, pushing him out of the way and offering his hand to her.

She cringed from the outstretched hand, backing away and scrambling to her feet.

Then Stafford started screaming. "Stop! Stop! We agree to all conditions. We agree to everything!"

And Mongril relaxed.

This little party was over.

It was time to make rules for a new game.

———

Later, Sandy waited at the water's edge while curfews were debated and conditions of the compromise were finalized. A feeling of *déjà vu* washed over her and she remembered her dream from the previous night, the dream that had ended with her on the beach and Mason closing in.

24.

Sandy and Stafford walked back together from the meeting on the beach and the silence between them was as palpable as a block of ice. They reached the Morelli ramp and Sandy was the first to try to melt it.

"Why did you do it?" she asked quietly.

Stafford stared past her. "If I didn't agree to their conditions, they'd have killed all of us."

"I'm not talking about the agreement," Sandy said. "I want to know why you didn't let me handle Mason like you promised."

"I was trying to help you," he said icily. "Thanks to me, at least you won't have to worry about Mason attacking you."

"Are you kidding? Thanks to you, I'll be a sitting duck whenever Mason decides to come and get me."

Stafford turned to her, his face rigid, expressionless. "He gave me his personal guarantee."

"His personal guarantee is a joke. You heard him with his 'It is written' speech. The man's insane!" Stafford's expression remained unchanged. "Naturally, I won't abandon you, Sandy. I'll keep an eye on your house at night, whenever I can."

"Well, hey, that's all right then," she said sarcastically. "I won't have a thing to worry me."

Stafford treated her to a frosty stare.

"And just what is your problem, anyway?" she asked angrily. "Why are you acting like you're mad at me?"

"I'm not mad," he insisted. "Annoyed, maybe—but not mad."

"Why?" she demanded.

Stafford raked his hands through his hair, started to turn away from her, then exploded.

"Because I don't appreciate you making a jerk out of me, that's why," he told her. "I asked you to stay in the background, to leave the negotiations to me, but no. You have to end up in the middle of a fight."

"But —"

"Mario was calling my name, not yours. You had no business interfering." He shook his head. "You made me look like a goddamned fool."

Sandy, speechless, stared at him, her mouth hanging open. Then she said, "You didn't look like a fool, Stafford. You looked like a goddamned coward." Stafford flushed a dark shade of red.

"You can blame me all you want, but you know, and I know, and everybody on that beach knows that you were too scared to do anything."

"The purpose of the committee was negotiations, not full scale war. I warned Mario about his knife."

"Negotiations, my ass," Sandy yelled. "Mario was protecting Donaldson. You didn't move when he called for help. So, don't be angry at me because I did."

Stafford looked ready to bust. "If it wasn't for you and your little problem with Mason — a problem that I tried to resolve for you — everything would have gone smoothly and violence would never have occurred."

"Thank you so much, Stafford," Sandy said bitterly. "Thanks for exchanging my little problem with Mason for a big problem. Thanks for everything."

She shoved her torch into his hand and raced up the Morelli ramp. At the front door, she turned back to look at him one more time. "Stay out of my life, Stafford. I don't need you to watch my house or protect me. It's too dangerous." She turned her back on him, opened the door, and rushed inside, before hot tears reached her cheeks.

Jesse stayed asleep, his hands tightly gripped around his bottle, on the short trek from the Morelli house to his house.

Sandy tucked him into bed and pushed his baby-fine hair from his forehead. Jesse nuzzled the bottle. *His thumb or his bottle*, she thought. *One or the other was forever stuffed into his mouth, poor baby.*

Stafford had been right about one thing: she should have stayed home and worried about her son, instead of trying to play hero.

After kissing Jesse good night, she padded upstairs and checked the doors and windows — not because they offered much protection, but because it gave her something to do while she waited out the night. She was not the least bit tired. She peered through an opening between the wood nailed across a window and surveyed the outside.

The street was dark and empty. There was no sign of anyone. It brought little comfort. Somewhere, unseen, Mason was out there. And this time she waited for him without any hope of escape or defense.

———

Across the street, Mason hid in the shadows and watched Cassie's house. This would be the hardest test of all. Every nerve ending in his body screamed for him to let go and run to her. The denial to do so was exhausting. He trembled from the incredible strain to keep his promise and pass the test.

"What's happening?"

Mason blinked at Mongril as if awakening from a dream. "What are you doing here?"

Mongril grinned. "Wanted to check out where you been spending your free time. I should have known that bitch had something to do with it. Want me to drag the whore out for you?"

With lightning speed, Mason gripped his hands around Mongril's neck and slammed him against a concrete bungalow wall.

"Leave her the fuck alone," Mason warned him. "You hear me?"

Mongril tried unsuccessfully to speak.

Mason raged on. "Remember what we did to Lou? Well, that ain't nothing compared to what I'll do to you, if you ever lay one grimy little pus-stained finger on her. Understand?"

"Hey, lay off, man," Mongril choked.

Mason slammed his head against concrete again, then let him go.

"Shit. I didn't mean nothing," Mongril whined.

"She's everything to me." Mason paced the sidewalk, struggling to regain control of his emotions. "And you fuck with her, you fuck with me. Understand?"

"Yeah, sure. Whatever you say. Only does this mean we're going to honor the compromise?" Mongril asked. "'Cause the goods have all been delivered and a raiding party's ready to roll."

Mason turned back to Cassie's house. He leaned back against the wall of a bungalow. "Tell them to proceed," he said. His gaze was fixated on her house again.

"But they're waiting for you."

"Tell them I said for you to lead them tonight," Mason said.

"Ah-right!"

"Only make sure they leave her house alone. Spread the word, understand? No one is to come anywhere near here."

"Yeah, sure. No problem. I'll tell them."

"One other thing," Mason added. "Before you start the raid, pack a box of supplies and bring it here to me."

Mongril cocked his head, trying to make sense out of his friend's requests. "Whatever you say. Mason. Oh, I almost forgot. I brought you these." He held out a fist full of multicolored pills. "Take 'em. They're from the new supplies."

Mason moved them away. "Don't need them," he said.

Mongril frowned, popped the pills into his own mouth, swallowed them, and headed back to the beach. As he plodded along, he scratched at the tumor that had grown over his green tattoo.

He could understand and respect Mason knocking him around. But turning down good shit was crazy. The dude was definitely becoming weird.

———

Vicky watched Mason from a few feet away.

Mason hadn't been the only one transfixed at the meeting. She hadn't recognized the slut until her attack on Mongril, but then it dawned on her. She was the one. She was the bitch who'd attacked her, who mutilated her face and killed her children. Mason was protecting her now, but she could wait. She could be patient.

Pushing her hair in front of her face, the rage inside her bubbled over with plans of revenge.

25.

Certain fragrances become deeply etched aromatic memories: a whiff of honeysuckle drifting through an open window; the smell of a freshly cut Christmas tree; homemade cinnamon bread baking in an oven; a chubby baby oiled and powdered after a bath; the smell of new shoes, new cars, or new money.

The smell of Sea Breeze Island was the fishy/sandy/salty smell of the sea. Standard activity for a walk on the boardwalk was a hands-on-railing pause to drink in the sights and sounds and smells of the ocean and to breathe clean, invigorating air.

By the end of July there was only the smell of decay on the island. Death permeated the air. Ocean breezes carried the stench of pustule-covered beachers who rested on the sand, preparing for their nightly attacks.

Professor Trifun and Al Granger were their first victims. Caught after sundown outside Al's gas station, where they'd lost track of time tinkering with a homemade battery, Al and the professor were hung upside down from engine hoists. The professor died immediately. Three hours later they took Al down and made him chug four gallons of antifreeze.

When he passed out on one of the lifts, Mongril covered him with a "Happy Motoring" banner and finished the antifreeze. He swore it tasted exactly like cherry soda pop.

In August, the police and remaining guards distributed handwritten notices to everyone on the island, warning them to stay inside after dark.

But temperatures reached the low hundreds. Without air conditioning, the bungalows were sweat boxes and the beachers had easy pickings.

A group of twenty former guards, ranging in age from nineteen to fifty, banded together to execute their own nightly raids. They stored their loot in the abandoned mansion near the armory ruins, and Mason and friends made a surprise call.

"I've heard that imitation is supposed to be a compliment," Mason told them, "but I'm not flattered."

"Yeah. We ain't fuckin' flattered at all," Mongril agreed.

Ernie, a guard who believed Dr. Jenkins when he'd assured him the beachers were mortal, pulled out a gun and began shooting. Ernie had also believed football games were never fixed and politicians were never crooked.

Ernie and the former guards believed only in pain by morning. Pain, and finally... death.

In September, thunderstorms brought clear, bitter-tasting rain and strong easterly winds. The foul stench would weaken occasionally, only to return with a rancidity that was dizzying.

The beachers, not content with curfew breakers and outlaws, attacked norms inside their homes.

By October the island was in chaos. Captain Cruthers was dragged from his bed, stripped naked, and paraded through the streets. Then his hands were tied, a straw-like tube was thrust in his mouth, and he was buried with Lou. He lived three days until Lou accidentally knocked out the straw.

On October 30, Mischief Night, the beachers carried the captain's corpse trick-or-treating with them until Vicky insisted they dump it at the town hall. The norms found him stuffed under a bench three days later. No one had noticed the odor because it smelled just like the rest of Sea Breeze Island air.

26.

It was November 7 and Sandy sat on the pier with Jesse and Beth.

Only one mile, Sandy thought. *One short mile across the bay and the world ended.* She felt a slight fluttering in her belly. It was a vague sensation, no greater than the flapping of butterfly wings, yet she was acutely aware of the movement and rubbed at it with the palm of her hand.

"You okay?" asked Beth.

"I'm fine," she answered.

"Is it...?"

"Yes."

"Are you sure?"

"Yes."

Sandy turned back to stare across the bay and Beth tried to interest Jesse in two sea shells she'd painted to look like small, flat-topped automobiles. Jesse refused to be sociable and hid his face in his mom's jacket.

Sandy quit rubbing her stomach and tousled his hair. "It's been four months now, and it never changes," she said.

"Jesse or the mainland?" Beth asked.

"Both," Sandy said. "Did anyone else go?"

"Not after last week," Beth replied. "Last I heard, they decided to cancel all runs until after Christmas."

The trips to the mainland—the runs, as Beth called them—always ended the same way. The boats would cross the water safely, arrive on land, someone would venture out to explore the black terrain—and eventually collapse.

Usually the entire crew would become violently ill before they rowed back to the island.

"How many died this time?"

"Only one—so far. The other crew members stayed in the boat. I guess they're finally getting it through their thick heads what Professor Trifun told them months ago: that the mainland is contaminated and it's suicide to keep going over there."

"Who was it that died?" Sandy asked softly.

"A guard named Dave. His family lived ten miles inland and he was desperate to go back there. He walked for about ten minutes before he..."

Sandy shook her head. The mainland looked like an evil, enchanted wasteland. It was lumps of dripping clay hardened into dark peaks and stringy black pinnacles. It was rock formations oozing with gray vapors. There was no sign of life, no sign of buildings, cars, flowers, fire hydrants, or trees. It was enveloped in smog — cold, impenetrable, surrealistic... deadly.

"Well, Dave lasted longer than anyone else who tried it," said Sandy. "Maybe that means the toxicity is easing off."

"Don't count on it. I saw the professor before he died. He kept talking about things like cell fusion and chemically induced electric fields. I didn't understand most of it, but I do remember him emphasizing that the only way for us to reach the outside world is by sailing down the coast as far away from here as possible. He said otherwise we'd better plan on our grandchildren greeting the first rescuers."

Sandy grimaced.

"You sure you're okay?" Beth asked again.

"I'm sure. Doctor Jenkins said I'm as healthy as a horse—a pregnant horse, that is. You would have to mention grandchildren."

"Sorry," Beth said quietly. "How many months are you?"

"Four."

"You didn't tell him who the father was, did you?"

"Shouldn't I?"

Beth shrugged. "It probably doesn't matter." She didn't sound convinced.

"I asked him if the baby would be okay — I mean, if Mason's condition was transmittable — but either he didn't know or he wouldn't say." She sighed deeply. "Actually, he acted annoyed I bothered him."

"Doctor Jenkins and his buddies are planning something big," Beth confided. She began packing their belongings into a plastic garbage bag. "They don't have time for health care or babies."

"What are they planning?" Sandy asked as the three of them headed back to the bungalow.

Beth smiled wryly. "They want an attack. They've argued about it for months, but Captain Cruthers' murder was the last straw. They want full-scale war, now."

"But that's impossible. The beachers can't be killed. They know that. Have you told your father?"

"No," Beth said, looking down at the sidewalk. "I couldn't do that. I love my father and I don't want anyone to hurt him, but he's changed, Sandy. He's different, now. If I told him about plans for an attack, he might hurt someone."

They reached Bay Boulevard. Sandy helped Jesse over a huge mound of garbage at the curb. In front of them, an old woman dressed in rags sifted through garbage. Sandy watched her find an empty cream of mushroom soup can, rip it open, and lick the inside of the can.

The woman saw Sandy staring at her and quickly clutched the precious can to her breast before hurrying away.

"Are food packages still delivered to your door?" Beth asked.

"Yes. Are you getting low? I can spare a can of peaches and some boxes of spaghetti. And there are still more jars of baby food, if you can stand them. Jesse hates the stuff."

"Anything," Beth said. "I'm sorry to keep begging you for food like this, but you know the system of food distribution at the town hall. There's no food left, except for a select few. I'd have starved months ago if it weren't for you."

"Don't thank me. Thank Stafford. If it wasn't for the food packages he leaves at my door, I'd be starving right along with you, or fighting that old woman for her soup can."

They reached the bungalow and Sandy bent down to carry Jesse up the stairs.

"You still haven't seen him?" Beth asked.

"No," said Sandy. She opened the door for Jesse to run inside, then turned back to Beth. "He leaves me food. He guards my house at night. But I haven't seen him once since our argument." Her eyes filled with tears.

"It's the compromise," Beth assured her. "He knows that if Mason ever caught him near you, he'd go berserk."

Sandy strained to hold back her tears. "I said such horrible things to him, Beth. If you see him, will you tell him how sorry I am?"

"Come to the town meeting this afternoon and you can tell him yourself. I'm sure he'll be there."

Sandy ducked inside the bungalow and returned with a paper bag filled with food. She waved away Beth's attempts to thank her. "Do you really think I should go to the meeting today? What about the conditions of the compromise?"

Beth flipped her long hair out of her eyes and smiled. "You don't have to worry. If the beachers are attacked, then there won't be a compromise."

—

It took three hours for Sandy to make up her mind to attend the meeting and an hour more to coax Jesse out the door. They reached the town hall and found the meeting in an uproar. Everyone was screaming. They were all out of their seats, waving their arms angrily, some calling out demands for food, for protection, or for a hearing of grievances suffered. Others screamed for the screamers to sit down, to calm down, and to stop screaming.

Mayor Raposo stood in the front of the room, trying unsuccessfully to quiet the audience. His appearance had changed drastically since the last town meeting. His hair stuck straight up in the air and masking tape was wrapped around the nose piece of his glasses. His clothes hung baggy and wrinkled on his thin frame.

Suddenly two shots were fired from a rifle and the room was silent.

"Next person opens their mouth out of turn, I aim for them instead of the ceiling," Mario said menacingly. Mario stood in the center of a group of guards near the windows. A moment of silence passed and he added, "We are not here to discuss food rations or garbage collection or any other minor complaints. Christ, you people act like a bunch of kids."

There was a murmuring of discontent at this remark. Sandy spotted Beth sitting two rows in front of her, raising her hand. Others soon had their hands raised, and the murmurings threatened to erupt into shouting dissent.

Mario fired two shots, waited until the room was absolutely quiet again, and then gestured for the mayor to sit down. Mario's movements were short and jerky as he took the floor. His face was angry.

"Fuck this shit," he said to the audience. "This is why we can't deal with the beachers. We've spent four months arguing among ourselves. This complaint, that complaint; civil rights, human rights. It's all bullshit.

"We talked ourselves into compromising and we're the only one getting compromised. Shit, the beacher freaks are picking us off one by one, and if we don't get our act together soon and start slaughtering them for a change, there won't be enough of us left to try." His remarks were met with scattered applause.

A senior citizen in the second row stood up. "I understand your anger," a familiar voice said. Sandy craned her neck and saw that it was Mrs. Morelli who had taken the floor. Mr. Morelli was sleeping in his wheelchair next to her. "I'm angry too. But my Danny, God bless him, isn't to blame. You call him a beach freak and you talk about slaughter. But you can't lump everyone together. My Danny hasn't attacked anyone. Why attack him? Bring the guilty to justice, sure, but not my Danny. Danny's innocent."

Beth jumped up before Mrs. Morelli sat down. "She's right. Why attack innocent beachers when only a handful of them may be guilty?"

Mario glared at Beth. "Nobody recognized you to speak. You're out of order."

"So are you," Beth retaliated. "Who recognized you as judge and jury around here? What right do you have to decide life and death?"

A grumbling of voices threatened to turn the meeting into chaos again, and Mario held up his gun, ready to fire it again.

Beth sat down.

"I'll tell you what right I have," Mario said when order was restored. "The right of the law of the jungle. The right to survive by protecting ourselves. And if there's anyone else who wants to argue further about it, kindly do us all a favor and come back tomorrow. I'll be more than happy to debate the legal issues with you, after the job is finished."

"Uh, if I might interject a thought here," Major Raposo said. "I might be open to a list of potential waivers for beacher friends or family members. Those interested, please see me after the meeting."

Sandy raised her hand as Mayor Raposo slipped back into his front row seat. "How do you plan to slaughter the beachers?" she asked.

Mario, scowling, addressed the audience again. "We've had four months to study them, to learn their habits and weaknesses. I'm not at liberty to discuss our tactics, but believe me, we won't fail. Our only problem is manpower so we can get the job done in one day."

"But how can you be so sure? Aren't you risking full-scale retaliation if your tactics do fail?" Sandy insisted. "After what I saw happen on the beach the night of the compromise, I think we're dealing with something that none of us can understand. Something outside the law of nature and your laws of the jungle. If we act rashly, we may all be destroyed."

No one jumped up to agree with her, but from the nodding of heads in her vicinity, Sandy felt their support.

Dr. Jenkins signaled for the floor. His face looked gray and haggard. Deep circles lined his eyes. "Nicely said," he commented, "but highly prejudicial, considering the fact that the one saying it is the mistress of the head beacher. She's four months pregnant with his kid. She isn't worried we'll all be destroyed. She's worried her boyfriend will be."

Sandy slumped back in her seat. She stared straight ahead, forcing herself to assume an unaffected look, but inside, she felt like all the air had just gushed from her body, leaving her empty and shamed.

Stafford raised his voice. "Why not have a contingency plan in case of a slipup? We can prepare the remaining boats on the island for an emergency evacuation."

"Emergency suicide," a guard snickered.

"No, not to sail the boats across the bay," Stafford corrected, "to sail the boats along the coast."

"We've tried it," the snickering guard complained. "Every boat we send comes back with the same information. The coastline is the same as the mainland across the bay. If you get too close to it, you're dead."

"Yes, but maybe we haven't sailed far enough. Look, I'm not saying it wouldn't be risky. But if we were forced to retreat, we might want to take the chance. At least, it's worth considering."

"And since retreat is your specialty," Mario said, "I'm sure you'll be happy to assemble the boats for us while the rest of us do the fighting. Is that the idea?" Stafford's face flushed crimson. He took a step toward Mario, but Donaldson held him back. The other guards howled.

Mario found the gavel inside a drawer in the judge's bench and slammed it down on the ebony block.

"Okay. It's all settled. Men meet here tomorrow morning at ten o'clock for specifics. Stafford will ready the boats, although I'm sure they won't be needed. Meeting adjourned."

Sandy moved to give Mrs. Morelli a hand with the wheelchair when Beth signaled to her, pointing to Stafford, who was sitting alone on the other side of the room.

"Go ahead," she whispered, "I'll take care of the Morellis."

Sandy smiled bravely and made her way to Stafford. Jesse trailed behind her.

"I've missed you," Sandy said when she reached his side.

Stafford said nothing. He continued staring into space. "Walk me home?" she asked.

Stafford blinked, as if noticing her for the first time.

"It's all right now. The compromise isn't in effect, is it?" she asked.

"I guess not." He sounded drugged or deeply depressed. His face was still flushed. His eyes were bloodshot and unfocused.

On the way home, Sandy thanked him for backing her up at the meeting. "I'm sorry, Stafford," she added. "I had no right to say the things I said to you that night. No right to doubt you."

"Didn't you?" he asked, still in a daze and looking straight ahead as they walked.

"No, I didn't, because you proved me wrong. You're no coward. Far from it. You've risked your life every night for four months protecting me. You brought me food." Sandy paused to look lovingly at him. "Jesse and I wouldn't be alive if it weren't for you."

Stafford stopped abruptly in his tracks. "I don't know what you're talking about, Sandy. I haven't been anywhere near your house in four months."

"But that's impossible."

Stafford's lips pressed together in a humorless smile. "It's not only possible, it happens to be the truth. The only place I've been is home in one long drunken stupor, and I'd still be there if the well hadn't run dry. Cops get special rations, remember?"

"But—"

"Except, as you have so recently witnessed, my influence with the other cops is nil. Point is, Sandy, whatever game you're playing, you're wasting your time."

Sandy blushed. "I'm not playing any game, Stafford. Someone's been leaving food at my door, and I thought it was you."

They reached the steps of Sandy's bungalow. Sandy touched his hand. "Do you want to come inside?"

He shook his head.

"Stafford, we're friends. I'm not out to get something from you."

"Good. Then maybe you'll be the first person I don't disappoint." Without further comment, he turned and walked back down the street.

27.

On the night of November 7th, Mason sat cross-legged in the shadows and stared at Cassie's house. His mind was still floating. A single beam of concentration focused on Cassie, his goddess. He thought of his devotion to her, of his endurance of the test and of his ultimate reward.

Nothing had changed inside him. His nightly vigil was his high mass. He had transcended his passion. He had kept his promise. But the sacrifice was great. His craving for Cassie remained. His need for her was the need of a man to be lover, rather than priest. None of that had changed.

Only outwardly had he changed; he barely resembled a man. His skin was gnarled, pitted, and dry. His left ear was gone; a flap of skin lifted up where his ear had been, exposing the white bone of his skull. His chest was an open cavity of shattered bone and blackened tissue.

His appearance was of no concern to him. He pushed the thought of it from his mind as he'd always pushed away unpleasantness, clearing his mind of everything but Cassie. It had been such a long time since he'd seen her. He'd give anything for just one look at her through an unbarricaded window.

Suddenly he felt something, the popping of a nail or miniature light bulb inside his head. He wasn't quite sure what was happening and then he felt another pop.

Across the street a section of paneling shifted from the inside of a window. A dim light inside Cassie's house became visible.

He had the strangest sensation that he'd experienced all this before, that all this was quite normal. And then he lost it. Reality was back. The sounds and the smells of the island reasserted themselves and he became aware of presences close to him.

He turned and found Mongril and Vicky staring at him.

"Hey, my man. What's happening?" Mongril asked.

"Did you see that board move?" Mason asked excitedly. "Did you hear anything pop?"

Mongril turned to Vicky. A knowing look passed between them before Mongril turned back to Mason. "No, we didn't see nothing. We just got here," he answered.

"Mason," Vicky asked softly, "can I talk to you?"

Mason sighed. He looked back longingly at Cassie's house before agreeing: "Okay, talk. But make it fast."

Vicky nodded to Mongril to leave before she settled on the sidewalk next to Mason. She played with the remaining strands of hair draped over her face as she talked. "You spend all of your time here," she said. "You're not interested in anything but staring at that house. You rarely go on raids with us anymore, and when you do go, you act different. You don't join in the games."

"The torture games?"

"Any games." Vicky moved closer to him. "Your friends are concerned, Mason. We miss you. We're worried about you."

Mason stared past her. The beachers rarely entered his thoughts. Sure, he spent his days, his "resting period," on the beach with them. Occasionally, he helped them plan an attack, more to satisfy a need for variety rather than victory. Victory was always assured. But the thought of friends made him laugh. He might as well be friends with the sidewalk or the street. They were background, a tool or weapon at the most.

"Tell all my friends not to worry," he told her. "And if they get lonely, tell them to catch a few norms to keep them company. Better yet, have Mongril dig up Lou again."

"Lou is up," Vicky said. Mason watched her play nervously with her hair as she talked. He found the habit extremely annoying. "Nobody got the chance to tell you, Mason. Lou digs himself out of the sand all the time now, with his hands and feet still tied. We can't figure out how he does it."

Mason decided the entire conversation was annoying. He would never get back to Cassie. "Look. Dig the hole deeper before you bury him. Or, better yet, dig one big hole and all the beachers can jump in. It really doesn't concern me. Go have your fun and let me be."

Vicky said nothing for a long time. Then, "Mason, remember the story I told on the first day we met? Remember the woman who killed my kids because she couldn't be bothered to open her fucking door?" Her voice broke with emotion.

"I've heard the story, Vicky. Find the bitch who did it to you and make an omelet out of her face. What else can I tell you?"

Vicky raised her arm and pointed across the street to Cassie's house. "I have found her. She's the one," she said. Her arm dropped to Mason's lap and she leaned her head against his shoulder. "She'll never love you. Mason. All the norms are revolted at the sight of us, so why torture yourself like this, night after night by staring at her house?"

Mason felt Vicky's claw on his leg, and a searing, hot rage rushed over him. His arms moved slowly to embrace her. His voice became smooth and soothing.

"Poor Vicky," he murmured. "Poor, poor baby." His hands stroked her hair. "Do you want me to kill her for you? Is that what you want? Lift up your face and let me kiss you, Vicky. Then tell me what you want to do."

Vicky raised her head. Her yellow eyes glowed with love. Mason brushed the hair from her scarred cheeks. He bent as if to kiss her — and then he struck.

His hands, already on her hair, grabbed handfuls of it and tore it from her scalp. Vicky screamed. Her hands flew to protect her hair, but she was powerless to stop him. And he pulled out two more handfuls. The hair pulled out easily, like dead plant stalks pulling out of loose, dry soil. Vicky howled. She struggled to get free.

Mason allowed her to untangle herself from him. She scrambled to her feet and ran several yards toward the beach. Then he pounced on her. She landed face down on the sidewalk and Mason straddled her. He twisted her arms behind her back, held them tight with one hand, while his other hand felt again for her hair.

"Please, Mason, please, not my hair."

Mason twirled a strand of hair around one finger. "See how foolish it was to worry about me, dear Vicky. I can still enjoy a good torture game now and then."

He twisted hair around a second finger and third finger. Then he bent down, close to her. "Not much hair left," he whispered. "You might be able to cover one eye, maybe, if you spread it thin."

She cried uncontrollably now. Her cries were the whining, whimpering sounds of an injured cat.

"You asked me why I sit here night after night," he said, "and I'll tell you. She's a goddess, something you could never understand. She's pure and holy and everything in this world that's good. And you foul the air she breathes."

As quickly as he pounced on her, he let her loose; she stumbled to her feet and backed away from him.

Tufts of spidery hair hung from Vicky's deformed face.

"You're wrong, Mason. Your goddess is a whore who'll lie and cheat to keep herself safe. I only hope I'm around the day you discover it for yourself."

Mason snorted at her contemptuously. "The day that happens, I'll gladly hand her over to you." He moved as if to pounce on her again, and Vicky turned and ran.

When she was no longer in sight, he brushed the hair from his jeans and resumed his cross-legged position in the shadows. He cleared his mind and focused on Cassie.

———

Sandy heard the angry voices outside her door and shivered in the dark. *Mason's out there*, she thought. *I know he's out there. I can feel him.*

How infuriating it was to be so stupid. She should have known Stafford wouldn't protect her. Something about his redheaded boyish looks had pulled at her heart, but underneath he was nothing but a weakling, a coward.

But she was worse than weak. She was a bird in a cage, Mason's pet parakeet that he kept fed and watered until he tired of playing and moved in for the kill. Or until she could find a way to break free.

She started back for the kitchen when something crashed in front of her. It sounded like furniture collapsing or a heavy object dropping to the floor. She remained very still, very quiet, but she wasn't terrified. Sounds in the dark didn't frighten her anymore. The bungalow was old and damp. Autumn winds rattled the windows and doors like old bones. Jesse would sometimes walk in his sleep. Wood across her windows would loosen. She was used to it all. If it wasn't for discovering the true identity of her "protector," she would scarcely notice one crash. Besides, she told herself, if Mason had decided to attack, he'd smash through the front door as he had the last time.

She listened and heard a yawning, creaking sound — a pop, a ping — then another crash.

She crept away from the porch and felt along the windows on the kitchen's outside walls. Her foot hit something hard and she reached down. It was a wooden plank that had fallen off a window.

She sighed, having known all along that her barricades had as much staying power as. pictures Scotch-taped to the wall. Then she heard a pop, two pops, three pops, and popping sounds all around her, like the uncorking of a hundred champagne bottles.

Something scraped along the wall, slid past her, and exploded. She jumped and backed away. She heard a crash in front of her and a clattering racket of crashes on the porch. The floors trembled. The walls were caving in. The house was coming apart. Sandy ran into the back bedroom, scooped Jesse into her arms, and ran through the cottage, sidestepping the falling walls like a soldier in a mine field.

She reached the front door, to find it disintegrated, ripped apart in exactly the same way Mason had smashed it months ago. Down the cement steps, hitting the sidewalk, and taking off like a shot down the street, she ran until she realized she had nowhere to go. There was no place to run. The street was darker than the inside of the bungalow, and Mason lurked nearby.

"Oh, Christ," she cried softly. She screeched to a stop, about-faced, gritted her teeth, and flew wildly in the opposite direction, past her house, up the Morelli's ramp, and finally through the door. Then she froze.

A haze of candlelight illuminated the kitchen table where two people sat hunched over their dinner plates. They turned to look at her.

"Sandy, I..." began Mrs. Morelli.

"No, Mother, let me:" Danny admonished. "So nice of you to drop in, Sandy. Why don't you and your son join us for a late supper?"

Danny's face was in shadows, but his eyes glowed with a burning yellow insanity. "Father, bring plates for our guest," he yelled. "Father, don't make me come and get you."

Danny grasped the armrests as if to lift himself out of his chair, when a stumbling, shuffling figure emerged from a darkened area of the room. Mr. Morelli pitched himself toward the table. His body leaned at a forty-five-degree angle to the floor. One foot caught the other and he slammed face down on the floor. The plates in his hand shattered into thousands of glass splinters.

Danny's eyes blazed with rage. He glared at his father, floundering in the glass. "He never did nothing for me. Nobody ever did nothing for me!"

Suddenly Mr. Morelli's body lurched upward. Feet together, knees straight, he flew into a standing position, rising from the floor as if he were a paper doll blowing in the wind.

And Sandy started screaming. Her eyes bugging out of her head, she screamed as the old man flailed his arms and legs, struggling to right himself in midair. She screamed as Danny's mutilated face convulsed with laughter. She screamed until she was hoarse, until Jesse started to scream too, and until Mrs. Morelli, crying continually, had her arms wrapped around her and Jesse, comforting them as she cried. Only then could Sandy close her eyes, stop screaming, and start to cry, too.

When she opened her eyes, Mr. Morelli was back on the floor. Danny was hunched over his supper. And she was too exhausted to care anymore.

Sometime during the night Mrs. Morelli gave her tea. She cared for Jesse. She begged Sandy to stay.

All through the night, Danny berated his father, cursing him to get up each time he fell, screaming orders at him, chores to do, items to fetch, tasks to perform, as Mrs. Morelli tried to soothe his anger. At dawn, Danny insisted that his father push him in the wheelchair to the front door. Then he left for the beach.

Mrs. Morelli collapsed into tears when he'd gone. "I should've told him to stay," she cried. "He'll be killed on the beach. I should've warned him."

Sandy was still numb from the shock.

"But I couldn't," Mrs. Morelli said, "God forgive me. I couldn't make myself do it."

Later, in the light of morning, Sandy returned to her bungalow. The house was standing. The walls were intact. Only the front door and barricades across the windows were destroyed. Wood and pieces of paneling lay in heaps on the porch and beneath the windows. And scattered across the floor were hundreds and hundreds of nails.

28.

The next morning at ten o'clock Stafford arrived at the town hall and was greeted by several of his former buddies.

"Sorry, Stafford," one of them yelled. "Only men allowed inside today. Women, children, and faggots got to wait outside."

"Hey, Stafford ain't no faggot," another guard chimed in. "He may be a goddamned pussy coward, but he ain't no faggot." Hoots and guffaws punctuated their remarks.

Stafford seethed. "Cute, real cute," he said. He pushed his way past them and entered the courtroom. Almost a hundred men were at the meeting. Some turned to look at him, but Stafford ignored them and quickly slid into the nearest bench.

In the front of the room, Mario emptied the contents of a cardboard box onto a table.

"Cleaned out my closet," Mario told the assembled volunteers. "I've got every kind of blade we need. You can all take your pick."

He spread the wide variety of cutlery on the surface of the table, holding up daggers, switchblades, and razors, Boy Scout knives, pen knives, and butcher knives. He chose a twelve-inch, serrated survivor blade and pitched it to Donaldson sitting in the front row. "Here you go, old-timer. This is one I use to clean my nails."

Donaldson jumped out of the way, and the knife hit the back of the bench before bouncing to the Door.

Mario snickered. So did several others in the room.

Unruffled, his voice calm, Donaldson said, "Thanks, but I'll stick to my gun." He retrieved the knife and placed it gently on the table.

Mario shook his head. "This is exactly what you guys have got to get into your heads. Guns are useless. They don't work at all against the beachers. The way I see it, there's only two things gonna do the job. Slicing 'em and burning 'em. We surprise them on the beach during the day, slice them up and burn them to ashes when they're weak as kittens—no way we can lose."

"You're gonna need a lot more than a couple of knives to kill all those beachers," someone yelled.

"Really?" Mario asked sarcastically. He gestured to a kinky-haired Italian bruiser standing by the window. "Joe Ab, give Doc Jenkins a hand bringing in the rest of the shit."

Minutes later, boxes of hatchets, sickles, cleavers, hacksaws, and all types of cutting tools were stacked along the back wall of the courtroom. Rolled-up fishing nets were dumped near the judge's bench.

The last thing carried in was a stack of papers.

"The mayor told me to give you these waiver lists," Dr. Jenkins said. A smirk curled his lips.

"We really gonna use those lists?" a guard yelled out.

"Absolutely," Mario answered, gesturing for the papers to be placed in front of him. "The mayor spent all night making copies for us. He's so exhausted from all that writing, he decided to remain with the escape boats instead of joining us for the attack."

"But how do the waiver lists work?" the guard insisted.

Mario smiled. "Glad you asked. Let me demonstrate how to use them." He searched in his pocket until he found his lighter, flicked it, and held the flame to the corner of a hand-copied list.

The courtroom was silent as they watched the paper burn.

"This waiver list makes the best kindling I've ever seen. Any more questions?"

Several men cheered.

"Okay," Mario said, his face beaming. "I'm gonna assign weapons to each of you, go over a little strategy, and then you'll take your positions. Let's start with the nets."

Two hours later the courtroom was empty except for Mario, three of his closest advisers, and Stafford.

Mario and friends headed for the door.

"Haven't you forgotten someone?" Stafford yelled.

Mario turned, squinting in his direction. "Hey, Stafford, old buddy. Where you been hiding yourself lately?" Muffled laughter from the three guards with them.

Stafford rested his arm along the top of his bench, maintaining casual. "I've been right here."

Mario nodded. "Yeh, well, the drinking and partying don't begin until after the attack is over." More snickering from the other guards. "Why don't you come back then?" He turned to go.

Stafford's body stiffened, but he willed himself to remain calm. "Stop with the jokes, Mario, and tell me what you want me to do."

Mario shrugged. "Take your pick. We got gasoline, torches, pitchforks, whatever you want. Or you can go help Raposo with the boats. That was your idea, wasn't it?"

Stafford stood up, his joints cracking from sitting so long, and strolled to the table in the front of the room.

He picked up the twelve-inch survivor blade. "This'll do."

Mario rolled his eyes. "Come off it, Stafford. You don't have to put on a show for us. We all know knives are not your thing. Better leave that for the big guys."

More laughter, and Stafford exploded. He knocked the table out of his way, tore across the courtroom, and grabbed Mario by his collar.

"You little shit," Stafford said between clenched teeth. He had the knife an inch from Mario's neck before the other guards stopped him. It took all three of them to hold him. The knife was knocked to the floor.

Mario, perspiring, his eyes flashing anger, brushed himself off and straightened his collar. "Sure. You're brave now, Stafford. Now, when it doesn't mean shit, you're raring to go. Real tough."

Stafford straggled against the guards who held him. "You want tough? Give me back the knife, and after I slice Mason, I'll take you on."

Mario pursed his lips. "First Mason, then me," he repeated. He grinned. "You got it." He retrieved the knife from the floor, flipped it into the air, caught it, and held it out to Stafford.

"Try not to swallow cement this time," Mario advised, and the guards started laughing. They were still laughing when Stafford broke free, grabbed the knife from Mario's hand, and ran from the courtroom.

———

On the beach, partially submerged in sand, Mason floated in a semiconscious dream state. It was the resting period, the daylight hours of inactivity, the time to recharge and rejuvenate the energy that surged through his body at night.

Mason's daily sleep took place a distance apart from Vicky, Mongril, and the other beachers. He was nearer the sea now, on the beach side of a sand dune at the water's edge. It was the same spot every day. Occasionally the waves trickled water over the sand dune. Sometimes a flood of salt water rushed over his body, wet sand and mud sliding into his clothes, over his arms, his legs, over his neck and his face. Those were special times and he would feel an inkling of a pleasure yet to come, a promise to be fulfilled, a unity with all creation to be attained.

Vicky and many of the Goon Squad members were grouped together in the center of the beach.

Mongril rested with them today, although usually he preferred a spot near the upturned lifeguard boat so he could gobble down handfuls of pills—any pills— that were stored in the boat. He liked the thought of taking them rather than enjoying their effect on him.

Other beachers insisted on pushing themselves beyond their daylight abilities. They resisted their need for rest and struggled to move from one area to another; No matter how hard they tried, continuous exertion always brought collapse until the night.

Old Man Simpson crept into view on the boardwalk, late again, from his daughter's house. Simpson resisted the pull of the beach, the pleasures of the sand, the way other beachers fought the loss of energy during the day.

Today, Simpson seemed frightened and excited. He waved his arms and screamed words Mason couldn't decipher.

Mason watched him tumble down the boardwalk ramp, hit the sand, and raise himself up on all fours to start screaming again. Mongril and several others turned sharply to stare at him.

Mason finally understood the words to be, "They're coming. They're coming," and suddenly norms flowed over the beach like one gigantic human wave.

———

Caught up with the mob, Stafford heard the battle roar as background to the rushing blood filling his brain, and he slammed his knife deep into the chest of the first beacher he encountered.

Head and arms quivered. Lips moved, then smirked.

Stafford disengaged the knife from the chest, grabbed a hunk of hair, pulled, and hacked at the neck. Several slices and the head almost detached. Another, stronger swipe... cracking bone... and the head pulled free.

Quickly he flung it away from him. He shaved off one arm, then the other, then both legs.

Liquid splattered over him as he worked. Body fluids and degenerating tissues dripped down his arm and sprayed across his face. He wiped it from his eyes wiped all thought of it from his mind. His only concern was the woodcutting job at hand.

When only a stump of the body remained, he cleaned his knife on his pants and headed toward the next creature.

———

Mason watched, as if in a trance, as the destruction progressed. Huge fishnets were strung across the beach, filled with bodies and body parts, doused with gasoline, and ignited. Bonfires sent black smoke spiraling up into the gray afternoon sky.

Vicky was one of the first to be set on fire. She lashed out frantically as a pitchfork-toting guard tossed her into a net. Then he soaked her with gasoline and threw a lit match at her. There was a loud thump, similar to the sound of a gas broiler being lit, and Vicky burst into flames. Carla, shrieking hysterically, crawled after her into the net and three beachers were thrown on top of them.

One norm was almost set aflame. Mason watched a long-haired norm burn her hands as she struggled to pull Old Man Simpson's blazing body from the nets.

Four norms had a hold on Mongril. They pinned him down while a fifth norm severed both of his hands from his wrists. They hacked off half of one arm. Then, tired of the exertion, they flung Mongril and his body parts into a net already partially in flames.

Mongril jumped up. Smoke rose from the sides of his head as if he were a fiery bull god, and Mason thought suddenly of Cassie, of how he'd caused the desecration of her altar by pulling the barricades from her windows. He'd sent her running into the streets. Could all this be part of it? Was this his punishment?

And vengeance is mine, saith the Lord... I will cast thee down into the fiery depths of Hades.

He watched the smoke curl around Mongril's face, billowing, intensifying, until a flame ignited the top of his head. Mongril's skin peeled, frizzled, blackened. Soon he joined the other corpses in their twisting writhing dances in the pit of flames.

Mason felt strangely numb. He was affected by Mongril's demise more than he thought possible. He felt almost sad, and sadness toward any person other than Cassie or himself was an entirely new experience. He inspected the emotion, examining it gently, rolling it over tentatively in his mind, and failed to see the approaching norm.

Stafford was almost blind with exhaustion as he headed toward the beacher. His gray parka was soaked and stuck to his skin. His mouth was filled with the taste of soot. He stood over the body, his knife posed above his head, ready to strike, and paused.

Gray eyes, surrounded by sand-crusted pustules stared back at him, and Stafford weaved. He recognized him. It was Mason, the head beacher, and for one brief moment he was sure his legs would buckle and he'd keel over and land on top of him. Then he thrust the blade deep into Mason's chest, pulled it out, and began hacking his neck. When the job was finished, he picked up the head and carried it over the sand dune.

He heard his name called, and he turned to see Mario and Donaldson smiling at him, holding their fists clasped together above their heads in a gesture of victory.

Stafford grinned back at them. Relief washed over him like a warm bath. For the first time in months, he felt wonderfully free of tension. The creatures were truly dead now, and he personally had destroyed their leader.

He walked into the surf, took a deep breath, and filled his lungs with clean, ocean air. Water splashed over his shoes, lapping at the cuffs of his pants. He had redeemed himself. He had nothing to fear and nothing of which to be ashamed. Swinging the severed head behind him, he pitched it as far as possible out to sea.

Mason's head landed past the breaking waves. It bobbed up and down as it drifted farther and farther from shore.

Stafford watched until it disappeared before he turned back to the beach.

29.

By 9:00, the victory block party had settled into a combination Fourth of July barbecue, firemen's parade, christening, and wedding reception. Rows of long picnic tables were piled high with food. Garbage cans overflowed with soiled paper plates. Beach chairs were clustered in small groups around the bonfire. An accordion played "Girls Just Wanna Have Fun." Spam stew simmered on a grill.

Sandy watched the festivities, surrounded by people laughing and enjoying themselves, and wondered why she felt less safe than all those nights she'd spent alone in the bungalow with Mason skulking around outside. It didn't make sense. There was no hint of danger or reason for fear, but an edgy feeling remained.

The day had passed quickly. She and Jesse had watched the mayor and his friends assemble a small fleet of boats, from Sun Fishes to thirty-foot cabin cruisers that would have to be pushed away from the pier with long poles. Mayor Raposo spent the afternoon hammering extensions to the standard paddles available on the island so that larger boats could be utilized without motors.

In the late afternoon, guards stopped by with stories to tell. From all reports, the attacks had been successful. One of the guards, Joe Ab, went so far as to say that the beachers had been "pulverized".

Sandy liked the word. It gave her a feeling of hope, if little comfort. Something still nagged at her. Something didn't set right.

She tried to come up with concrete reasons for her uneasiness, but couldn't. There was only this vague suspicion that something was wrong. She knew that Mason wasn't dead.

———

Across the street from Sandy, Stafford grabbed a brown Tupperware pitcher of wine, held it between two hands, and drank heartily. Mario slapped him on the back and the wine flew back the way it came. Stafford coughed, sputtered, tried to keep it in his mouth and not to laugh, and the wine sprayed out of his nose, splashing his pants, dribbling down his chin. He and Mario shook with laughter.

"Hey, let's not waste it;" Stafford said between convulsions. "This stuff is gold."

"Stafford, old buddy, you can drink as much as you want. You deserve it. Besides..."Mario waved drunkenly for Stafford to lean closer to him, "There's plenty more where that came from. The beachers hardly touched the supplies we gave them. I only took enough for tonight's party. Tomorrow, we clean out everything they got stored in the amusement pier. They sure as hell won't be needing it. Hey, buddy?" He punched Stafford's right arm, catching him in midswallow, and the wine spewed from his mouth, sending them into another fit of laughter.

The party was in full swing.

Children chased one another in and out of the dance area. One couple had passed out, their heads leaning against each other as they slept. Another couple argued.

Joe Ab yelled, "Get the hell out of my face. You don't know what you're talking about," before his wife threw a paper cup of wine in his face.

Stafford watched Mrs. Ab's speedy retreat, with Joe Ab in hot pursuit. "Ain't love grand?" he asked Mario.

"You said it," Mario agreed.

After gulping the last of the wine in his pitcher, Mario glanced around for his wife, a nervous mouse of a woman who wore a brown quilted down coat.

She'd been sitting with a group of women, and her eyes darted up, startled, when he looked at her. Mario held up his empty pitcher and she immediately scurried over to refill it.

"His too," Mario told her. They were the only two words he spoke to her, and she quickly complied with his wishes before returning to the group of women across the street.

Stafford saw Sandy. Her chair was set on the edge of the women's group, and Jesse played at her feet. He noticed that she wasn't involved in the conversations of the women near her. She seemed preoccupied and tense, always looking over her shoulder into the darkness beyond the party.

"Broads," Mario said when he saw the object of Stafford's attention. "They're nothing but trouble."

"You said it," Stafford agreed. They both laughed.

"You're all right, Stafford," Mario said. "You took care of that sucker with no help from anyone. Sliced the sucker's head off clean as a whistle, and I'm proud of you." He slapped him on the back again. "What do you say we get our fight out of the way right now? First one empties his pitcher is the toughest."

"I like it. Let's drink to it," Stafford agreed, turning his attention away from Sandy.

They clinked pitchers, then emptied them.

———

Hours later, at a minute past midnight, the beach began to tremble. Flakes of black ash made a papery, rustling sound as they swirled across the sand. A bone teetered. A handful of dry, brittle hair fluttered against the burned remains of a scalp.

The only sound was the rush of waves on the shore.

There was no life... and yet in the dark, in the shadows within shadows, energies rippled and bulged above the sand. There were rumblings in the air and movement all around. Lightning flashed across the sky.

A severed hand reached out of the sand. Its fingers uncurled. A skull whipped frantically from side to side. Skeletons of bones and matted flesh stretched their arms as if awakening from a deep, refreshing sleep.

Mongril was the first to recover. He pulled himself up from the ashes and raised himself into a standing position. Black pulp meshed to his bones. His face bulged, changing shape, until his original tumors and pustules were in place again. Black ash eyelids opened, revealing white gelatinous masses, and he shook his head, surveying the scene around him.

Behind Mongril, Vicky snapped awake. During the fire, she'd protected her face by submerging it in the sand. It was still snaked with glass-pocked cysts, but was free of the scorching that had turned the rest of her body into caked cinder.

Carla crawled next to Vicky and was the first to make a sound. Flaked skin peeled away from her mouth, her jaw dropped, and she let out one long searing scream.

It was as if an alarm had been sounded. Suddenly, all the beachers began to move. Arms and legs reassembled. Bones meshed. What was left of skin and ash solidified. On the other side of a sand dune, a headless torso waded in the surf, paused, and bent down to retrieve the head that had been washed ashore.

Mason adjusted the water-bloated head pulp on his neck and without further thought climbed back over the sand dune to walk to the center of the beach.

Lightning flashed and the beach lit up, on and off, several times.

Mason raised his arms away from his limp body. The fingers on his hand were spread wide. His eyes were still closed.

Another lightning bolt zigzagged across the sky. And slowly, Mason's body began to rise several inches off the beach.

The beachers surrounded him, assembling themselves into a silent, waiting army. And Mason opened his eyes and gave him the signal to move.

———

Sandy heard a loud noise. Jesse was in her lap and she was halfway out of her chair before she realized the noise was thunder.

"Sounds like rain."

Sandy jumped again at the sound of the voice behind her, then turned and relaxed.

"Beth, where were you? I've been looking for you."

"We could have used the rain this afternoon," she said. She knelt beside Sandy's chair, staring straight ahead at the bonfire, as if transfixed. Streaks of soot stained her face.

"Beth, what's wrong?" Sandy asked gently. She reached out to comfort her, touched her wrist, and Beth flinched; Sandy saw that her hands were covered with blisters.

"Beth, what happened to your hands?"

"They built a fire like that on the beach," she said, staring at the bonfire. "And they threw my father into it. They burned him alive." Her voice wavered. "I tried to pull him free, to put out the fire... I..." She looked at her hands, then at Sandy. "I couldn't save him." Her face contorted. Tears streamed down her cheeks.

"Beth," Sandy soothed, "You did everything you could."

"I warned him," she said. "I knew the waiver list was a fraud and I begged him not to go to the beach, but he insisted. He kept spending more and more of his time with the beachers." Her bottom lip quivered and she started crying again. "We were so close once. Did I ever tell you what he had painted on his pickup? 'J. Simpson and Daughter, Beverage Distributors, Inc.'

Can you imagine that? And if we weren't making deliveries together, he was checking in on the CB after every stop."

Thunder rumbled in the sky.

"Beth, I'm sorry."

Suddenly a scream rang out from far across the island, and lightning crackled above them.

Sandy turned and saw Donaldson glance nervously at Mario.

There was another streak of lightning followed by a scream louder 'and more piercing than the previous one.

Mario gestured for everyone to remain calm.

"Listen, people, it's nothing but a storm. Nothing to worry about. And that scream you heard just means Joe Ab finally caught his wife."

There was halfhearted chuckling at his last remark, but several women began folding beach chairs, packing to leave. A few husbands joined them.

"Hey, if you bunch of pussies are scared of a little storm, I say go on home. Who needs you?" Mario shouted at them. He stood on top of his beach chair and guzzled his wine defiantly.

"Let's go," Sandy said, breaking out of her paralysis. She lifted Jesse higher on her chest and started toward the bay. Ten feet later she realized Beth wasn't following her. "Come on Beth. Let's go for the boats."

Beth stared past her, the grief on her face giving way to wide-eyed wonder. "It couldn't be," she said softly. "They couldn't still be alive. It's not possible."

"Please, Beth. Let's grab a boat and sail out to sea like Professor Trifun advised."

"I can't, Sandy. If the beachers are alive, if somehow my father survived, then I have to go to him."

More bloodcurdling screams were audible, and suddenly the beachers crashed the victory party and everyone was on the move.

Sandy felt someone brush against her. She tripped and was almost trampled by the crowd. She grabbed hold of her chair, Jesse holding tightly on to her, and pulled herself upright.

Someone screamed her name.

She turned, straining to look over the heads of the norms racing past her, and saw Beth. Two beachers were dragging her into the bonfire.

Sandy moved toward her, but was caught up in the flow of norms streaming to the boats. She tried to go against the current, but it was all she could do to stay on her feet. Jesse was hit on the head and Sandy finally stopped struggling. Soon she was being carried along with the crowd.

Beth's father was with her when Sandy caught a last glimpse. He was helping the other two beachers keep her in the flames.

When Sandy reached the bay, all the boats were filled. There were torches lit, but Sandy saw only darkness —dark water, dark sky, and dark backs of people rushing past her. She heard screams and a baby crying, and splashes in the water.

She stepped away from the crowd and ran along the bay's edge until she was parallel to several boats rowing out to sea. "Hey! Take us, too," she yelled. "You have room for two more." She waved frantically and continued running along the shore, but was ignored.

There was a loud explosion. Sandy looked back to see part of the pier in flames. Smaller flames shot into the bay and Sandy realized it was bodies on fire, jumping into the water. She heard continuous screaming, continuous splashing, and agonizing cries. Fire drifted on the water like floating candles in a dark pool.

The light from one fire illuminated the sky and Sandy saw an empty rowboat caught in the weeds in front of her. She stepped into the cold water, holding Jesse tightly with one hand, and climbed into the boat. Miraculously, the oars were intact. She tried to lower Jesse to the bottom, but he refused to let go of her.

Sandy grabbed an oar and thrust it into the water. The small boat began to circle, heading farther into the weeds, instead of out of them. The bottom of the boat scraped sand.

Running feet hit the ground on the other side of the weeds. Boats in flames drifted nearby.

Sandy tried again to east Jesse from her chest. His grip tightened and he refused to budge.

More feet pounded. A man and a woman, both dark-haired, both in their early twenties, spotted Sandy and her beached rowboat. They ran toward her.

"Please, the boat's stuck. There's room for both of you if you'll push it out from the weeds," she told them.

Shell-shocked, their faces rigid with fear, the couple pushed the boat free of the weeds and sand and dived in.

Others saw them. A husky man dashed into the water and held tightly to the side of the boat screaming for his two children to follow him. The boat nearly capsized before all three had climbed aboard.

"No more," screamed the man in his early twenties behind her. "We're overloaded as it is."

He grabbed the oar from Sandy and aimed for a man swimming toward them.

The oar slashed at the water. The boat rocked violently from side to side.

"Sit down, we'll tip," Sandy screamed.

The swimmer's hands clutched at the side of the boat and an oar cracked down on them.

"No, please," the swimmer begged, and Sandy recognized Dr. Jenkins. He held out his hand to her for help and Sandy reached instinctively for them.

"There are too many. You'll kill us all," the man screamed behind her and then suddenly she was pulled into the water, tumbling into the cold, murky bay, and Dr. Jenkins was scrambling over her body to take her place in the boat.

She surfaced, Jesse coughing up water, but holding tightly to her. There was debris everywhere in the water — bags of garbage, chunks of wood, abandoned rafts, and sections of canvas sail. She dog-paddled, begging the people in the boat to help her, but they had the oars in place and ignored her cries.

She made a futile swipe at the boat as it glided past her. Dr. Jenkins bared his teeth, grabbed an oar, and threatened to strike her.

Resigned, Sandy retreated.

She was tired and out of breath from treading water with Jesse high on her chest. She saw a raft, and hoping for a moment's rest, she grabbed for it.

The raft collapsed in her hand. It made a squishy sound when she touched it.

She let go.

The raft drifted in a circular motion and a hand floated into her face.

She screamed. She recoiled from it.

The raft was a down coat. It was the corpse of Mario's wife floating face down in the water.

Lightning flashed and Sandy saw that she was surrounded by floating corpses. They knocked against her and against one another like trees in a lumber-packed logging stream.

She screamed again and pushed away from them.

They bobbed back. Their mouths gaped open like dead fish. Their eyes stared at her accusingly. Blood seeped from recent wounds.

Sandy gagged. She choked on the bloody water entering her mouth when she tried to scream and swim at the same time. She slammed a fist at the corpses blocking her way to the shore. She shoved corpses violently out of her way and swam through them.

Coughing, sputtering, she felt her feet touch ground. She stood and the water was waist deep. She was almost to the shore. More corpses floated toward her. Blackened bodies of norms burned in fires on the pier or in boats. She hurried through them, hating to touch them, but hating it more when their cold flesh grazed her arms or their dead fingers snagged her jacket. So she knocked them away from her until finally she reached land and dragged Jesse and herself out of the water.

Her clothes were heavy and dripping. Her teeth rattled and she shivered continuously.

Jesse coughed up more water. His face looked bluish-white and Sandy wrapped her arms tightly around him. He didn't cry.

All around her there was frenzied activity: people running in the dark, explosions, screams, panic, brutality.

Sandy had no choice now — no other option. Even if another boat would take them, she and Jesse would freeze to death in their wet clothes.

She saw corpses of norms along the edge of the pier, corpses in the streets, wounded norms crawling over corpses on the sidewalks. Beachers were everywhere.

Sandy mumbled a prayer and ran toward the cottage, staying close to buildings and ducking into alleys along the way.

Half-running, half-falling, she stumbled up the cottage steps and hurled through the broken front door. She tiptoed over the debris on the porch, heading for the back bedroom and dry clothes, when a hand reached out from the shadows and grabbed her.

30.

That same night, Mason prowled the island with a small band of beachers, exacting vengeance for atrocities suffered.

His mind raced at fever pitch. His feet touched the ground now. But sometimes, when he grabbed hold of a victim and his fury threatened to explode inside his head, he could feel himself rise off the ground again. Or his victim would fly out of his hands and slam into a wall. Some were bludgeoned with pieces of wood or stones without his hands ever touching a weapon.

He reached the bay and watched the pitiful norms panic at the sight of him. Many of them dived into the water, and Mongril and the members of Mason's squad dived in after them.

Two norms made a wild dash, trying to escape by running past him. Mason grabbed one with each hand and cracked their heads together until their bodies fell limply at his feet.

"Hey, one of them ain't dead yet," Mongril yelled, coming out of the water empty-handed.

Mason looked down and saw the man at his left foot trying to stand. He pulled him up by his hair until his feet dangled above the ground. After examining him, he smiled. "This norm look familiar to you?" he asked.

Mongril snickered. "Oh, wow! You got the prize, Mason. He's the dude who led the attack. He's Mario something or other. What you gonna do to him?"

"Not what," Mason corrected, still smiling. "The question is *how*. Bring me a torch, Mongril."

While Mongril went for the torch, Mario regained full consciousness and found himself hanging by his hair, Mason grinning at him. Mario beat the air with his fists, frantically trying to save himself.

"Don't wear yourself out," Mason advised. "You'll spoil all the fun."

Mario spit in Mason's face. "Fuck you," he screamed as Mongril came running back with a torch.

Mason's face contorted with rage. He felt the saliva run down his cheeks and suddenly the torch flew out of Mongril's hand into Mario's face.

Mario ducked and his hair caught fire. His ears sizzled. His arms and legs jerked spastically in the air as if he were a dancing clown, in a shadowbox.

Mason's hands started to burn, and he threw the body on the ground.

Mario shrieked hysterically. He rolled violently from side to side, writhing in pain. He tore at his face with his hands, trying to rip the fire from his skin.

Mongril watched the flames consume Mario's head. "Aw, it's all over." Mongril pouted.

"Come on, I'll find you another one." Mason held out his hand and the lit torch flew to him.

"How do you do that?" Mongril asked.

"Don't know yet," Mason answered, but all at once he did know.

The power had been there all along. He'd been using it unconsciously since the rain first hit. He remembered the handles of the black doctor bag moving around in the sand, the first day after the rain stopped. He thought of how many times he'd felt suspended in the air when his energy surged at night. He remembered gaining control of his body the day after the beachers' first attack. And he remembered Mongril's words of advice. "Go with the flow," he mumbled.

"Huh?"

Mason saw the look of confusion on Mongril's blackened face.

"That's advice you gave me once," Mason explained. "Only now take it one step further. Empty your mind of everything—which shouldn't be hard for you to do—then focus and let it happen."

Mason stared at the burning torch in his hand, released it, and the torch flew to Mongril.

"But—"

"Practice," Mason advised. Then he took off down a darkened street, leaving Mongril to figure it out for himself.

"Practice," Mongril repeated after Mason had left. He stared at the torch in his hand, held it out in front of him, then closed his eyes and scrunched up his face.

Slowly, he opened his hand.

The torch dropped on Mario's corpse.

"Shit," Mongril said when he opened his eyes and saw Mario's clothes burning. He picked up the torch and tried again.

———

Mason ran through the streets and his feet kept flying off the ground. He hadn't told Mongril all of it. He'd explained the how but not the why. He was the only person who understood why they'd been blessed with such powers.

"I am the resurrection and the life," his father had quoted from the Bible in his sermons. "He that believeth in me, though he were dead, yet shall he live."

He had passed the tests. He had sacrificed all for Cassie and been found worthy, and now his reward was at hand.

———

Sandy's hand shook as she lit the oil lamp. Her watch read 2:30. She was still shivering in her wet clothes as she carried the lamp into the back bedroom.

"Sandy, say something," Stafford pleaded. He trailed after her and watched as she set the lamp on top of the bureau. "Haven't you heard a word I've said?"

Sandy rummaged inside a drawer and pulled out a diaper, jeans, polo shirt, sweatshirt; and two pairs of socks for Jesse. In another drawer, she found clothes for herself.

"I'm sorry I scared you. I didn't want the beachers to hear me. They're tearing the island apart, killing everyone they find."

Sandy changed Jesse and propped his small, limp body against a pillow in the middle of the bed. She moved to the door and he blocked it.

"Sandy, they killed Beth. They burned her alive. There are bodies all over the streets. By tomorrow morning —"

"Stop it. I don't want to hear any more. I know how rough the situation is. That's why as soon as I change my clothes I'm going back out there to find a boat so I can get the hell off this island."

Before he could argue further, she pushed him out of the way, stepped inside the bathroom, and closed the door.

He knocked softly. "Sandy, there are no boats left on the island. Every boat's been burned or demolished. That's why they're tearing up the streets. They've smashed porches, garages, sheds, and even outdoor showers looking for hidden boats. They don't want anyone to escape. They've even burned the model of the old sailing schooner that hung over the bar at Surf Side Bar and Grill. By tomorrow morning you'll be lucky to find a rubber raft still intact."

The bathroom door swung open and Sandy was dressed in an old pair of jeans and her father's Giants football jersey. "No rafts," she said emphatically, the thought of Mario's wife still vivid in her mind. "I need a boat. There must be one left somewhere on the island. I'll find one."

Stafford placed his hands gently on her arms.

"But that's why I came here. You do have a choice. Maybe all of us do. I was thinking about it while I was on the run tonight. About the food you thought I'd left for you, about you being protected all those months, and I figured it out. It's been Mason. He's been watching out for you all along." He paused. "Well, don't you see? We don't have to find a boat to go anywhere. We can be safe right here if you'll talk to Mason."

"Talk to him? I don't understand."

"Sure you do. Mason loves you. He'll do anything for you. If you ask him to stop the killing, he will."

"Stafford, we already tried a compromise with the beachers. It didn't work then. Why should it work now?"

"Because this time you'll be the negotiator. He'll listen to you. He wants to protect you. Why else do you think this house hasn't been raided when everything else is in ruins? Christ, you don't have a front door, but your house is the safest place on the island."

"Then why was the door smashed?" She shook her head very slowly back and forth. "You're forgetting that four months ago Mason broke into this bungalow twice, and attacked me. Last night — I don't know how — he ripped all the barricades off the windows. If you call that safe, fine. You stay here. Be my guest. But I'm going."

She pulled out of his arms and hurried to the back bedroom for Jesse. Almost to the bed, she heard screams and the sound of breaking glass. Her eye shifted to the window and Mr. Morelli's bedroom across the alley.

The room was brightly lit. The window was broken. Mrs. Morelli was flattened against the back wall, screaming hysterically.

Sandy rushed to her window and opened it.

Mrs. Morelli's screams intensified. Her hands were pressed against the sides of her head in tight fists. Her eyes were open wide, staring downward.

Sandy opened her mouth to yell, to ask Mrs. Morelli what was wrong.

Then Danny reared into view. His flesh was partially burned — scabious, a mass of gnarled flesh. His lipless mouth had peeled away from teeth clenched in rage as he dragged a bundle across the room.

He heaved the bundle to the windowsill and Mrs. Morelli flew from the wall and tried to pull the bundle from him. She cried, begging him to stop. Danny shoved his mother out of his way. He raised the bundle in view of the window and Sandy stood rooted to the spot.

The bundle was Mr. Morelli, and Danny's hands were clenched around his neck, strangling him. Mr. Morelli's arms twitched at his sides. His eyes bulged from their sockets. His mouth was stretched open wide, gasping, straining for a last breath of air. Finally, when the twitching and the straining stopped, Danny let the body drop to the floor, and he walked away from it.

Mrs. Morelli's screams changed to cries of despair. She approached her husband slowly, falling to her knees when she reached him. Sandy could see only the top of her head, but she could tell from the wailing cries that Mr. Morelli was dead.

Danny stood in the back of the bedroom. His mangled face grinned with smug satisfaction, then grew rigid. Narrowed eye slits stared at his mother and the fury seemed to consume him again: He took a step toward her.

"His mother'll be next," Stafford Said, leaning over Sandy's shoulders.

The sound of his voice shocked Sandy into action. "Mrs. Morelli, watch out!" she screamed.

Danny's head jerked up, his eyes searching for the caller, and a low, guttural growl 'escaped from his lipless mouth. He lunged toward the broken window, facing Sandy and Stafford.

Behind Danny, Mrs. Morelli stood up. Her face looked tearstained and confused.

"Now! Run now," Sandy screamed.

Mrs. Morelli jolted, as if an electrical current had passed through her body. Finally, she ran, racing to the bedroom door and out of Sandy's field of vision. At the sound of his mother's retreat, Danny tore himself away from the window and bolted from the room.

Sandy slammed the window closed and hurried to the front of the cottage as Mrs. Morelli came through her front door. Sandy helped her over the debris and brought her into the kitchen.

"You're okay now," Sandy said, easing her into a chair. "You're safe here."

Mrs. Morelli gripped Sandy's hands tightly and started to cry. Sandy rocked her in her arms, crying with her in a shared grief that words could not express.

Stafford entered the room, one hand carrying Jesse, the other hand carrying the oil lamp. He placed the lamp on the table, moved to Sandy, put his arm around her, and the four of them huddled together in the kitchen.

"You're the only one who can help us," Stafford said softly. "Please, Sandy. Talk to Mason."

Outside the bungalow, Mason stared through Cassie's window and watched her embrace the devil.

"Seen enough?" Vicky asked. "What do you think of your goddess now?"

Danny and a group of beachers waited at the foot of Cassie's cement stairs. They were excited, anxious to begin as soon as someone gave the word.

Vicky gloated. "Come on, Mason, don't take it so hard. We all make mistakes." She moved closer to him and ran her sticky-thin fingers lightly down his arm. The stub of her burned tongue licked her dry, flaked lips. "But we can also be very forgiving."

Mason grew rigid. He stared coldly at her, his face filled with revulsion. He walked stiffly to the stairs.

Vicky seethed with rage. "Just remember what you promised me, Mason. The bitch is mine to torture. You owe me that much. You hear me, Mason?"

Mason heard her words like one would hear a fly batting itself against a window on the other side of a room. His mind was in turmoil now. His world cracked open. Nothing else mattered but this time, this moment, this confrontation with Cassie.

He climbed the stairs, walked into the house, and faced her.

31.

Sandy saw Mason approach and prickles of terror ran up and down her spine. Mason's face was bloated. It was greenish-gray and his skin looked soft and spongy in patches, like sinkholes in a swamp.

Stafford backed away from Sandy. He carried Jesse to the far end of the kitchen. Quickly the room was filled with beachers.

Sandy's eyes darted from one face to another. Some of the beachers were as burned as shiny pieces of charred wood. Some had faces pieced together like a child's first jigsaw puzzle, with deep gorges from the knives and hatchets that had sliced into them. All the beachers were misshapen, all were hideously deformed, and all had the same glazed lust for torture in their eyes.

All except Mason. Mason's eyes were accusatory, expressing deep pain and deep betrayal.

"What do you want, Mason?" Sandy asked in a small, childlike voice. She looked away from him when she talked.

"What do you think he wants, bitch? He wants to see you bleed. He wants to see you burn," Vicky said.

Sandy heard the venomous reply and turned quickly to look at the beacher woman with the wispy black hair. "Mason promised not to hurt me," she said softly.

Vicky sauntered over to her and brought her scarred face within inches of Sandy's face. "And you, bitch, promised no interaction with your redheaded boyfriend over there," she said, gesturing toward Stafford.

"But he wasn't..." she said hurriedly, turning to Mason. "I mean I —"

"I'm only here because she wants to make a deal with you concerning all of us," Stafford said.

Vicky started laughing. "What did I tell you? Do you need further proof of her loyalty?" she asked Mason. "If she's a goddess, I'm Little Bo Peep."

Mason turned quickly and walked out of the room. He paused at Sandy's front door, unable to remain looking at her but unable to leave.

"What's wrong, Mason? What did I do?" Sandy called out to him.

"No more talk," Vicky said, fingering Sandy's blond hair as she spoke to her. "Now it's time to play. Don't you love playing games? Kids love games. My kids always did." She let go of Sandy's hair and walked to Stafford. "This kid like games?" she asked, snatching Jesse out of Stafford's arms:

Stafford tried to grab him back, but a beacher elbowed him in the stomach while another locked hands and smashed them into the back of Stafford's neck.

Mrs. Morelli screamed, and a beacher knocked her to the floor. Danny, giggling to himself, stood over her body, then propped her back up into her chair.

Jesse moaned weakly in Vicky's hands and Sandy flew across the room. She lunged for him; Vicky shoved her back against a table and laughed.

"You are rude. Where are your manners? You have to wait your turn if you want to play." She made a move to throw Jesse at her, then faked a half turn and threw him to Danny. He caught him on the fly.

Sandy screamed, rushed at Danny, and Danny threw Jesse back to Vicky.

"Gee, isn't this fun?" Vicky exclaimed. "It's like playing monkey-in-the-middle — or maybe we should call it goddess-in-the-middle." Sandy charged and Vicky sent her reeling into a wall. "Too bad Mongril isn't here. He'd enjoy this. Somebody run and find Mongril." She pointed at two Goon Squad members. "And bring torches on your way back," she called after them. "It's so dark in here, people are walking into walls."

Sandy shook her head, trying to clear it. Her vision blurred, then focused, and she saw Jesse in midair.

She dived for him.

Vicky wrenched him out of her reach.

Sandy tripped, landing hard on her knees. She cried, watching helplessly as Jesse was tossed from one hulking creature to another, around and around the room. She heard glass shatter and two ghouls dragged her off the floor.

Vicky walked toward her, holding a jagged-edged broken soda bottle in one hand and Jesse in the other. "Here's a game you taught me, bitch. Remember?"

Vicky stood in front of her and brought the jagged glass toward Jesse.

Sandy screamed, struggling to free herself from the beachers that held her.

From the front door came the sound of crunching wood, then footsteps. It was Mongril, carrying a torch and grinning like a blackened Halloween pumpkin.

"Hey, dudes, what's happening?"

Vicky paused, the glass an inch from Jesse's neck. "You're just in time. We're gonna paint the town red, only we're short on red paint so I thought I'd use blood."

The glass touched Jesse's skin and he yelped.

Sandy screamed, straining against her captors.

"Wait," Mongril yelled. "I got a better idea."

Vicky pulled out the glass and there was a pinpoint of red on Jesse's neck.

"What's your idea?"

"Bring the brat here," Mongril said. "I want to show you something."

Vicky carried Jesse to Mongril, who placed him in the center of the kitchen table.

Jesse moaned weakly, rolled over, and sucked his thumb. His other arm stretched out to Sandy, beseeching her to help him.

Mongril stepped back and held the lit torch in front of him. "Watch this," he said, and closing his eyes, grunting, squishing his features together as if he were going to lift a thousand pounds, he concentrated. He opened his blackened fingers. The torch dropped to the floor.

"Mongril, what the hell are you trying to do?" Vicky asked. She bent to pick up the torch, but Mongril plucked it from the floor before she reached it.

"Wait. I can do it. I been practicing all night. One more try."

Before Vicky could protest, he clamped his eyes shut, concentrated, inhaled, exhaled loudly, and let go.

The torch wobbled, unsupported, but suspended in midair.

Mongril grunted again. His blackened features were pulsating from the strain.

The torch drifted slowly, if somewhat jerkily, to the kitchen table. It floated over Jesse.

"Incredible," Vicky told him. "How did you do it?" The torch dropped and Vicky snatched it from the air before it fell on Jesse.

Sandy gasped.

"It's easy," Mongril bragged. "Wanna see it again?"
"Sure," Vicky agreed. "Only this time see if you can lift the kid and fly him over to the flame."

"No problem."

Mongril assumed a Buddha position on the floor and shut his eyes.

Vicky grabbed a toaster, flung it on the table, and propped up the torch in a bread slot. She lifted Jesse and held him at arm's length, facing away from her. The torch spewed flames on the table.

"Ready?" Vicky called out.

Sandy jerked violently to free herself from the ghouls holding her. Mrs. Morelli, conscious again, cried softly. Stafford remained knocked out on the floor.

"Go!" Vicky shouted, and she let Jesse fall.

Sandy shrieked. She shut her eyes as he dropped.

But when there was no crash, no new wailing of pain from Jesse, she opened her eyes and relief washed over her.

Jesse hovered a few inches above the floor. Then he started to rise.

"You did it," Vicky told Mongril. "Now keep it going. Keep bringing him up... higher... higher... That's it."

"No more," Sandy cried as she watched her son rise.

"Mason, please, wherever you are, don't let him do this anymore. Mason, please!"

"Forget Mason," Vicky sneered. "He don't go for tarnished goddesses. He found out you're no better than anybody else."

Jesse whimpered like a frightened puppy. His arms flailed wildly at his sides.

When he reached the level of the blazing torch, he wobbled in place.

"Perfect," Vicky shouted to Mongril. "Now bring him across, closer to the flames."

Vicky's eyes gleamed yellow. Her pleasure was almost sexual as the small boy's body stopped wobbling and lurched forward like an old train moving straight toward the fire.

Tears streamed down Sandy's face. She had stopped struggling, stopped trying to tear herself free. Her mind was a whirlwind of emotion and narrowly focused drives.

The drive was to save Jesse.

The focus was on Mason to do it.

"Mason, help me," she begged. "If you ever loved me, prove it to me now."

Jesse's body inched slowly toward the flame. The fingers of his outstretched hand touched fire.

Jesse squealed. He jerked his hand away and stuck his fingers into his mouth and howled.

Sandy clenched her fingers tightly together, as if she felt the pain with him.

"Save him, Mason. For the sake of our unborn child, the child that is growing inside of me this very moment, the child that is a product of... of... our love together."

Now a strand of Jesse's hair was licked by the flames. The hair caught fire and Sandy and Jesse screamed.

"Mason, please! I'm not a goddess. I never said I was. I'm just a woman, but that's what you really want anyway. It's what you wanted when we first met and what you want now."

More of Jesse's hair sizzled.

"Mason! For our child. For our love. For our life together!"

She flung herself from side to side, wailing, beyond words now, beyond pleas.

Mason watched her from the doorway that led into the kitchen, staring at his Cassie — loving her, forgiving her, wanting her.

There was a swooshing sound in the room, the sound of rushing air, and Jesse flew away from the flames.

The beachers fell away, releasing their hold on her, and she pulled Jesse close to her, smothering the burnt hair strands. She rocked and cuddled him to her breast until his whimpering ceased.

Vicky flew into a rage. She shrieked, denouncing Mason, screaming at the other beachers to help her. She cursed them when they refused and snarled at Sandy like a mad dog while Mason kept her at bay. He laughed at her. Then he concentrated his energy on pushing her out of the house and back to the beach.

After Vicky, the other beachers were easy for him. No energy was heeded. One look at Vicky cartwheeling down the sidewalk and they shrank from any confrontation with him.

"Wait for me outside," he told them, and they slithered out the door obediently. "And take him with you," he added, pointing to Stafford, who was still passed out on the floor.

Sandy looked up from Jesse and watched Stafford regain consciousness as the beachers dragged him to the door. Stafford was dazed. He blinked, saw Sandy, and called her name.

Mrs. Morelli moved next to Sandy and held her hand.

Mason leaned against a window and stared at the darkness. It was four o'clock, more than two hours until daybreak, but he felt weak. He felt like the sun was already starting to rise.

He turned to Cassie and held out his hand to her.

She rose, handed Jesse to Mrs. Morelli, and walked over to him.

Mason smiled. The swelling of his face had eased. Water oozed from the fetid craters in his face, giving the greenish-gray flesh a moist, wet sheen. Where flesh was eaten away, the bones of his skull gleamed brightly in the torch-lit room. A deep black scar ringed his neck.

"I love you, Cassie," he whispered. "I'll always love you." He touched her cheek.

Sandy held her breath as his skeletal fingers lightly touched her skin. Her hands squeezed together tightly, but she forced herself not to flinch.

"I love you, too," Sandy said flatly. She paused, trying to think of words that would convince him to stop the attacks. "But, Mason, all this killing and torturing is wrong. The killing has got to stop. Do you understand?"

"Our baby," he murmured. He reached out and touched her belly.

Sandy willed herself not to move.

"I will do anything for you, Cassie," he said.

"Will you promise me that no one else will be killed?"

"Yes, I promise you."

"Thank you, Mason," Sandy said, but before she could turn to leave him, Mason grabbed hold of her hands, refusing to let her go.

"And now you must promise me, Cassie, to love me and to live here as my wife forever."   .

Sandy gazed into his eyes. The meaning of his words was clear. Her fancy phrases had meant nothing. It was a bargain, plain and simple. Her life, Jesse's life, the lives of her friends, and the lives of all other norms on the island, in exchange for...

Sandy shuddered. She couldn't do it. She stared at his watery pustule-riddled face, the tufts of hair that remained on his scalp, the exposed skull, and the jagged scar where Stafford had decapitated him. She remembered the rape and the feel of his dead flesh against her and inside her. Her stomach heaved.

But then she thought of Jesse — with his hair singed, with his face close to the flames. And the decision was made.

"I promise." Her voice was barely above a whisper. Mason brought her hands to his face and kissed them. "Until tomorrow night," he promised her, and he walked slowly to the door.

"Hey, how am I doing?" Mongril called.

Mason snapped around to see Mongril, still sitting like Buddha, in a corner of the room. The toaster hovered in the air above him, the lit torch still jammed into the one-slice slot.

Mason's eyes narrowed and the toaster crashed to the floor. "You're doing fine, buddy," Mason told him. "Come on, let's go."

Mongril opened his eyes. "Did you see it, Mason? Did you see how long I kept that kid in the air? Hey, where'd everybody go?"

Mason leaned against the door frame and gestured for Mongril to join him. "Come on. I'll tell you all about it."

Mongril stood up, almost fell, and then weaved drunkenly to Mason's side. "I'm tired. Is it morning yet?"

"No, but don't worry. We'll feel recharged by tomorrow night."

"You sure?"

"Positive."

"Okay. Let's hit the beach."

"Sure, only I've got a little job for you first."

"Anything, Mason. You name it."

"I want you to organize some of the Goon Squad and have them pass the word. Starting now, the norms are strictly off limits. Nobody touches them. Understand?"

Sandy listened to Mason outline his plans to protect the norms, and her head started pounding with the worst headache she'd ever experienced. She felt dizzy with exhaustion, yet she doubted she'd be able to fall asleep.

Mason was planning to protect the lives of everyone on the island. He was keeping his promise to her. And tomorrow night, after darkness descended on the island, she would have to keep her promise to him.

32.

After sunset on November 9, Sandy sat quietly at the kitchen table. Her hands were folded primly in her lap. The front door — the door she'd spent all day piecing together with some of the wood used as barricades — was unlocked. Jesse was next door, spending the night with Mrs. Morelli, and Sandy waited for Mason.

True to his word, Mason had arranged for the security of the norms. He'd placed them in protective custody within a two-block area that surrounded the town hall. There weren't many norms left — maybe two or three hundred, but no one felt like counting. That afternoon, Sandy had walked with Jesse to the norms' restricted area but the remains of the people slain the previous night had soon sent her reeling with horror, and she hurried back to the bungalow to get ready for Mason, her husband.

Mason had told Mongril that only Mrs. Morelli and Sandy were allowed to keep their houses. No one else would be protected outside the town hall area or would be provided with rations of food and water. Her rations would be provided by Mason, her husband, her lover, who would soon come to claim her.

She straightened her costume, a long white nightgown and a pink-and-white rosebud-patterned duster that had belonged to her mother. She insisted on thinking of it as a costume because it was the only way she could go through with it and still retain her sanity. This was an acting role, nothing more.

All day long she had prepared for it. She'd stretched her mind and envisioned tonight's scene from the audience's point of view. She'd drilled her concentration and practiced her breathing exercises: take deep breaths, deep breaths, and let it out slowly; feel your toes, and your toes and your feet, and your toes and your feet and your ankles; now retain this focus of feeling as you move up and add the rest of your body... inhale... exhale... relax.

Sandy refolded her hands in her lap and rehearsed the scene in her mind. It was a love scene that required elaborate costumes. Tonight's play was set in prehistoric times and her leading man's costume was most cumbersome. Oh, well, she'd get through it somehow, no matter how distracting or odious the costume proved to be. The pay was worth it.

She heard footsteps coming up her steps. She wet her lips and straightened her costume. Yes, she'd think of the pay, she reminded herself, taking a deep breath to quell the panic rising in her throat. It was the highest pay any actor or actress had ever received. Higher than Sylvester Stallone or Eddie Murphy. Higher than Marilyn Monroe, if Hollywood could coax her back from the dead.

The door opened and Mason entered the bungalow. Slowly, he walked over to her, and Sandy visualized the dimming of the lights, the raising of the curtain, and the hush falling over the audience.

She smiled at him, and he drew her into his arms.

The pay was the sum worth of her life, and Jesse's life, and the lives of all the norms.

The dead, cold flesh pressed against her lips. Sandy needed every ounce of strength to keep from screaming out in horror and disgust. He tasted of finely ground dust, and his coldness chilled her deep within the marrow of her bones.

Rotting fingers brushed against her face, down her throat, and lingered at the top buttons of her mother's duster. She squeezed her eyes shut tightly, willing herself not to flinch, not to breathe, not. to move; the duster soon fell to the floor.

His stench was dizzying. Somehow she kept herself from gagging, but she couldn't keep her knees from weakening. The room was spinning all around her. She started to fall and Mason caught her, lifting her up into his arms and carrying her into the back bedroom.

"Rest now, darling Cassie," she heard him say. "There's no hurry. We have all night to make love and the rest of our lives to be together."

He placed her gently on the bed and one small tear traveled down her cheek. Mason reached down and brushed it away gently. And the corpse, her leading man, her husband, her lover, continued to undress her.

33.

In the following months, psychic power crackled in the air above the beach at night. Lightning zigzagged across the sky and rumblings deep below the ocean floor shot water up like oil gushers.

Mongril was the first one, after Mason, to perfect his new skills. In November, he delighted his fellow beachers with floating torches, swirling sands, juggling and balancing acts. He learned to lift himself off the ground, but it made him dizzy, so he restricted his lifting to objects and occasionally his fellow beachers.

Vicky convinced him to share his expertise. By December he was giving lessons to all the beachers, and the island shook from their practice lessons. The norms, segregated in their two-block area, huddled together in the town hall until the earthquakes subsided. They were increasingly becoming a hotly debated issue. Vicky argued vehemently that norms were valuable test subjects on which to practice their growing powers. Other beachers agreed with her.

Mason forbade it. Intent on pleasing Cassie, he cleaned up the island and dug a mass grave for the norm corpses that littered the streets. He allowed no beacher but himself to go near a norm, delivering food and water rations to them each night before his visit to Cassie. Several beachers grumbled. None openly opposed him.

Beachers had no need for food and water, and less and less desire to continue the rituals of eating. They were interested in entertainments now, displays of talents and powers. They were interested in arousing fear.

On Christmas Eve, Vicky awoke at nightfall imbued with Christmas spirit. She waited until Mason departed for his nightly sojourn, then assembled the beachers.

"Since Christmas is a time for giving, I think we should give the norms a party." Her yellow eyes twinkled with delight. "A surprise reunion between friends and family."

Her suggestion was met with grumblings and hostility.

"What family are you talking about?" asked Mongril. "I know I ain't related to no norm. Besides, Mason said—"

"Mason," Vicky interrupted, spitting his name out with contempt, "is so occupied with his whore, he'll never notice a thing."

"But Mason said we ain't allowed to touch them," Mongril insisted.

"That's the beauty of my plan," she insisted. "We won't do anything directly to them, at all."

Later, when Mason heard screams echoing across the island, be left Sandy, rushed to the town hall area, and found it in chaos. Norms were hysterical, running wildly in the streets, yet no one beacher could be found.

The bedlam had been created by a bombardment of norm corpses that were removed from their mass graves and animated by beacher power, in order to torment surviving norm relatives and friends.

Mason, enraged, delivered a stern verbal reprimand, warning of dire consequences if beachers attempted similar stunts in the future.

The beachers were stunned into silence, not by his lecture, but by Cassie's Christmas gift to him: a stocking hat made of a white gauze material that fit snugly over his head.

In January, the beachers knew the boundaries and limitations of their power abilities. It was a talent, like painting or singing, that not all possessed in equal measure. Lou, who had displayed his sand burrowing skill so much earlier than the others, never learned to move anything but sand. And Carla couldn't move anything at all. Conversely, Mongril possessed a natural gift. Vicky's theory was that Mongril's mind, unspoiled by intellectual growth, was like a plain of fertile, virgin soil for psychic abilities to take root and grow.

By February, the beachers were cantankerous and unruly. Their bodies were little more than bones, eyes, and patches of skin. Short-fused tempers ignited easily and violent arguments broke out among them. With Vicky's prodding, they began questioning Mason's authority, and raids were planned against the norm compound.

To forestall full-scale rebellion, Mason relaxed the rules concerning norms. They could not be killed, but they could occasionally be utilized for "psychic research."

A huge cage was constructed on the beach using the chicken wire lining the boardwalk railing. The norms were transferred into it and the beachers became obsessed with taunting them. It was their one abiding pleasure, their only release from boredom.

More important, torturing norms blocked out the memories of what they had been and the reality of what they had become.

FOUR

KINGDOM COME

34.

On February 24, Mongril and Vicky sat together on a broken boardwalk bench. The night sky above them was painted in hues of deep purple and vibrant red. A crescent of a moon accentuated a kaleidoscope of color patterns.

Vicky and Mongril were oblivious to the spectacle. "Mason leave?" Vicky asked.

"Yeah," said Mongril.

"You talk to him?"

"Yeah."

"Well, what did he say?"

Mongril scratched his scalp. Much of the skin had deteriorated on his hands and face. The dry, flaky patches that remained itched ferociously as they pulled from his skull.

"He said he'll think about it and let me know," Mongril answered.

Vicky made a sound that reminded Mongril of a conch shell pressed against his ear.

"Christ. I told you to go ahead and do it and not ask his permission. What right does he have to object to you taking a norm out of the cage for your personal use?"

"He didn't say I couldn't take one out. Only that he had to think about letting me keep one for myself."

"So, in other words, only Mason, our illustrious lord and master, is allowed to set up house with one."

"He ain't our lord and master and he didn't say that, Vicky. He said—"

"Christ," Vicky muttered, cutting him off with a wave of her hand. She made the conch shell sound again. "Fuck it."

She shoved herself up from the bench and paced the area. She wore a sleek black dress she'd unearthed from the ruins of a boutique on Bay Boulevard. A black shoulder-length wig was set forward on her skull and she patted it to keep it in place while she walked. From the back, with her long, bone-tight dress and her black hair blowing in the wind, she resembled a Vogue model. When she turned around, her attire was in shocking contrast to the acid-eaten horror that was her face.

Vicky quit pacing and headed toward the beach.

"Where you going?" Mongril asked.

"To the cage," she answered without looking back.

Mongril bounded after her.

The cage was constructed like an enclosure for a lion act in a circus. There was a locked gate entrance and only Mason and Mongril possessed keys, but almost any beacher could "think" it open if they dared. So far, no one had dared.

"Why are you so afraid of Mason?" Vicky asked as they neared the cage.

Mongril shook his head. "Not afraid."

"Yes you are. Last week you lit up an entire video arcade. You had every machine running."

Mongril grinned. "Yeah. It was beautiful."

"Sure it was. And it took an enormous amount of power to do something like that."

"Shit," Mongril agreed. "I couldn't move for the rest of the night."

"I bet it took more power than Mason's got."

Mongril dropped the grin and shook his head. "Not really. Mason's pretty strong. He swept that kid away from me and I didn't feel a thing."

"Shit. That was four months ago. You were still learning, then. Now he wouldn't stand a chance against you."

Mongril scratched at his scalp again. "Aw, Mason's all right."

Vicky sighed her loud, conch shell sigh. "Why am I wasting my time talking to you? You're like all the rest of the idiots around here, hanging around with nothing to do until Mason gives you permission to have fun."

She turned from him and leaned against the cage. The beachers pursued the same activities every night. Lou burrowed in the sand and popped up inside the norm enclosure, hoping to startle the norms. Danny pestered his mother. Carla laughed at the sea. Mongril blindly enforced Mason's rules. Vicky complained about them.

Other beachers got a big kick out of rattling the norms' cage, grabbing at them through the spaces in the chicken wire, growling at them, or teasing them with bits of food that they'd float too high for the norms to reach.

The norms had quickly learned to stay clear of the bars after dark. They wrapped themselves in ratty little blankets and huddled together in the center of the cage all night. The highlight of the evening was watching them slop up their food, which Mason dumped in a trough.

"Hey, maybe Mason'll let you feed them tonight," Mongril said as if reading her thoughts.

Vicky glared at him.

"Want me to light up the video arcade again?"

Vicky shook her head. "When was the last time we did something interesting?" Before he could answer, she told him. "Christmas, that's when. Remember how the norms squealed when those stiffs started chasing them down the streets?"

Mongril giggled.

"And remember how we made Mario's body break dance in front of the town hall?"

"Yeah," Mongril said, laughing. "I was watching from a rooftop. I laughed so hard I almost fell off."

"And remember how the norms were so terrified, some of them threw themselves in the bay and drowned?"

"Yeah, yeah, yeah." Mongril laughed and then abruptly stopped. "But Mason got pretty pissed about that trick."

"Fuck Mason!"

"And besides, there ain't no more bodies to scare anybody. Mason dumped them in the ocean."

"Fuck the bodies. There are other ways to use the norms."

Mongril looked at her sharply. "Whatever you got in mind, I don't think Mason's gonna like it."

"Quit worrying about Mason. Do you think he worries about you? Every night he's at the slut's house. He never spends any part of the night with us anymore. He's changed, Mongril, and the sooner you realize it, the better off you'll be. Christ, he doesn't even look like us anymore. He started with that hat the whore made for him and now she's got him trussed up in bandages like he's some kind of mummy." "Yeah, but—"

Vicky's yellow eyes flashed, reflecting her anger and a tinge of the purple sky. "I'm bored with Mason and I'm bored with his goddamned rules. We need some excitement around here, some fun. And I've got a terrific idea."

Mongril looked at her uneasily. "I don't think Mason's gonna like this."

"A race," Vicky said innocently. "A simple little race. Now how could Mason possibly object to the norms running a little race?"

She smiled at him, revealing the rotten yellow stubs of her remaining teeth. "You'll love it. The first thing we do..."

———

She knew Mason watched her as she crossed the kitchen carrying a bowl of hot soup. She walked with a slight waddle. Her steps were heavy and slow.

"Let me help you," he said, jumping up and taking the soup from her hands. "Sit down, Cassie. Please, rest awhile."

She lowered herself slowly into a chair. Her complexion was pale. Her hair was limp. She wore no makeup. And she was all belly, late in her seventh month of pregnancy, but Mason acted like she'd never looked lovelier. He raced across the table and held her hand in his bandaged one.

Sandy shuddered.

"Are you cold?" he asked. "Maybe the fireplace isn't working. Maybe I should—"

"No. I'm fine. Thank you." She closed her eyes and concentrated on mentally separating her hand from the rest of her body.

"Eat your soup," he advised. "It'll warm you." He placed a spoon in her hand and gently wrapped her fingers around it. Then he pushed the bowl of soup in front of her. "Eat."

"Hmmm? Oh, no, I changed my mind. I'm not hungry anymore."

She dropped the spoon as she turned from him and stared down at her bulging belly. The baby seemed lower than it had been last week, and less active. Maybe it would come early, she thought. Jesse had been one week early, so it was a definite possibility. Please God, she prayed, please make it soon.

Sandy had two fears that obsessed her now. One was going into labor all alone, with no one to help her, no one to cut the cord. The second fear was not going into labor for another month, which might seriously delay her escape plans. She looked up at Mason, at his white gauze bandages that she convinced him he should wear to "protect himself" from further deterioration. It made it easier to look at him but did nothing to change the disgust she felt for him, or her eagerness to leave the island.

"Mason," she said, "I was walking along the boardwalk yesterday and I noticed how thin the norms look."

"Please, Cassie, I've asked you so many times. Don't go up there. It's too dangerous."

"I only go during the day. Walking is good exercise, especially good for going into labor. It limbers up the body. Exercises the muscles. It's healthy."

"Eating is also healthy," he reminded her. He picked up her spoon, dipped it into the soup, and brought it to her lips. "Open wide."

"No... please, don't baby me, Mason," she said, pushing the spoon away. "Besides, how can I eat when the norms on the beach are starving?"

"Is that why you sneak food to them?"

Sandy's head jerked to look at him, surprised he knew about it. "Some of those people are my friends," she said.

"Is the red devil a friend?"

"Mason, I told you before, he's not a devil, he's not even a friend. He's an acquaintance. He was nice to me and—"

"Let's not fight. The island doesn't have unlimited food supplies and I'm only trying to save what we do have for you and the kids in the years to come." He smiled and leaned over to pat her tummy. "Kids. I can't believe how happy I am."

He massaged her belly with wide, circular strokes. Sandy's body stiffened. Her hand gripped the edge of the table as she struggled not to protest.

"I think I hear Jesse," she lied, unable to tolerate his hand on her any longer. She jumped up from the table. "I'll be right back."

"No, let me," Mason insisted, and he hurried to the back bedroom where Jesse slept.

Sandy sank back in her chair. She felt on edge, almost to the breaking point. She could not keep her true feelings bottled inside of her much longer.

Please God, make it soon.

"He was awake," Mason said, interrupting her prayers. A sleepy-eyed Jesse was in his arms.

"He was?" Sandy asked, surprised.

"Well, actually he was awake after I picked him up out of bed." Mason ruffled Jesse's hair affectionately. Jesse grinned. "G'morning, Mommy."

"Never mind, good morning. Back to bed, buster." She held out her arms to carry him to bed.

"No-o-o," he moaned. He slipped his arm around Mason's neck. "Me stay, Mason."

"Forget it." Sandy told him. "Back to bed."

"No."

"Let me do it," Mason said. He turned to look at Jesse. "How about a horsie ride?"

Jesse's eyes lit up. "Yeah!"

"Okay, get ready."

Jesse put his hands out in front of him, holding imaginary reins as Mason turned him around so that he faced away from him.

"Ready... set... go," he yelled, and suddenly Jesse was flying in midair, across the kitchen toward his bedroom.

"Don't do that," Sandy screamed. She jumped out of her chair to where Jesse floated and snatched him out of the air. "You could have killed him," she screamed at Mason.

Startled by her action, Jesse howled.

Mason stared at her, dumbfounded. "Cassie, I always play horsie with Jesse like that. He loves it."

"Poor baby," Sandy murmured to her son. "Mommy's poor, poor little boy."

Mason listened to the child's whimpering. He watched Cassie carry her son back into his bedroom. It was all so confusing to him. The way he felt, the way to act, the things that made her happy, and the. things that angered her were all so alien to him. Mason tucked in part of the bandage around his face that had loosened. It was like having to learn a new set of rules for a game he'd been playing all his life.

Vicky watched as Mongril unlocked the cage and threw the racing participants at her feet. The six men, all former guards or policemen, quickly scrambled into a line. They were emaciated, unshaven, dressed in rags, and bleary-eyed, but there was still a look of contempt in the way they looked at her.

Her hands on the hips of her slinky long black dress, the wind whipping the black wig hair around her face, she ordered them to undress. "Everything," she commanded, cackling at their uneasiness.

She walked slowly in front of the men and in back of them as they complied with her orders, stopping to run her hands over one of them, slapping another one on his bare buttocks, wagging the burned remains of her tongue lasciviously at another.

When all six were naked, she marched them single file to a torch-lit circular track that had been blasted into the sand. The track was packed with beacher spectators — boisterous, rowdy, and eager for the night's entertainment. Vicky eyed her six racers and prepared them for the show.

"I want a good race from all of you. No slouching and no pussyfooting around," Vicky told them. Then she smiled mockingly. "The winner will be rewarded in more ways than one."

Turning from them, she signaled to Mongril, "Tell the trainers they may dress their animals. The dog race will begin immediately."

Stafford, one of the six racers, looked up into the face of his trainer, a charred, rotting skull whose gleaming eyes were full of hate and full of malice. A yellow silk bathing suit was thrown at him.

"Put 'em on," his trainer ordered. Flags with the number five were tied around his waist, and spiked bands were fastened on his wrists and ankles. Finally, the trainer dangled one last brown leather band in front of him. It was decorated with long, sharp nails.

"Your dog collar," the trainer explained; enjoying Stafford's incomprehension.

"What's it for?" Stafford ventured to ask.

The gleaming eyes flashed and an arm smashed into his face.

"Put 'em on," the grinning corpse repeated, and Stafford, dazed from the blow and numb from the cold and the fear, quickly obeyed.

Minutes later, a leash was clicked onto his collar and he was walked to the entrance of the racetrack.

Vicky stood on top of the lifeguard, chair near the starting line. She clutched a garden hose whip in her hand. Behind her, ocean waves eight feet high crashed to shore. She waited until all the racing "dogs" were assembled and the crowd of beachers grew quiet. "Gentlemen, display your animals," she ordered. Stafford was knocked to his knees and forced to crawl on all fours, leading the promenade onto the track.

The spectators went wild, convulsing with laughter, catcalling, shouting obscenities, and making known their approval or disapproval of each contestant.

After the walk around the track, the dogs were lined up at the starting line.

Stafford looked to his right and saw that Donaldson, wearing orange trunks and the number four, waited next to him. Donaldson's midriff was a corset of spikes and a helmet with a long pointed metal file protruded from the top of it, like an antenna.

Donaldson turned to look at Stafford. They stared at each other briefly. And Stafford saw in his eyes a mirror image of his own shock and humiliation.

Then a sharp kick in his rear sent Stafford face down in the sand.

"Pay attention, dog," his trainer warned. "You may wanna win this race when you hear all the rules."

". . . and the first dog once around the track and in possession of the prize, will get to keep it," Vicky held up a canned ham that had been magic-markered with eyes, nose, whiskers, and ears to look like the face of a cat.

The crowd of spectators roared.

Vicky continued. "Dogs must remain on all fours at all times. Dogs are not to be aided by outside help, physically, mentally, or any other way, or they're disqualified. And finally..."

She grinned at the humbled dogs shivering at her feet. "There will be only one winner of this game. Only one dog will be returned to the cage tonight. Therefore, dogs may use any means to capture the prize before or after they cross the finish line. Any dog disqualified or still alive after a winner is declared will be duly executed."

Beachers cheered, applauding the final rule.

Mongril tugged at Vicky's dress, trying unsuccessfully to make himself heard over the noise of the crowd. Vicky bent down to him, whispered in his ear, and handed the canned ham and the whip to him. Mongril stared at the items, hesitating, trying to come to a decision. Then he grinned and sent the canned ham sailing through the air. It landed twenty feet in front of the racers.

Vicky blew a kiss to him before turning back to the racers. "Gentlemen, unleash your animals." She paused. "On your marks. Get set." Another dramatic pause, glancing sideways at Mongril, and seeing him nod, "Go!"

Mongril snapped the whip and the crowd cheered.

The race was on.

None of the dogs moved.

Stafford felt a kick in his side. "Take off, dog!" his enraged trainer yelled. Stafford crawled forward several feet, then looked around for his fellow racers. Donaldson was behind him. His eyes were opened wide, full of panic. He was frozen to the starting line. Another racer crawled sideways, toward the crowd. One crawled backward. Two racers sat on the sand, staring at each other.

Vicky was livid. She shrieked with rage at the trainers, and Stafford felt a barrage of kicks. He sunk down into the sand and covered his head, determined to take the beating and not budge.

Then he felt a sting across the back of his neck. He felt a slash behind his ear, and a fire burned the back of his head. His hands rushed to smother the flames, but there were none. There was only wetness and a huge gash made by the whip. Another burning slash; this time it was across his unprotected face. Stafford lurched forward, toward the magic-markered canned ham in front of him.

Behind him, the snapping of the whip sliced through the deafening noise of the crowd. Arid one by one the racers were forced to move.

Stafford was out in front.

The cat-faced ham was located only several arm's lengths away. He reached for it, and another "dog", responding to a severe flogging, pulled at his feet and yanked his knees from under him.

Stafford ate sand.

The racer wearing neon blue trunks plowed over him, his spike-studded belt cutting into Stafford's back. Stafford tried pushing him off, but the nails on his collar had flattened when he'd fallen on them, twisting the collar tightly around his neck. He raised his head and choked. Blue Trunks, scrambling away from him, kicked him in the mouth, and Stafford tasted his own blood. He spit it out and part of a tooth was expelled with the thick fluid.

He shook his head. The beach was swimming all around him, waves of sand billowing everywhere he looked. He felt the air rush past him and then suddenly the whip exploded across his back. His hair was yanked back and a fist full of small objects were dumped into his mouth before he was released.

"Swallow 'em," rasped a voice behind him.

Stafford's tongue identified the objects as tablets and capsules. Immediately he began to spit them out. Again, his hair was pulled back.

"I said swallow 'em."

Stafford's eyes: looked upward into the tunnel-eyed beacher with the whip. He swallowed and his hair was released again. A whip lash against the back of his legs set him in motion.

Booing and shouts of "Foul" greeted Mongril's return to Vicky's side. He motioned for one of the trainers to take over his whipping duties and pulled himself up into the lifeguard chair to sit beside her.

Vicky slid to one side to make room for him. "You did good, Mongril," she said with a gaping grin. "You did real good. How did it feel?"

Mongril nodded his head up and down several times, then started to giggle. It was a lewd, humorless laugh.

And Vicky knew the answer.

The crowd worked itself up into a frenzy, screaming loudly for the racer of their choice.

Blue Trunks, in the lead, retained possession of the prize. All dogs but Stafford were in sight of the finish line. Then Blue Trunks slipped, and the dogs at his heels fell on top of him. The canned ham flew into the air.

Stafford quickened his pace. Sand and broken shells grated into his knees as he crawled to where the can had landed. He passed the pileup as two racers peeled off the top of the heap. While they searched the surrounding area, Stafford moved directly to the half-submerged can, faking a fall on top of it. He howled, as if he'd been hurt, bellowing with his faked injury as he slowly inched the can away from the others.

The beacher audience, aware of Stafford's ploy, screamed the information to the other racers, but their combined voices made it impossible for their words to be understood.

Stafford slid to within a foot of the finish line with the can under his chest when suddenly the beach beneath him caved in. The canned ham shot out from beneath him, and Lou was standing over him.

The audience jeered.

Lou pranced around the track, taking bows and dodging the racers and the trainers like Charlie Chaplin dodging the Keystone Cops.

Vicky signaled Mongril to intervene, and the canned ham flew from Lou's hands and hovered over the center of the track.

Lou burrowed out of sight.

The can dropped to the sand.

The racers, spread all over the track, turned toward center and headed for the prize.

The beachers pressed closer to the action, overflowing onto the track, shoving one another out of the way, jockeying for front row views. They hurled garbage at the racers—bottles, cans, shells, rocks, anything they carried with them. Fights broke out between them. Soon there were as many beachers crawling as there were watching the race.

Stafford ducked from a flying beer can and touched the canned ham prize with his fingertips, only to have it snatched from his reach by Blue Trunks, lucky number seven. Uttering a guttural cry, Stafford lunged at him. Something exploded in his head. It was four months ago and he was slicing up the beachers.

But this time it was easier; this was more satisfying.

When the job was finished, the sound of the crowd was a dull roar in his ears and three racers lay in a dead heap.

Stafford watched Donaldson disengage the spike of his helmet from his adversary's heart. The two men faced each other.

Recognition, or a last spark of humanity, flickered briefly in Donaldson's eyes. Then he attacked, head down like a bull, his spiked helmet dripping blood, aiming straight for Stafford.

His first charge was easily averted. Stafford rolled out of Donaldson's path and scrambled for the prize that was only a short distance from him.

Donaldson changed direction, charged again, and this time his spiked helmet sliced into Stafford's foot.

Stafford yowled. He kicked at Donaldson with one leg and knocked him out of his helmet. The spike remained lodged in his foot. Stafford propelled himself forward, screaming with rage and dragging the helmet with him. He attacked. His hands closed around Donaldson's throat, squeezing for an eternity, until the life was wrung out of him.

A throng of beachers rushed to him, sweeping him onto their shoulders for a victory lap around the track. He pulled the spike out of his foot and put Donaldson's helmet on his head as they carried him. The beachers thrust the canned ham into his arms and he held it in the air as if it were a loving cup trophy. Blood from the spike dripped down his face.

———

At the first hint of morning, Stafford and his trophy were dumped back into the cage. Other norms eyed the ham hungrily, but a flash of Stafford's spiked arm and ankle bands was all that was needed to convince the others to let him be. He hurried into a corner and turned the can over and over in his hands.

The metal key was missing.

He pulled a nail from his dog collar and used it to wind the metal strip from around the can. It detached easily — too easily. The metal strip had been glued to the can and inside was nothing but packed wet sand.

Stafford stared at the mud, unable to believe his eyes. He raked the mud in a manic attempt to find something; hidden in it — something edible, something of value...

There was nothing — nothing but the mud.

Stafford threw the can violently against the bars of the cage and sank into the sand. His insides rumbled. His stomach reacted violently to the drugs that had been given to him during the race, and his bowels exploded.

A flurry of snowflakes coated him as he slept.

35.

February 25th dawned cold and gray. The light snowstorm ended at daybreak, leaving a thin crust on bungalows and island streets. Jesse awoke to see the glittering outside his window. He squealed with delight.

"Mommy, it's snow outside. Mommy, getty up. Snow!"

Sandy rolled over, protecting her belly as Jesse executed his daily saddle-jumping maneuver.

"Can we make a snowman, Mommy, ple-e-e-ase?"

"A snowman?"

Sandy raised herself up into a sitting position and looked out the window. "Honey, I don't think there's enough snow out there to make a snowball."

"Ple-e-e-ase."

"Jesse, listen. By the time we get dressed and have breakfast, the snow will be melted."

"No, won't."

"Snow never lasts long this close to the ocean."

"Why?"

Sandy sighed, rubbed her eyes, and tried to wake up.

"Why, Mommy, why?"

"I don't know," Sandy answered. "It must have something to do with salt in the air. Now, no more questions. Let's concentrate on breakfast."

Sandy heaved her body into a standing position. Once she was standing, her extra bulk was no strain. She had gained only eighteen pounds so far, ten pounds less than she'd gained expecting Jesse. But the weight was all baby, all wrapped up and neatly tied into a little basketball that hung front and center at her navel. With Jesse, the weight had been spread around: hips, thighs, face, ankles, stomach, everywhere. Labor with Jesse had lasted six hours.

Please God, don't let it last long and please—don't let me be alone.

"Mommy, me talking to you," Jesse said, interrupting her thoughts. He threw a Little Golden storybook at her. "Me make a snowman like this." He pointed to a picture of a snowman on the cover. "See?"

Sandy took the book from him and moved to the cooking grill and fireplace Mason had fashioned in place of her electric stove. The fireplace supplied heat to the kitchen and back bedroom, and cooking on its grill was much easier than standing outside or near a window to cook on the barbecue.

After lighting the fire, she put water on to boil and turned back to the book. It was unfamiliar to her. After eight months, she thought she'd seen every nut, button, and bobby pin in the cottage at least a hundred times.

"Where'd you get the book?" she asked Jesse.

"Mason gave it to me."

She should have guessed. She took cereal out of a cabinet, poured it into a bowl, added water, and placed it in front of Jesse.

Soon, she told herself. Soon she'd be away from Mason. Away from his gifts, his presence, his loving concern, and away from the touch of his sickening bandage-covered flesh.

Her escape plans were set. Everything was packed including a map of the coastline she'd extracted from a glass-framed wall hanging in the town hall. The boat, of course, had been the hardest thing to acquire. She had spotted it almost two months ago, right after Christmas.

When she and Jesse were on the pier washing clothes, she noticed a rope tied around a wood piling. She'd probably seen the rope on previous visits, but on this particular day it suddenly clicked into place. This was the rope tied to Lenny's sinking boat, according to the story Stafford had told her.

Two weeks were spent pulling on the rope. She climbed into the black mud silt that formed the bottom of the bay, stumbling over beer cans and broken shells as she worked the skiff loose. She finally dragged it to shore.

Lenny's skull was still stuck in the bow. She dislodged it with a hammer, but the worst part was picking it up with her bare hands. The act seemed on par with fondling spiders. The absurdity of her squeamishness struck her and she almost fell into the water laughing. Tears streamed down her face. What was picking up a skull compared to the acts she'd performed and withstood for Mason's pleasure?

Line up the spiders, she thought. After kissing Mason, she could kiss a hundred black widows. *Bring on bloodsuckers*. She could undulate with pleasure with an army of leeches feeding on her. Send in head lice and wood ticks, and worms and snakes of every size and variety. She could lie motionless without uttering a solitary word of protest while they crawled and skittered freely across her flesh.

In the weeks that followed, she patched two holes in the bow of the boat according to instructions in an old copy of Canoe Times she'd found in Dr. Jenkin's waiting room: Sandy had gone there looking for a book on natural childbirth, but she hadn't found one. She figured she'd have to rely on Mrs. Morelli to help her with the delivery.

She turned back to Jesse. "If you hurry up and eat your cereal, you can visit with Mrs. Morelli today."

"No. Make snowman," he insisted.

"Okay, okay. We'll make a snowman first and then you can stay with Mrs. Morelli."

Satisfied, Jesse finished gobbling his cereal while Sandy searched for his clothes. She dressed him in two summer jackets, cutoff red sweatpants, and a summer hat-and-kerchief combination tied around his head. She put socks on his hands for mittens.

It was after twelve o'clock when they headed outside. "Too cold, Mommy," he announced when they were two steps away from the front door.

Sandy scooped up a handful of icy mush that was all that remained of last night's snowfall and held it out to him.

"Here. Let's get started on your snowman."

Jesse shook his head and held his arms stiffly at his sides. "Too cold," he repeated. "Mommy make snowman."

Sandy laughed. She threw the slush at him, then picked him up when he squealed, and carried him up the Morelli ramp.

The tip of his cold nose touched hers as they ran.

"I love you, baby."

"Love you too, Mommy."

She put him down at the top of the ramp and he planted a juicy, cold kiss on her cheek before hurrying inside.

Minutes later, she was meandering through a wonderland of snow-capped bungalows on the way to the bay. The boat was concealed beneath a pile of trash near the pier, and she checked on the water jugs, the food secured in double plastic bags, the patches still smooth and uncracked, and the antique oars, dismantled from above a fireplace display. Blankets were rolled and tied. Under the wooden plank seats were four bright-orange life jackets — one each for Mrs. Morelli, Jesse, herself, and Stafford.

Stafford!

Sandy glanced at her wristwatch. It was two o'clock. She had more than enough time to visit Stafford on the beach.

Quickly, she covered the boat with pieces of burned wood and other garbage that had been washed ashore. She stopped home for a box of saltines and a jar of peanut butter, hid them inside her jacket, and hurried to the cage. There was no snow anywhere in sight when she reached the boardwalk and ho sigh of beachers.

The beach looked deserted, but Sandy knew it wasn't. The beachers were resting, concealed beneath small mounds of sand that dotted the beach. Mason had told her the custom had grown steadily in the last four months. The sand was soothing, he'd said, and it protected them from the sun.

Sandy hadn't understood but she'd been grateful for the improvement in the scenery. Then the norm cage had been constructed and put to use.

No one noticed her approach. The sand mounds were clustered in small groups near the water's edge. The norms, accustomed to her daily visits, were beyond noticing anything. There were no children among them, and very few elderly people. The ones remaining were painfully thin and dressed in rags. They paced constantly back and forth, up and down the length of the cage, or they leaned against the bars trying to sleep. They rarely talked.

Aside from pacing and sleeping, their main activity seemed to be digging with shells, forever searching the sand for a cigarette butt to smoke or an old candy wrapper to suck.

Sandy reached the boardwalk area overlooking the cage and leaned over the railing, searching for Stafford's red hair. When at last she saw him, coated with sand and huddled in a corner, she called out softly to get his attention, but he didn't respond.

"Stafford." This time she used a loud stage whisper, and his head moved. His hand scratched his back and Sandy saw that underneath the sand was bare skin.

"Stafford, behind you."

He heard her and turned around. She gasped. His neck and half his face were swollen and streaked with blood. Deep, long gashes snaked across most of his body.

Sandy plodded through the sand until she stood only inches away from him, on the outside of the cage. "Stafford, what happened?"

His dazed eyes looked up at her. "I won a race." His voice was a hoarse whisper.

Sandy reached through the bars to touch him, to reassure him. He flinched back from the pain.

"Sorry," she whispered. Her face was a grimace, reflecting the pain she knew he must be feeling. "I can run home and bring you back some first aid cream for those wounds, some bandages, and some clothes."

Stafford shook his head slowly. "Too dangerous."

"But I can be back within an hour if I hurry.",

"No," Stafford cried out. "Stay away. You shouldn't even be on the sand."

Sandy heard the catch in his voice. She knelt to his level and saw the tears wetting his face. "I don't care how dangerous it is for me. You'll freeze to death out here in the cold."

Stafford looked directly into her eyes and Sandy was surprised to see hate mixed with his fear. The hate seemed to be directed at her.

"Can't you let me be a hero just once? Can't you let me die thinking I saved someone from pain, that I thought of something else besides my own worthless life?"

"But, Stafford," she whispered, clutching the bars with two hands. "You don't have to think about dying. I have a plan for us to escape. A good plan. I was waiting until the baby was born to tell you, but maybe you need to know about it now, so you can hold on... just a little longer."

Stafford shook his head again, side to side. "Too late, Sandy. Too many things have happened."

"Wait, you don't understand." She looked over, her shoulders to make sure no one was listening before she continued.

"I have a boat,", she whispered. "It's hidden near the pier on the bay and it's stacked with food and water and everything we need. All we have to do —"

"No, Sandy," he exploded. "You're the one who doesn't understand. I don't want to escape. I want to die. Save yourself and the kid, but leave me out of it." He turned away.

"Please Stafford. You don't know what you're saying," Sandy cried. "Here. I almost forgot to give you this." She extracted the jar of peanut butter from her jacket and held it out to him.

Stafford turned and solemnly appraised the offering. "Keep it. I'm not hungry. I had a canned ham for breakfast."

"Stafford, please. For me?" she begged.

He sank against the bars of the cage, head down and indecisive. Finally, he spoke. "You win, Sandy." His voice was flat and emotionless. He slipped his hand between the bars and grabbed the jar out of her hands. Unscrewing the top, he jabbed his hand into the peanut butter and shoveled it into his mouth as quickly as possible.

"I'll be back tomorrow," Sandy whispered, pushing the box of saltines into the cage. When he neither raised his head nor acknowledged her farewell, she smiled weakly, then departed.

Stafford finished the peanut butter and threw the empty jar to the sand behind him. Six cell mates who hovered nearby, hoping for that particular action, dived for the jar.

Stafford pulled his stained blanket from the sand, wrapped it around his shoulders, and tore into the box of saltines.

Lou rested beneath the sand floor of the cage and giggled to himself. Vicky was a personal friend of his. He was confident she'd be immensely interested in an escape plan devised by Mason's concubine.

Heads will roll, he thought gleefully. *Heads will roll.*

36.

Late afternoon on February 25, Mason lay buried between cool, comforting sheets of sand. He heard the rumblings of waves rushing to the shore above him and he felt peaceful yet tense, fulfilled yet frustrated. Sand filled his eyes, his ears, his mouth. Grains slipped between his bandages and meshed with his skin and bone, and soon he was spreading, flattening out like, rays of dawning sun on the water, before gradually gaining speed, accelerating, intensifying. He was almost there, almost at the top, the bottom, the end... only to lose it and drop back to the beach, back into the wet gravelly sand.

Understanding of the situation eluded him. At times, he felt wild excitement, but there was also sadness and depression. He still felt a oneness with the universe, but only fleetingly, only at the first touch of the cool sand, or at the last touch, at the falling away when he rose at night from his daytime grave.

His love for Cassie remained unchanged, but all other physical needs and passions were in turmoil. Something was missing. Something wasn't happening. He felt like an insomniac, or a chick stuck inside a steel eggshell. He was always in flux, an eternal wheel that rolled on and on and on and arrived nowhere.

That night when he lifted from the sand, he was greeted by Vicky and a small group of beachers.

"We've got something to tell you," Vicky said with a mysterious smile.

"I'll bet you do," Mason snarled. "The beach reeks of last night's dirty little entertainments and five norms are missing from the cage. I know I'm going to enjoy hearing your explanations, Vicky."

"You're going to enjoy hearing this even more," she told him. She pulled Lou from the group behind her and pushed him toward Mason.

"Tell him," she ordered. "Tell him about the escape plan the slut has. Go ahead."

Mason stood mute, frozen to the spot, as Lou hesitantly, and then with obvious enthusiasm, related the discussion he'd overheard between Cassie and the prisoner who'd won the race.

Vicky smirked as each aspect of the betrayal was analyzed by Lou. Other beachers watched Mason's face, the expression in his eyes. There was excitement building, and more beachers gathered near them as they waited for Mason's explosion and the plan of vengeance to be wrought on the guilty betrayer.

The story ended and Mason's face remained stone. Vicky raged. "She's been using you, Mason. The bitch has been fooling you all along." The beachers behind her snickered.

"You mean nothing at all to her. You never did. She can't wait to get away from you."

Mason remained immobile except for his eyes, which seemed to swell, bulging out of the eye openings in his bandages.

"Love," Vicky sneered. "You honestly thought she loved you, and all the while she couldn't stand the sight of you." Vicky laughed. "She covered you with bandages so she wouldn't have to look at you, or feel the touch of your —"

"Shut up." Mason whispered. "Don't say another word." Slowly, rigidly, he began walking through the crowd of beachers toward a ramp exit off the beach.

"The hell, I will," Vicky snarled. "Four months ago the bitch broke the agreement — your agreement — and you let her get away with it. Now she's made a total ass out of all of us, and she must be punished."

Mason ignored her and kept walking.

"Mason!" Vicky screeched. "You can't protect her any longer. It's out of your hands." She waved her hand. Her eyes flashed. And a sand wall formed in front of Mason, blocking his way.

Mason smashed the wall with his fist and it crumbled into dust.

"It's not that easy," Vicky screamed. "There's too many of us now. We're too strong for you."

At the nod of her head, the beachers moved apart and concentrated their energy in Mason's vicinity. Sand walls sprang up all around him. His fists became like battering rams and he easily dispersed them.

Vicky laughed and boards from the exit ramp flung themselves into a stockade surrounding him. Seconds later, Mason raised himself into the air and floated out of the top of the stockade to directly above Vicky.

Vicky shrieked. Mason dropped to the sand in front of her and grabbed her by the collar of her slinky black dress to. bring her to within inches of his face.

"Go ahead," she screamed at him. "Do what you want to me now. But remember. You'll get tired. Eventually, your energy will drain. That's when we'll move in on the slut and her kid."

Mason glared at her. He threw her into the air, forcing her to rise into the sky. Vicky howled. She flung her arms and legs about her, trying to control her body.

"Take him for me, Mongril," she screamed. "Send him out to sea or drill him into a hole all the way to Australia."

Mongril stepped out from behind a group of beachers. He looked at Mason, then stared up at Vicky.

She hovered thirty feet above the beach. "What are you waiting for? Take him!"

Mongril turned from Vicky back to Mason. "Are you through with the norm broad?"

Mason concentrated on Vicky. "That's none of your concern."

"Bullshit, man. It's all our concern. We need to know what side you're on," said Mongril.

"He's on the slut's side, can't you tell? Otherwise he'd punish her and her kid right now, in front of all of us."

"Shut up, Vicky. I want to hear it from Mason," Mongril said. "Answer me, man."

Mason tore his eyes from Vicky and she crashed to the sand, a pile of jumbled bones and thrashing arms.

"What's it gonna be?" Mongril insisted.

Mason looked at Mongril and the other beachers waiting silently for his answer. There was no sound but the grating roar of the ocean behind him, the slapping waves, and the hissing surf. Even Vicky had stopped screaming, focusing all her attention on mending her bones.

Mason felt tired, more exhausted than he'd ever been in his life — and more alone.

"I'll take care of it," he said quietly.

"Make him tell you how," screamed Vicky, squatting on the sand behind him.

"How?" Mongril insisted.

Mason could barely speak. "First the kid," he whispered. "The kid and the boat will be destroyed." He choked on the next words. "And then... Cassie."

"Right," Mongril agreed. "But you get it over with. You do it all tonight. Agreed?"

"Agreed," Mason answered. Then he seemed to rise above the weakness of his emotions. "And let's celebrate the occasion. Let's party tonight as we've never partied before."

He turned around in the sand and focused on the boardwalk. Lights flashed. Concession stands started to shed their locks. Sluggishly, resembling the start-up sounds a needle makes on an old Victrola, the boardwalk came to life.

"Ah-RIGHT!" Mongril whopped at Mason's side. "Let's party. Par-ty. Par-ty. Par-ty."

The beachers joined Mongril in the chant and more of the boardwalk sparkled with neon lights. A bell rang from inside an arcade. Game wheels flapped against steel pins as they began to turn. The Wild Mouse on the amusement pier squealed on its tracks. There was a crash. The norm cage collapsed. Beachers chased norms as they scurried in all directions.

Mason stood silently, his mind as confused as the growing disorder of sights and sounds around him. He saw Vicky glaring at him, her face a skeletal mask of hate and vengeance. He had to think. He had to get away from Vicky and the others. He had to take off alone and sort things out, figure it all out for himself. And if what they said was true, he would have to do the right thing, no matter how much it hurt him to do it.

At seven forty-five, Jesse was asleep in the back bedroom and Sandy sat at the kitchen table, waiting for Mason and trying to remain calm. The noise that drifted through the bungalow was unsettling. It was eerie. Twice she had poked her head out the door to see what looked like electric lights flashing along the boardwalk. She heard loudspeakers and blasts of music with a heavy metal cadence.

It was impossible, her mind insisted. How could the electricity be restored? Excited, she flicked several light switches in the bungalow and was surprised when they didn't work.

She heard a knock at the front door — and another surprise. Mrs. Morelli, not Mason, walked inside.

"It's late. I hope I'm not disturbing you," Mrs. Morelli apologized. She looked fearfully from side to side as she walked across the kitchen floor.

"Mason's not here yet," Sandy said, allaying her neighbor's fears.

Mrs. Morelli's apprehension lessened, but her hands remained fidgety, clutching and unclutching a book she held in her hand. They sat down at the kitchen table.

"Sandy," Mrs. Morelli said, keeping her eyes lowered, "I wanted to give you this tonight."

She slid the book across the table to her. Sandy squinted in the candlelight to read the title: *Thank You, Dr. Lamaze.*

"Oh thank you, Mrs. Morelli! Where did you find this? I've searched the entire island for something on natural childbirth."

Mrs. Morelli blushed. "I took it from a friend's house. Her daughter was expecting last year and... Well, I didn't think she'd mind if I borrowed it... Oh, Sandy, I'm so sorry, but I don't think I can make it much longer." Her eyes filled with tears. Elbows propped up on the table, she leaned her head against her hands. "I've tried so hard to remain strong for your sake, for the little one's sake..."

She collapsed into tears and Sandy leaned over, patting her hair, trying to comfort her.

"What's wrong?" Sandy asked gently. "Is it Danny? Has he been bothering you again? I'll tell Mason to —"

"No, no," Mrs. Morelli interrupted. "It's not Danny's fault. What Danny said months ago was true. God forgive us, he did sacrifice his life for his parents. He had to help care for his father for forty-five years. Who can blame him for being bitter? He never had a life of his own."

"But that's not true," Sandy argued. "Sure, he had responsibilities because of his father's disability, but sacrifice his whole life? That's ridiculous! He had a job, he was a volunteer fireman, he had friends."

She lifted Mrs. Morelli's chin. "And he had a mother who cooked and cleaned and worried about him, a mother who dearly loved him."

Mrs. Morelli shook her head. She dabbed at her nose with a balled-up handkerchief. "It's God's will and I just have to accept it."

There was a loud crash, like the sound a heavy steel ball makes when it knocks down part of a building. Mrs. Morelli and Sandy jumped up, startled. Sandy rushed to the front door and was momentarily relieved that the attack was not against her house.

Then came another thundering crash! Pieces of wood flew down the Morelli ramp.

"It's Danny," Mrs. Morelli said in a voice drained of emotion.

As if to verify her statement, a voice bellowed, "Mother, get me out of this bed. I've been in this bed all night. Mother, where are you?"

Sandy held Mrs. Morelli's arm to dissuade her from investigating. "Don't go. Wait until Mason comes. Let him take care of it."

"Mother," the voice hollered. "You don't do nothing for me. Nobody ever did nothing for me. I've been in this bed all day, all my life, and nobody cares if I live or die."

"Please... wait," Sandy begged, but Mrs. Morelli, with a muffled cry of despair, shoved past Sandy and hurried next door. She stood on her steps watching helplessly as Mrs. Morelli disappeared up the ramp.

She heard snapping, crunching sounds that could have been Mrs. Morelli's footsteps over fallen debris. Then all sounds were drowned out by the screams and laughter emanating from the boardwalk and amusement pier.

Sandy debated with herself. She was frightened for Mrs. Morelli. She should run next door to make sure she was all right. But she couldn't bring herself to take one step off her stoop. The night was too forbidding, the dark too cold, too enveloping, and she was so vulnerable.

Her stomach lurched and a spasm of pain jabbed at her side. Sandy's hand flew to the spot and she massaged the pain away. A gust of wind snatched her front door, catching her off guard and almost knocking her down the steps. She held on to the door tightly and regained her balance. Resolved, she stepped back into the house and closed the door.

She made herself a cup of tea and paced the floor inside the cottage. Wandering into the back bedroom where Jesse slept, she peered through the window at the Morelli house across the alley. The Morellis' back bedroom was obscured by darkness. She saw nothing to relieve her uneasiness, but fortunately nothing to increase it. She pushed away from the window and heard Jesse rustling in his bed.

"What doing, Mommy?"

Sandy sat down next to him and stroked the hair back from his forehead. "I'm going crazy. What are you doing?"

"Me waiting for Mason."

Sandy sighed and tucked the covers around him. "Forget Mason. He could have killed you with his horsie ride. I don't ever want you playing that game again. You understand?"

"Okay, Mommy," he agreed cheerfully.

His quick agreement knocked the wind out of her sails and she fell silent. Then she smiled, leaned over him, and tapped him on the nose with her finger. "I love you, Jesse."

"Love you too, Mommy."

"Why?" she asked him suddenly. "Why do you love Mommy?"

"'Cause you crazy," he said, and grabbing her around the neck, he kissed her smack on the cheek.

An hour later, Mason stood listlessly on the pier, his arms hanging heavy at his side, his shoulders stooped. His eyes stared at the tortured moonscape across the bay, but he saw nothing. He felt nothing. He wanted nothing.

The boat and its pitiful provisions lay uncovered several feet away from him. He visualized Cassie's hands as she packed the plastic bags, as she filled the water jugs, as she smoothed the putty on the patched holes.

Tears wouldn't come; neither would anger. He knew everything Vicky said was true. It was as if a knob had been turned and the pictures of his memories had been brought sharply into focus. He saw the expression on her face when he at last held her in his arms. He saw her eyes when she greeted him at the door. They were always filled with her fear and hatred and disgust for him.

The firing of the gun came back to him, and her satisfaction when she thought he was dead.

Their reunion... he realized with a start how she had interpreted their lovemaking. What were her words to him? Yes, now he remembered. "Please, Mason, no more," she'd begged him. Why had he blocked it out for so long? Why had he deluded himself?

Tears still wouldn't come, but Mason's body heaved with dry sobs. He loved her so completely. It seemed incomprehensible that the passion he felt for her existed alone, without being fueled by any love from her. The spark that had ignited his love must have existed at one time. He remembered their first night making love together on the sand and a twinge of uncertainty, a glimmer of hope that he was wrong to doubt her flared briefly.

He'd give her one last chance, he decided, one final chance to prove she really loved him. If she failed, the alternative was available.

Mason turned from the boat, his eyes resting briefly on the bay, and realized other eyes were staring at him. Mongril was eyeing him from the other side of the dock.

"What's happening?" Mongril asked in a strained, casual voice.

Mason regarded Mongril's scorched, patched face. "Vicky send you down here to spy on me?"

Mongril raised blackened skeleton hands in a no-contest gesture. Several of his fingers had disintegrated.

"I only rolled on over to give you a hand, if you need it. What's left of my hand, that is," he joked.

Mason didn't laugh. "I don't need help, thank you. So why don't you roll on back to the party on the boards?"

"Party's just warming up. Vicky and I got the norms having all kinds of fun. We got some tied to the front of the Bumper Cars, and some sliding down the Wild Mouse without a car. We're using them in place of the water balloons on the Balloon Bust stand and strung up with lights as decorations on the Ferris wheel."

"Sounds like your kind of gig."

"For sure, man."

"So what the fuck are you doing here bothering me instead of laughing your sick head off on the boards?"

Mongril's eyes narrowed. His voice lost all hint of humor. "We've been tight since day one," he said. "But Vicky says you've changed and maybe she's right. Vicky says the broad's fried your brains and you ain't gonna punish her like she deserves."

"Vicky's a shithead."

"Yeah," Mongril agreed. "We're all shitheads. But if she's right, I want you to know that it's over between us. All debts are paid."

"I'll remember that."

"You're on your own."

"I'll try to survive."

"Let it go, Mason. The bitch ain't worth it."

"Fuck off, Mongril. I said it on the beach and I'll say it one more time: I'll take care of it."

"Okay, then." Mongril took a few steps back. "That's all you had to say. Handle it any way you want. It's up to you. Only you'd better do the job quick before the rest of us do it for you."

37.

By ten p.m., a façade of normalcy was restored to Sea Breeze Island. Strings of garish lights lined the boardwalk. Red and blue lights flashed "Play Scillo" and "Lucky Larry's Arcade." Loudspeakers blasted last summer's rock hits. Carousel organ music drifted from the amusement pier arcade. There was a whiff of cotton candy on the breeze, a trace of Piña Colada-scented suntan oil intertwined with the stink of damp rot and mildew.

A mechanical barker yelled, "One win, choice of the stand."

All of the boardwalk stands were open. The shooting gallery guns popped continuously at rotating targets. Stale, colored popcorn burned in their transparent warmers. The pull-string bells on the kiddie fire engines clanged in the distance. Every light was flashing, every ride moving. Everyone was a winner.

Outside the ride-through Fun House, a laughing, barrel-bellied, mechanical clown waved at prospective customers. Elaborately scrawled coach cars were lined up on a conveyor belt to enter the gaping clown mouth forming the entrance to the attraction.

Carla stood outside the Fun House, transfixed by the rollicking, high-pitched canned laughter and the squirming female norm that was tied to the first coach car in line. A group of beachers crowded past Carla, dragging another two captured norms with them. Vicky separated from the group and approached her.

"Go on," Vicky urged. "Try it. Send the norm into the Fun House."

Carla's eyes remained glued to the laughing clowns and the norm, as if unaware of Vicky's presence. Then with a sharp pull, the conveyor belt began to move. The car and its prisoner headed into the clown-mouth tunnel. The norm stopped twisting to free herself. Aware of the slow, jerky movement, she stared at Carla and Vicky with wild terror filling her eyes. Her lips mouthed words begging them to let her live.

The car moved into the clown-mouth entrance and stopped. Vicky looked at Carla expectantly, then turned back to the Fun House. Her eyes narrowed.

The clown mouth started to split. Hairline cracks zig-zagged through the lips, spreading to the red bulbous nose and star-rimmed eyes. The upper part of the mouth broke free, peeling red paint and blowing white asbestos smoke as it chomped down on the car. The norm prisoner screamed, and the plaster lips moved apart to come crashing down again and again on the scrolled coach car and its passenger.

The norm was tossed side to side as the plaster chewed into her body. Her head hit the rim of the car and rivulets of blood streamed down her face. She shrieked. Her piercing scream cut through the canned laughter that played incessantly in the background.

The barrel-bellied laughing clowns continued to wave at prospective customers. The scrolled coaches remained lined up on the conveyor belt, awaiting their turn.

Suddenly the norm's scream was cut off as the plaster mouth bit down on her skull and cracked it in half as if it were nothing more than a candy-coated mint or a chocolate-covered cherry.

Vicky closed her eyes and the plaster mouth was still. "Show's over. I'm getting pooped. You'll have to learn to entertain yourself."

Vicky took a last look at the vociferous laughing clown. The norm, legs tied at the ankles, hung out of the shattered mouth like a limp cigar. Blood drooled from the corners of its fragmented lips.

"That clown is one messy eater," Vicky said, shaking her head.

Carla began to laugh. Her skeletal face squealed with the delight of a child unwrapping a new toy. When Vicky left her, she was already seeking another victim.

Vicky passed other friends playing with their toys.

Lou rode up and down the Big Zipper to get bird's eye view of trussed-up norms flopping around helplessly in cages that whirled upside down and sideways, fifty feet off the ground.

Old Man Simpson liked the microphone on the Himalayan bobsled ride. It reminded him of the CB in his old pickup. "Do you want to go faster? How fast do you want to go?"

Vicky watched the circular spinning ride and thought of the tiger who had turned to butter while running around the tree, in a story book she used to read to her kids.

Vicky continued walking along the amusement pier. The party was in full swing. Every beacher was having quite a time.

Everyone but her. There was only one thing that would put her in a party mood tonight, only one norm she'd get any delight out of torturing.

"Where is she?" Vicky asked after finding Mongril outside the bumper car attraction. Norms decorated the fronts of the cars like figureheads on the bows of ships.

Mongril directed his norm-car into a low spectator wall. A splash of flesh shot out, drenching two beachers watching the action.

Mongril grinned, then turned his attention to Vicky. "Mason said he'll kill her."

"When?" Vicky demanded.

"Tonight."

"What happens if he doesn't come through?"

"Then we finish the job for him. No problem." Mongril turned his bumper car back toward a head-on collision with another norm spear-headed car. His aim was perfect.

Sandy turned away from the fireplace and carried another cup of tea to the table. It was ten-thirty. The room was dark. A curl of smoke was all that remained of her candle.

She lit a match to light an oil lamp. And then she saw him.

Mason stood in the shadows of her front door staring at her. He stood absolutely still, without movement, without noise. The light of the newly lit oil lamp fluttered shadows across Mason's gray-white bandages. The openings for his eyes, nose, and mouth appeared so dark in contrast that they were like empty black holes in his skull.

"You startled me, Mason. It's so late, I was starting to wonder where you were. There's all that noise coming from the boardwalk. And so many lights. And Mrs. Morelli's Danny started calling for her. I couldn't stop her from going to him and I'm worried about her now. Maybe later you could check on her for me..." She stopped talking to clear her throat. Her mouth was dry. Her hands clasped together nervously. She looked down at her hands, relaxed them, and glanced back self-consciously at Mason.

"Why are you staring at me like that? Why don't you say something?"

Mason remained silent and Sandy sensed the tension in the air. Something was wrong. A hollowness opened inside of her. Her hands clasped together tightly again.

She managed to keep her voice subdued. "Mason, won't you tell me what's wrong?"

When he finally spoke, his voice seemed to come from far away, and it was almost indiscernible, like a whisper on the wind.

"Do you love me?" he whispered.

Sandy exhaled. The hollowness began to fill. It was only the same old problem—the same old insecurities, the same old Mason.

"Of course," she answered flippantly.

"Do you love me?" he whispered again.

"Yes, Mason, I love you. I always will." The words sounded flat, even to her ears. She struggled to ease back into the role of a dutiful robot.

"Me, Cassie. Do you love me?"

"Yes, Mason. I do." Flatness disappeared. Her words swelled with just the right amount of sincerity.

Mason took a step out of the shadows. "Show me," he said.

"How? How can I show you, Mason?" She was back in the swing again. The rest of the night's performance would be clear sailing.

"Take off my bandages, Cassie."

"Soon, my darling. As soon as the baby's born we'll—"

"Take them off now!" His voice had become loud. He took another step forward, toward her.

"Of course, darling. We'll take them off now and put on fresh ones. Let me get: the scissors and—" Mason grabbed the clipped ends of a bandage around his face and ripped it free. He handed the end to her.

Sandy felt the hollowness open up again. She became light-headed and dizzy, but she maintained control. It was dark, she told herself. She could stand unwrapping him in the dark. She'd stood much worse.

Gently, she lifted the first layer of gauze from his skin. The smell hit her in the face like air from a deflating balloon. The smell was rancid and suffocating, like rotten eggs and spoiled meat left festering in a small enclosed container. She gagged, she began choking. Her eyes teared.

"Take them off," Mason repeated, aware of her discomfort, but determined to continue.

Sandy regained her composure and tried breathing through her mouth instead of her nose. She felt weak-kneed, and the baby lurched inside her, but she went on unwrapping the bandages from the lower half of his face and his neck, consoling herself that at least it was dark in the room. At least, she didn't have to see him as clearly as she smelled him.

The end of the first bandage was stuck and she pulled hard to free it, until it finally loosened and tore off. She fell to her feet.

Mason unbuttoned his shirt. She waited patiently for him to dislodge a second bandage, remaining very still and controlled, but as mentally removed as possible while still functioning.

Mason placed the end in the palm of her hand and she felt a dampness, a sticky wetness that coated the gauze. She held it between two fingers and walked around him unwinding the soiled covering and dumping it on the floor.

This time the bandage made a Velcro scraping sound as the final section peeled free of his body. The cloth felt heavier and there was a slight thud when it hit the floor.

Sandy groped toward her kitchen table and sank into a chair. "Let me rest one second and I'll get the new bandages," she begged.

Mason was dimly visible in the shadows.

The top half of his body was free of bandages. The bottom half remained concealed in jeans.

"Do you love me?" he whispered again.

"Yes," Sandy said. She was exhausted now and the smell was still making her dizzy.

He moved toward her.

"Love me, Cassie," he said. "Show me that you love me."

"I do, Mason. I..."

And then she felt his arms touching her, lifting her out of the chair. She felt the cold, gelatinous feel of his flesh. She felt bones. She tasted ash and gravelly sand and something else, unrecognizable, that was bitterly foul and nauseating. She tried to spit it out but her mouth was pressed hard against the stickiness and the bones.

She tried to move, but she was caught in an iron grip. She felt pawing against her breasts, and her clothes slid from her body. She cried out. She screamed. The sound was muffled when more of his flesh entered her mouth and the mucus slid down her throat.

She gagged. She began to choke.

He released her then and sat her back down in the chair, until the gagging and choking stopped.

And then, when she thought it was over, when she thought it was finally over, all the lights in the cottage clicked on, brighter than daylight, and Sandy had to look at him standing next to her.

Mason was emulsified flesh. He was white bones and greenish-black tissue. His facial features had blurred into a muddy pulp. Eyes looked out at her from deep within sunken sockets. His mouth was an empty hole unframed by lips. And his chest and arms were oozing flesh and bone skeleton.

He unzipped his jeans.

She cringed. She was no longer able to maintain any semblance of compliance. And yet there was no escape, no chance that he couldn't overpower her.

His dripping hand stroked her hair.

She huddled at the table, head down, arms around her stomach, crying, "Please, Mason. Don't do this to me... please, please!"

The hands lifted her head. They raised her chin. Sandy squeezed her eyes shut and continued to beg; her voice was childlike and broken with tears. "You'll hurt the baby. Please, Mason, don't hurt your baby. I love you, Mason. I promise I love you. Please don't hurt the baby."

Rank breath washed over her face as he whispered to her. "All right, Cassie. We won't hurt the baby. Just kiss me like you love me and I'll go."

When she opened her eyes, she saw that Mason's rotted corpse was reaching for her again. He grabbed her by the arms and pulled her body tightly against his brackish, liquifying flesh as he moaned with pleasure.

His cadaverous head tilted toward her. He moved to kiss her. His lipless cavity began to drool, and the stubby remains of a tumor-riddled tongue flickered hungrily for her as his mouth sought hers.

She balked. "I won't," she screamed at him. She shoved him violently away. Her features contorted with rage. "Go ahead. Kill me, goddammit! Murder me if you have to—at least I won't have to touch you again."

Her eyes flashed anger. She stepped backward, against the chair, and shoved it out of her way, knocking it to the floor. She was breathing heavily now, her hands clenched into fists at her sides, her chin up as she faced him.

"You talk about love. How much you love me... how much you want me to love you. But what kind of goddamned fucking love is it to torture someone? To keep them a prisoner like some goddamned fucking slave?"

"I've always loved you, Cassie," he said in a small voice.

Sandy stared at him in disbelief. "Jesus Christ! Why won't you listen to me for once? Why won't you see how I really feel? You don't even know me. First you thought I was a goddess. Then you treat me like I'm some kind of toy. I'm forced to act like a robot around you and you don't even notice."

"I never forced you, Cassie."

"You never did anything but force me," she shouted. "Do you honestly think there was one second I didn't find you utterly and totally repulsive? Look at yourself, Mason. Find a mirror somewhere and take a good look at what you've become."

"But, Cassie—"

"And my name is Sandy, not Cassie. You made up a nickname for me, just like you made up a personality that was supposed to be me. But I'm not that person. I'm not Cassie. I'm Sandy!"

"You said you'd always love me."

Sandy laughed, aware that her bitter sarcastic laugh would affect him more than her angry words. "I would have said I loved Godzilla to keep Jesse and myself alive." Sandy shook her head. "I have only contempt for you, Mason, and not because of the state of your miserable body. I loathe you because of your lack of feeling, your total lack of concern for anything in this world but yourself. I loathe your sappy emotionalism. But most of all, I loathe your driveling need to obliterate the personality of another person, so that you can make yourself believe you're in love.

"So go ahead. Kill me, you bastard. Kill me right now or I'll tear you apart with my bare hands. And if you come back from the dead again tomorrow night, I'll do it again and again and again..."

She lunged at him, slamming her fists into his chest, pounding at him, scratching at the runny flesh, kicking him, tearing at him with all the built-up rage inside of her.

Mason took it. He offered no resistance. He didn't back away or crumble, and he didn't retaliate or make her stop. He stood firm until the onslaught was finished, until her anger was spent, and she collapsed into tears on the kitchen floor.

———

Sandy remembered the lights clicking off. She'd heard footsteps and the sound of the front door slamming shut. She'd heard all these things through her tears, but they registered in her brain like echoes down a long corridor in an Alfred Hitchcock movie as she spiraled away from the grief and despair—to sleep.

———

Mason waited outside Cassie's front door and listened to her cry. Her sobs were nails driven into his body, but he remained on her stoop until the weeping subsided. Then he crept into the alley and slid the bedroom window open, inch by silent inch. A brief second of concentration and he raised himself into Jesse's bedroom. The boy remained asleep until he gathered him in a blanket and carried him to the window.

"What doing?" Jesse asked sleepily. His lids fluttered as he opened his eyes.

Mason raised a blackened finger to the hole that was his mouth. "Shhh..." he whispered. "It's Mason, Jesse. I'm taking you for a horsie ride."

Satisfied, Jesse closed his eyes, sighed and cuddled closer to Mason's chest.

Halfway out the window. Mason noticed the oval mirror hanging above the bureau. He paused, debating with himself, then decided against it and continued out the window.

At the pier, he wrapped the sleeping boy tightly in his blanket, swaddling him like an Indian papoose with a piece of rope he'd found in the boat.

Jesse's eyes jerked open and this time he didn't ask questions. He cried out in fear. Mason tried to soothe him, but his words had no effect. Jesse squealed and tried to twist free. His face was wet with tears. Mason placed him into the bottom of the boat and tied him to the center wooden seat. Jesse's cries changed to a high-pitched whimpering. Mason was relieved he wouldn't have to gag the boy and he jumped into the boat behind him. Soon they were floating away from the pier.

His plans crystallized. He'd sail around the island and head for the House of Mirrors on the amusement pier. Maybe if he saw himself as Cassie did, he'd finally be able to finish it with her.

38.

At a few minutes after midnight, Sandy jolted awake and found herself on the cold, linoleum floor. She shook her head, dazed, wondering briefly how she came to be there. Then her body stiffened as she remembered the way Mason looked, the way his flesh felt against her skin, and the way his kiss tasted.

Quickly she scanned the dimly lit room. Then she sighed with relief. There was no sign of Mason anywhere in the bungalow.

But what would happen when he returned?

She shivered. A cold breeze blew through the cottage. A draft of cold air was coming from Jesse's room.

When she went to investigate, she found Jesse's window open so she rushed across the room and leaned over the bed to close it. She'd slammed the window shut before she noticed. Her stomach did an elevator drop to the bottom floor.

The bed was empty.

Sandy felt along the surface of the mattress. She ripped off the blankets and sheets, tossed them on the floor, and searched the mattress again. She looked around and under the bed. She got down on her hands and searched for him on the floor. She couldn't find him.

Quickly, scrambling to her feet, she crossed the room to the crib, thinking, *That's where he is. He knew how to climb out, maybe he wanted to try climbing back in.*

But he wasn't in the crib, or behind the stuffed animals, or in the closet, or on the floor, and the panic flowed over her body as she tried to look in all directions at once. She raced from the bedroom into the kitchen to grab the oil lamp from the table. Her heart was pounding louder than the footsteps that slapped on the linoleum as she ran from room to room, upstairs and downstairs, searching every nook and cranny in the bungalow looking for him.

But he was nowhere to be found.

Suddenly she remembered the open window. Why hadn't she thought of it before? She rushed to open it and pictures of Jesse flashed in her mind: Jesse bleeding in the alley, Jesse reaching out for her, Jesse screaming in pain, Jesse dying.

She was almost unable to shine the light out the window. But she did. And he wasn't there. The alley was deserted, except for a ball of paper rustling in the wind as it rolled toward the street.

Part of her wanted desperately to dash out of the house, run wildly down the streets, from bungalow to bungalow, to the boardwalk, to the pier, tearing up the island to find him. But another part of her knew it was Mason. He was punishing her for what she had said. It was all her goddamned fault.

But where would Mason take him?' What would he do to him? Mason had seemed to genuinely like Jesse, but she remembered what the other beachers had tried to do to him. And what about the way Danny looked at her the night he killed his father?

She made her decision.

Grabbing a jacket from the pile of coats on the floor, she raced to the Morelli house. The front door was merely splinters. Sandy stepped over the debris and walked into the kitchen. She was breathing hard, still trembling, her hand pressed against a pain in her back as she peered into the darkness.

"Mrs. Morelli?"

The wind whistled through the rooms. Lace doilies and dried flowers swirled against her feet. Cabinet doors banged open and shut. She heard the faraway tinkling of wind chimes and the creaking, moaning sounds of the floorboards under her feet.

"Mrs. Morelli, it's me, Sandy."

She cursed herself for not bringing the oil lamp with her. Then she remembered that Mrs. Morelli kept candles near the sink. She moved slowly, blindly, toward the kitchen.

A door slammed shut in front of her. It made her jump, but she continued to move forward into the room. Pieces of glass crunched under her feet. Her hip banged into the corner of a table.

"Ouch. Dammit."

Miraculously, she found the sink, and her hands quickly closed on a book of matches. She lit one match and saw the candles on the floor.

The room was in chaos. There were broken lamps, shattered end tables, and upturned bureau drawers with their contents strewn across the floor. Mr. Morelli's old wheelchair was jammed headlong into the coat closet. Clothes were scattered everywhere. The rocking chair was overturned near her. A lit candle in hand, she stepped over it, and moved to the back bedroom door.

"Mrs. Morelli?"

The bedroom was empty. The bed was stained with a black, grease-like substance. Her candle flickered from the breeze blowing in through the broken window and she cupped her hands around the flame.

She turned away from the bedroom and heard something creak across the room. She moved to investigate, stumbled over the rocking chair, and only then, in breaking her fall, did she notice Mrs. Morelli on the floor. Her body was still in the chair. Her face was covered by a pillow. Sandy removed it and let out a cry.

Mrs. Morelli had not died easily. Rigor mortis had set in and her face was frozen in a contorted, agonizing scream.

Across the room, something creaked again. Sandy turned from Mrs. Morelli, held the candle out in front of her, and the wheelchair backed out of the closet. It rolled toward her, whirled around, and Danny bobbed up his head to look at her. He grinned.

"Get me out of this chair. I been in this chair all day."

Danny was white skeleton and burned coal. Half of his face was eaten away. One eye was a hollow cavity. The other eye hung out of its eye socket, a white gelatinous glob with a black pupil that was fixated on her.

She backed away from him, inching toward the front of the house. But she knew she couldn't leave without knowing, without making sure.

"Where's Jesse?" she hissed. "What have you done to him?"

The wheelchair came to a halt and Danny's cadaverous grin stretched wider. "Jesse never did nothing to me. I never did nothing to Jesse. But Mason did."

He shrieked with laughter at his joke, his hanging eye shimmering in the dim candlelight, his mouth opening wider. And as he laughed, sand crabs and black beetles crawled out of his mouth. A gray-white maggot slithered out from his empty eye socket. Then, Danny stopped laughing and the wheelchair started to move again, rolling closer to her. He reached for her, insects coating his face and hands.

Sandy bolted. She stumbled over the debris to the front porch, tripping and falling over splintered wood, and raced down the ramp. Behind her, she heard Danny's cackle echoing in the darkness, but she didn't look back. She didn't stop to think.

She ran toward the lights of the boardwalk, tearing through deserted streets, toward the music and laughter drifting from the amusement pier. She ran toward the beachers and toward Mason and, hopefully, toward Jesse. She had to beg Mason to forgive her and make him forget everything she'd said. Whatever he wanted in exchange for her son's life would be worth it. She'd perform without complaining as long as Jesse was safe.

A block from the amusement pier, she crept up a ramp and waited on hands and knees, while two beachers walked past her, dragging a norm between them. The beachers didn't notice her, but the norm did. Their eyes locked, staring at each other for several long seconds before he was dragged away.

It was Stafford. His face was swollen and his body smeared with blood. But his physical condition wasn't what startled her. What startled her was Stafford's reaction when he saw her. He'd winked, smiling at her as they dragged him away.

She crept closer to the amusement pier and watched the beachers carry Stafford up the elevated trestle of the Wild Mouse roller coaster ride. They tied him to the tracks and a car began its elevated climb. Sandy averted her eyes, thinking of his smile when the Wild Mouse car sliced through his body. And she had the distinct impression after the car hit, that Stafford had been laughing.

Mason strolled along the amusement pier as images and sounds rushed past him. There were the screams of the norms and the splattered blood of their wounds. There was the churning on and off of machinery and the flashing colored lights of the rides. He heard blasts of music, shrill laughter, buzzers, ringing bells, and a rumbling of feet as a group of beachers moved past him. Heightened energy and excitement swelled around him, but he didn't share it.

When he reached the House of Mirrors, he stared through its transparent facade, and paused. Bright lights and mirror slats waited for him, and he tried to work up the courage to walk inside.

Jesse was nowhere. Ignoring the steadily increasing pain in her back, Sandy crept along the dark rim of the amusement pier, searching for him in the crowd of beachers above her.

There was room to stand closer to the water. She hobbled beneath the pier through a jungle of thick wooden pilings. The dark, wet sand at her feet was slashed by light filtering through the boardwalk slats.

She saw legs shuffling above her. They were bones smeared with emulsified flesh and bits of cloth; the bones scraped the boardwalk when they walked. Some beachers wore shoes, but most feet were bare, blackened, and leathery. Many feet were missing toes and those remaining were shriveled strands of flesh. Occasionally, she saw a norm through the slats, or she heard one scream. Screams were the hardest to take because they emphasized why she had to find Jesse as quickly as possible.

She doubled back, and the sand rose slowly, away from the water, climbing like a pyramid until it was less than a foot from the bottom of the pier. Sandy found crawling easier than walking now. Her legs were bloated. They felt ready to explode, and her back screamed out in pain at every move she made.

She pushed herself, crawling as low as possible under the pier, peering through the boards and listening for some sign of Jesse or Mason above. But there was none at all. And there was nothing else to do but crawl back and try searching in another direction.

She held her wristwatch in a shaft of light and saw that it was 1:15. Then something brushed against her hair. The top of her head was only inches from the floor of the pier and she turned quickly to see a small black hook with a strand of her hair wrapped around it.

She pulled up to remove it—and the hook began to squirm in her hand. She gasped and pulled away but the hook held firm, resisting her efforts to pull free. She let the hair rip, biting her lips to keep from screaming as hair was torn out of her scalp.

Then she panicked, scrambling away from the hook, only to be hooked again, on her jacket, and on another strand of hair. And suddenly they weren't hooks, but fingers, sliding through the cracks in the boardwalk. Long blackened fingers wriggling like worms hung from the boardwalk everywhere she looked. She whacked off the fingers hooked on her jacket, lost another patch of hair, and dropped to her side as flat on the ground as possible.

A stabbing pain in her lower abdomen protested the position, so she shifted onto her back, digging her heels in the sand, kicking, trying to propel herself away from the fingers.

There was a crackling, splintering sound of wood above her and the fingers became hands and arms, reaching for her, grabbing at her clothes, her hair, her face—fingers scratching at her.

Sandy screamed. She lurched in one direction, then another. She slapped at the hands, kicked them, bit them, their ash taste filling her mouth. One hand groped for her eyes. She jerked away, shielding her face with her arms.

The hands reached deeper for her, the boardwalk buckling under the strain. Boards cracked. Some split in half. Cold, decaying fingers slipped around her neck. She began to choke, flailing at the hands trying to wrench free. She couldn't breathe. Her eyes bulged. The world became filled with blurry lights, swirling colored lights and then lights with no color... and then blackness.

When she woke up, she was lying next to a hole on the top of the amusement pier, beachers crowding around her. She saw Vicky. Her rotted skull was draped with black hair. Her sunken yellow eyes were gleaming.

Then Sandy's water broke. She felt the throbbing ache of her first contraction, and her labor began.

39.

All the light bulbs were lit in the House of Mirrors. Mason stood in front of a mirror and stared into his eyes, deep into the speck of light in his pupils. He focused on this light and on all the lights around him and tried to see the person Cassie saw.

He turned slightly and his face doubled; he stared at two exact images of himself. He turned again and the images tripled and then quadrupled. He twirled around and around and saw reflections within reflections, a multitude of Masons, their faces all screaming at him to close his eyes and not to look.

He refused. He started to run. The light bulbs glared brightly all around him. The bulbs were smoking hot and made a hissing sound when he passed them. He ran from mirror to mirror, lurching away from one to go crashing into another in a frenzied whirling dance. His hands slapped against the glass. He left smeared hand prints and fragments of flesh on every mirror he touched.

A light bulb popped.

A dull desperate moan escaped from him now as he ran. He reached the center of the maze, turned, and the mirrors surrounded him. Openings were sealed.

Cracks between mirrors disappeared. He was trapped in reflections with no place to hide, no way to escape.

And finally, he saw the reflection Cassie saw—the decay, the thick rot slipping from the bones, the cold, cold hollowness.

He screamed and light bulbs exploded all around him. They shattered into a thousand tiny particles of glass that filled the air.

When it was over and he finally stopped screaming, every bulb had been destroyed. The mirrors, intact, slid away from him.

And he heard Cassie calling for him.

———

The pier was in shambles. Many of the rides lay in pieces. Other rides twisted and whipped the corpses of norms they carried as passengers. Strings of broken colored lights blinked off and on. Many boardwalk stands were demolished. Many beachers were exhausted now. They leaned against the bodies of dead norms, content to watch and be entertained by the beachers still active.

Mason walked through the rubble in the direction of Cassie's scream and found only four beachers fighting over her. Vicky clutched her hair. Danny had hold of one leg. Two former Goon Squad members pulled at her clothes.

"Put her down," Mason ordered.

Heads swiveled around to face him. The tug-of-war paused.

Cassie stared at him, her face twisted in pain. "Mason, please help me. I'm sorry for what I said. I didn't mean it. I swear I didn't."

"Get away from here, Mason," Vicky screamed. Her black wig had shifted to the back of her scalp. Her dress was in rags and splattered with blood. "The bitch belongs to us now. We'll finish the job you couldn't do."

Mason concentrated his rage on Vicky and. a lightning bolt singed her hands. Her dry skin sizzled, curling and withering like strips of fried bacon. Vicky screamed and let go of Cassie. The other beachers did the same.

Mason caught Cassie with his mind before she hit the pier and flew her gently into his arms.

"Jesse," she whispered weakly to him. "Where's Jesse?"

"Gone."

Sandy stared at him in disbelief. Her eyes were glazed and she cried out in pain.

"No. Where is he? What have you done to him?"

"The same thing he should have done to you," Vicky shrieked. She attacked. Electricity shot out of her blackened fingers radiating toward Mason.

Mason's mind blocked the attack. The electricity hit an invisible shield, and the current splintered upward into the sky, where it crackled and fizzled out. Vicky grunted. She seemed to be straining as a lightning bolt zigzagged across the sky at him. Mason adjusted his shield and the bolt was reflected back to her. It lifted her off the ground, twitching and twisting at her body. Puffs of black smoke, escaped into the air. Her wig burst into flames and she fell.to the ground.

Cassie twisted in his arms. "Is it true?" she cried. "Is Jesse..." She couldn't bring herself to say it.

"Does it matter?" Mason asked.

Cassie's eyes blazed with anger as they had earlier in the evening. "Yes, it matters. If you killed Jesse, I swear... Her body contracted and she lurched from the pain. "Put me down, goddammit. Get away from me."

Mason lifted her up into the air and let her float free of his arms. "Did you really mean the things you said tonight? That you never loved me? That you've always despised me?"

When the contraction passed, Cassie stared at him. Her clothes were torn and soiled. Her eyelids drooped from fatigue. Her hair was drenched with sweat. It took all her strength to lift her head. "If Jesse's dead, I meant every word of it," she whispered hoarsely.

Then the pain overwhelmed her again.

Mason flew her to the beach and dropped her gently to the sand. He was overwhelmed with sadness. The plan would have to be carried out. He had no other choice.

Vicky rushed to the railing on the pier to see where Cassie landed, and Mason turned his attention back to her.

"Is that it?" Mason asked. "Was that the best you could do? I think you're tired, Vicky. I think what you need is a long rest. You look worn to a frazzle."

Vicky threw off her smoldering wig and rallied the other beachers. "Come on, stand with me. He can be defeated if we unite against him."

Several beachers stood up, fanning out to surround him. Mason's attitude remained smirkingly casual, but his body tensed, anticipating the next assault.

It came from the edge of the pier. Suddenly the Himalayan ride reared off its track, the long train of cars bearing down on him at a hundred miles an hour. His mind leapt and his feet followed only seconds before the train would have plowed through him. He glimpsed Old Man Simpson, a conductor's hat cocked to one side of his skull, in the front car of the ride. It passed under him, swerved through a railing, and crashed into the ocean.

Mason felt a rush of air coming at him. He ducked and a spinning Lucky Larry number wheel whizzed past his head. Kiddie airplanes painted a bright-cherry red, swooped down on him. He grabbed the wing of the closest one, snatching it out of the air to send it crashing to the ground as if he were King Kong on the Empire State Building.

"Come on," he screamed at the beachers still circling around him. "Is this all you can do? I think you're all tired."

The Big Zipper churned into action. It's huge hammer arm slammed into the pier, shaking the boards beneath Mason's feet. Carla perched on top of the Zipper's tower, shrieking hysterically as she aimed the hammer at Mason's head.

The fifteen-foot statue of Paul Bunyan staggered onto the pier. Sliding forward, one side at a time, it was energized by Danny straddling its shoulders. Mason darted from the hammer, shot through Paul Bunyan's arched legs, and laughed When the hammer collided with Big Paul instead of him.

Danny fell to the pier. Carla and the Zipper's tower crashed down on top of him.

Mason was tired now. The House of Mirrors and his defensive maneuvers had zapped much of his strength, but he dared not show any sign of weakness. Let the others tire themselves out with their fancy tricks, he decided. It took much less power to circumvent them. Hopefully they'd give up now. They'd figure he was too strong for them, and they'd be bluffed into backing down.

"Don't tell me that's all," he screamed at the beachers who were collapsed around him. "I'm just starting to enjoy myself. Doesn't anybody want to play anymore?"

Beachers that were still standing backed away from him. Others averted their eyes. Vicky screamed for another attack, but her appeals fell on dead ears. She slithered toward him, her eyes bulging with hate. But even she hesitated, finding herself alone, confronting Mason's cavalier taunts.

Then a voice behind him said, "I'll play," and Mongril joined the battle.

Mason faced him and saw immediately that Mongril was neither tired nor the least bit intimidated by him. He remembered the feeling of regret he'd experienced the night Mongril burned in the fire. He was the closest thing to a friend he'd ever had.

"We were buddies," Mason said.

Mongril scratched at his skull, which was now completely free of any hair or skin. "You slipped up, man," he said casually. "You lied to Mongril about the broad."

"I lied about nothing. I said I'd get rid of her and I will— but I'll do it *my* way, when I decide to do it. That's a commander's prerogative."

"Maybe it's time to change commanders," Mongril said.

Mason's lipless mouth twisted into a smile.. "Sure you can handle it?"

Mongril matched his smile. "No problem."

And suddenly all the rides on the pier came alive again.

———

Sandy lay curled in a ball on the beach. She was in agony. She was in the center of a small black universe whose boundaries extended only inches from her body. This universe included the sand beneath her, her torn, wet clothes, and anything within her reach. But the substance of the universe, the inner core, was a pulsating, shrieking pain.

At times, she dug her fingernails so deep into the palms of her hands that blood dripped down her wrists. Other times she clutched at her clothes, pulling pieces of cloth off in her hands. Her lips and the insides of her cheeks were bitten raw. Her eyes stung. Her teeth were clenched together when they weren't chattering. And sometimes the shrieking pain reached all the way to the top of her head, vibrating for an eternity.

This was nothing like Jesse's birth. Besides the obvious lack of comforts like hospital and doctors, clean sheets and a warm bed, the labor itself was different: Labor pains with Jesse had come in waves, rising and falling in an ever-increasing crescendo. There had been breathing spaces, pain free moments here and there to catch her breath, build up strength, and make preparations for the next wave.

But this labor was the top of the mountain all the way. It had a beginning—that seemed to have occurred years ago—but there were no valleys, no small hilly areas to practice on, no resting plateaus. There was only the peak, the high note of the song that shrilled on and on, tuning out the wind, the ocean, the cold, and the crashing destruction on the pier.

Yet, occasionally she could pick out a stray voice. She distinctly heard Mason say he would get rid of her in his own way, but she hadn't heard him say anything else. And once she thought she heard Jesse's voice crying for her. She kept absolutely still, straining to hear it again, but she never did. The hopelessness of finding her son only intensified her misery. Her head slammed into the sand. Tears drenched her face, and the pain reached the point where she'd do anything to stop it—she'd kill herself or tear the baby out. She didn't care anymore. She had to end the torture.

She took a deep breath and pushed as hard as she could, bearing down, grunting. She was straining, maybe tearing herself, but she didn't care. She felt a ripping inside and thousands of dull knives slicing into her and finally a gushing release.

Minutes later she realized it was all for nothing.

The baby wasn't breathing.

On top of the pier, Mongril continued the attack. Log flumes, carousel horses, fire engines, and Tilt-a-Whirl cars were fired at Mason.

Mongril had the abandonment of a hyperactive two-year-old set free in Toys R Us. Nothing escaped his fancy. His mind pulled out every attraction on the pier—pokeno machines from the penny arcade, stuffed animals, T-shirts, beach towels—nothing was too ludicrous to use as ammunition against Mason.

With little power left, Mason withstood the bombard-ments, sidestepped projectiles, and saved his energy to redirect larger, more dangerous items. The caterpillar ride's orange canvas top flapped open and closed as it aimed for him. Mason focused on it and his mind felt like it was being squeezed in a vise. When the caterpillar sideswiped him, the canvas top caught on his hand and almost ripped his arm off, before it drove off the end of the pier, crashing into the Himalayan ride.

"What's wrong?" Mongril mimicked. "You getting tired?"

"I'm not the least bit tired. I can go on forever," Mason screamed back at him, and then he heard a thundering behind him. He turned and was knocked off his feet and mowed over by the Ferris wheel turning on its side. He saw crisscrossed steel and bodies of dead norms dangling from light strips. He banged against a chair, bounced from safety rail to footrest, flew into the air, and dropped to the pier. Then he was crunched.

The Ferris wheel rolled to a clattering, clanging stop on top of him, and Mason was pinned to the pier. He made no effort to get up.

The beachers cheered. They surrounded Mongril and congratulated him.

Through jagged steel. Mason watched Vicky move through the crowd and whisper into Mongril's ear. Mongril grinned, and together they walked to the railing that over-looked the beach.

It was almost dawn. But Mason realized there was still plenty of time for them to hurt Cassie.

———

Sandy blew air into the baby's mouth. She remembered when her worst fear had been being alone, with no one to cut the cord. The fear seemed so inconsequential now. What was biting the cord with her teeth compared to struggling to make her baby breathe?

He was a beautiful infant, perfectly formed in every way. But he wasn't moving. And he was turning blue. Sandy wrapped him in her jacket and held him against her breast to warm him. It wasn't fair. She'd lost Jesse and now this little one, too.

She checked him again for the hundredth time to make sure his nose and mouth were clear. She went back to forcing air into his lungs when she heard them. They were chuckling.

The light was dim and Sandy didn't want to pause from what she was doing, but she gave a quick look up toward the pier and saw shapes pointing toward her. Suddenly she was lifted up several inches from the sand away from the baby and toward the pier. She screamed, her arms flailing. She tried to crawl away or hold on to the sand. She rose five feet into the air, and then ten feet above the pier. And in the growing lightness, she saw the eaten-away faces of the beachers as they reached for her.

———

Mason looked up from beneath the Ferris wheel to see Cassie floundering in the air above the beachers. She was screaming, trying to escape. The beachers drew her to them as she scratched the air to pull away.

Mason focused his mind to wrench her free and a sledgehammer pain numbed his brain. He couldn't save her. The pain was too great and there was nothing left in him.

Cassie started to drop into the waiting arms of the beachers, and he knew that soon they would tear into her. Soon they would be ripping her clothes, clawing her skin, pounding on her, and he knew he had to try again, no matter how bad it hurt. He focused. And this time he concentrated on pushing her away, sending her onto a breeze. He heaved.

The beachers struggled against him, trying to maintain their hold. Mason trembled. His head was being squeezed by the strain. He pushed her. Something exploded in his brain.

He held on, straining not to let go, and Cassie flew from within the beachers' grasp and shot out, up into the air. The beachers screamed, tried to pull her back, mentally tugging at Mason for control of her.

But dawn was breaking and they were weakened by the all night partying so Mason was able to keep Cassie from them. He floated her over the railing and underneath the amusement pier where he'd hidden Jesse and the boat.

There was a sound growing inside his head, the sound of screeching subway brakes. And he knew he had to put on the brakes himself or he'd burst. But he held on, train sounds squealing through his mind... until Cassie reached the sand near the boat... until he was sure she was safe with her son and sailing out of his life forever.

His head was vibrating now. Train noise was drowned out by jackhammer drilling of cement.

Movement was all around him. The beachers wormed their way through the spokes of the Ferris wheel, crawling over him, determined to claim a victim. He couldn't stop them, just like he couldn't stop the speeding train or the drilling jackhammer that splintered his brain into a thousand hairline cracks.

Until suddenly he was shattering... exploding like the light bulbs in the house of mirrors... bursting into specks of light and ground glass and a billion particles of matter.

There was no more pain now, and no more fear. It came to him that this was the fulfillment eluding him for so long. This was dying. He felt himself spreading out from the pier, merging with the sand and water, dissolving into the sunlight that was shining down on Cassie. Although he knew she couldn't hear him, he whispered to her as he filled the air around her.

I love you, Cassie, I'll always love you. And death will never part us.

EPILOGUE

She stopped rowing and rested her hands.

Jesse smiled at her and offered her a saltine. "Where going, Mommy?"

"Not sure yet," she answered. "But don't worry. Fearless Mom has got everything under control. We'll be fine."

Sea Breeze Island was many hours behind them. They'd traveled down the Jersey coast passing Ship Bottom, Brigantine, Atlantic City, and Wildwood. So far, land had been the same wherever they'd looked— black rock landscapes, deserted and lifeless. But she wasn't worried. They had enough food and water to last for weeks, and blankets to keep them warm.

They had each other.

"Mommy, what's this?"

Sandy looked to where he pointed and saw a bundle of rags on the floor of the boat. She lifted it and realized it was her jacket with her stillborn infant wrapped inside of it. Mason must have sent it along when he'd saved her life.

Jesse stared at her, ready with another question. "It's only Mommy's jacket," she told him before he asked again. "Now put those crackers away before you eat all our food in one day."

"Okay, Mommy."

She waited until it was dark and Jesse was asleep before she decided to lower the small body over the sides. A tear in her eye, she unwrapped her jacket and took one last look at him. He had such beautiful blond curls. She hadn't noticed it before, but the child looked very much like

Mason when she'd first met him — same hair, same finely chiseled features, if only she could have done something to save him...

Her breasts, engorged with milk, ached when she looked at him. She reached under her blanket and felt the wetness on her skin. Her flannel shirt, already torn, was now drenched with milk. She moved to grab a cloth to dry herself, and suddenly the infant in her arms opened his eyes. She gasped, frozen with shock, and almost dropped him on the floor of the boat.

His eyes were gray and speckled with gold. She leaned over to get a closer look at him. The dead infant opened his mouth and licked his tiny dead lips. He nuzzled her breasts and began to suckle.

ABOUT THE AUTHOR

Candace Caponegro was born and raised in New Jersey. She has held many jobs including actress, cashier, director, bookkeeper, insurance underwriter, waitress, jewelry clerk, gas station attendant, and English teacher. She is currently lecturing on cruise ships with her husband, Sam.

WELCOME TO THE BLACK
MOUNTAIN CAMP FOR BOYS!

Summer,1989. It is a time for splashing in the lake and exploring the wilderness, for nine teenagers to bond together and create friendships that could last the rest of their lives.
But among this group there is a young man with a secret--a secret that, in this time and place, is unthinkable to his peers.
When the others discover the truth, it will change each of them forever. They will all have blood on their hands.

ODD MAN OUT is a heart-wrenching tale of bullies and bigotry, a story that explores what happens when good people don't stand up for what's right. It is a tale of how far we have come... and how far we still have left to go.

Available in paperback or Kindle on Amazon.com
ISBN-13: 978-0998067919

Welcome to the small Midwestern town of Belford, Ohio. It's summer vacation and fourteen-year-old Toby Fairchild is looking forward to spending a lazy, carefree summer playing basketball, staying up late watching monster movies, and camping out in his backyard with his best friend, Frankie.

But then tragedy strikes. And out of this tragedy an unlikely friendship develops between Toby and the local bogeyman, a strange old man across the street named Mr. Joseph. Over the course of a tumultuous summer, Toby will be faced with pain and death, the excitement of his first love, and the underlying racism of the townsfolk, all while learning about the value of freedom at the hands of a kind but cursed old man.

Every town has a dark side. And in Belford, the local bogeyman has a story to tell.

Available in paperback or Kindle on Amazon.com

ISBN-13: 978-0692730980

ON THE HORIZON FROM
BLOODSHOT BOOKS

2017*

Abode – Morgan Sylvia
The Raggedy Man – Christopher Collins
Those Who Follow – Michelle Garza & Melissa Lason
Sinkhole – Ken Goldman
Dust to Dust – M.C. Norris
White Death – Christine Morgan
Red Diamond – Michales Joy
The Organ Donor – Matthew Warner
What Hides Within – Jason Parent
It Sustains – Mark Morris
Blood Mother: A Novel of Terror – Pete Kahle

2018*

Victoria (What Hides Within #2) – Jason Parent
Happy Cage – Gene Lazuta
The Winter Tree – Mark Morris
The Abomination (The Riders Saga #2) – Pete Kahle
The Horsemen (The Riders Saga #3) – Pete Kahle
Not Your Average Monster, Volume 3

* other titles to be added when confirmed

BLOODSHOT BOOKS

READ UNTIL YOU BLEED!